To N...

Praise t...

Is New York Burning?

Love v.

Arty Madhu:

22/9/04

"The great return of the Lapierre and Collins duo with a
new bestseller, based on a staggering research.
A great piece of fiction more real than reality."

Paris Match (No. 1 News Magazine in France)

⌐

"A showdown from the headlines between democracy
and terrorism... a novel written at a breathtaking pace,
a thriller to give you chills."

Le Point (No. 2 News Magazine in France)

⌐

"A superb novel of political fiction."

Le Figaro

⌐

"A book full of scoops and revelations which
will leave the reader speechless."

Valeurs Actuelles

⌐

"A hair raising thriller which is already rocketing
to No.1 on all bestselling lists."

Panorama (No. 1 News Magazine in Italy)

Is New York Burning?

A FULL CIRCLE BOOK

Books by the same authors

- Is Paris Burning?
- … Or I'll Dress You In Mourning
- O Jerusalem
- Freedom At Midnight
- The Fifth Horseman

LARRY COLLINS

- Fall from Grace
- Maze
- Black Eagles
- The Day of Miracles
- The Road to Armageddon

DOMINIQUE LAPIERRE

- The City of Joy
- Beyond Love
- A Thousand Suns
- Five Past Midnight in Bhopal (*with Javier Moro*)

Is New York Burning?

Dominique Lapierre
Larry Collins

FULL
CIRCLE

This book is a piece of political fiction and does not relate to any factual events and/or incidents. The authors have conceived/visualized a tale that they wish to share with the reader.

Names of characters as used are purely fictional.

IS NEW YORK BURNING?
Copyright © Dominique Lapierre & Larry Collins, 2004
First Paperback Indian Edition, 2004
ISBN 81-7621-157-5

Published by arrangement with the authors

Published in French as NEW YORK BRÛLE-T-IL?
by Robert Laffont

Published by **FULL CIRCLE**
J-40, Jorbagh Lane, New Delhi-110003
Tel: 24620063, 55654197 • Fax: 24645795
E-mail: fullcircle@vsnl.com • website: www.atfullcircle.com

Typesetting: SCANSET
J-40, Jorbagh Lane, New Delhi-110003
Tel: 24620063, 55654197 • Fax: 24645795

Printed at Nice Printing Press, Delhi-110052

PRINTED IN INDIA
04/04/01/05/11/SCANSET/TP/NPP/MBB

To the victims of terrorism of all forms,
and to the men and women of good faith
who strive for truth, justice and peace.

Contents

1

Northwestern Iraq

Early Spring, 2003

The black Cadillac, its window shades drawn, sped through the moonless night along the hard packed desert road that, since Biblical times, has been the principal link between the cities of the caliphs, Damascus and Baghdad. The car was one of the personal vehicles of Iraqi Dictator Saddam Hussein. With the American invasion of Iraq seeming increasingly certain, it was equipped with electronic devices capable of jamming the radars of any American fighter jets seeking to perturb the 435-mile (700-kilometer) journey of its occupant.

On the outskirts of the Iraqi capital, the car pulled to a halt in front of a palatial residence. That was not, however, to be the destination of the car's passenger. A pair of uniformed guards escorted him to a second

Cadillac which set out immediately for another palatial residence where the process was repeated a second and yet, a third time. Like the first vehicle, the second and third Cadillacs were equipped with tightly drawn window shutters.

In these tense days, visitors to Saddam Hussein were not going to be able to identify in which of the dictator's many residences and offices their meeting had taken place, for the benefit of any American agents. To further that effort, Saddam made it a point to never receive visitors during the hours of daylight.

The visitor's lengthy journey finally came to an end at the guard post of yet another imposing palace, where half a dozen security officers in black combat gear took him into a small ante-room. There, much to his distaste, they performed a full-body search and strip on him. That completed, he was turned over to six officers of Saddam's personal body-guard in olive green uniforms. They escorted him down a long corridor, its walls decorated with yellow and blue mosaics of the famed lions of Babylon and the ancient capital's great monuments.

At the end of the corridor, they entered a small private elevator. While its downward journey lasted only seconds, the plunge was so swift and steep, the visitor's ears popped as they might in an airplane coming in for a landing.

The elevator's door opened onto a communications center, full of computers, radios, television screens and telephones. The visitor was now placed in an electric cart, similar to those used to shuttle disabled passengers around an airport and, accompanied by another pair of armed guards, trundled down another seemingly interminable corridor lined with still more mosaics of ancient Babylonian vistas.

Finally, they stopped before a locked door which gave onto another locked door which led, at last, to a large office. At the head of a long table of highly polished oak, sat the Iraqi dictator. He was wearing the olive green, jacketless uniform in which he had become familiar to television viewers around the world. Unlike many dictators who were forever awarding themselves decorations for wars in which they had not fought, no battle ribbons adorned the dictator's blouse. His only identifying marks were a pair of gold eagles on his shoulder boards and the dark blue tatoo of his Tikriti tribe on the back of his right hand.

He beckoned to his guest to be seated. "May Allah shower His blessings upon you, brother," he said in a greeting that was for him more ritual than religious. "Thank you for paying me the honor of accepting my invitation to visit me here in Baghdad in these perilous times."

The visitor laughed. "It is a privilege *Ya Sidi* (Yes, Sir). The real honor was in being shown just how well protected you are here."

Saddam smiled in return. "Bush and his American jackals are preparing to invade my nation. It is their goal to capture or kill me. Believe me, I shall not make their task easy."

"They will need much more than their Boy Scout skills to find you," the visitor laughed in return.

Saddam smiled. "I asked you to undertake this difficult trip because I have something very important to give you, my brother, and I know of no one who will know how to use it better than you will."

The visitor acknowledged his words with a kind of half bow.

He was a 43-year-old Lebanese born Shiite Moslem of Palestinian descent. His name was Imad Mugniyeh and until 9/11, he had been for the CIA, America's Most Wanted War Criminal. Indeed, the ghastly death toll of 9/11 aside, no one was responsible for as many American or Western deaths as Mugniyeh. Sixty three Americans killed in the bombing of the U.S. embassy in Beirut in 1983, 241 U.S. marines and 58 French Foreign Legionnaires blown apart in their Lebanese barracks a few months later, 114 victims in the bombings of the Israeli embassy in 1992 and Jewish Community Center in Buenos Aires, Argentina in 1994, 19 American airmen at their Khobar Tower barracks in 1996 – all of those bloody incidents were the work of this slightly built terrorist.

Mugniyeh avoided publicity as a cat avoids water. Not for him interviews on Al Jazeera television or videotapes smuggled to Lebanese TV channels. Indeed, western intelligence agencies possessed only two small photographs of the man, a thick mop of hair pushing over his forehead, a sparse beard encircling his chin.

Born in a village near the Lebanese coastal seaport of Tyre, he had enrolled at an early age in the training camps of Yasser Arafat's Al Fatah, learning his trade alongside kamikazes of Japan's Red Army, the Shiite warriors bent on overthrowing the Shah of Iran and fellow Palestinians dedicated to the destruction of Israel. His enthusiasm, his aptitude for violence, caught Arafat's attention. The PLO chief assigned him to his elite bodyguard unit, Force 17.

With Israel's invasion of Lebanon in 1982 and the PLO's expulsion from the country, Mugniyeh signed on with the Islamic Jihad and became one of the founders of the Iranian inspired Hezbollah. He was instrumental in developing the organization's use of suicide bombers against southern Lebanon's Israeli occupiers. He was also the architect of the wave of kidnappings in the Beirut of the 1980s, criminal actions which led to the seizure of people like the Archbishop of Canterbury's envoy Terry Waite, American journalist Terry Anderson and the torture and murder of CIA agent, William Buckley.

The CIA, Britain's MI6, France's SDEC, Israel's Mossad, had all pursued him with no success. He was just a myth invented by the Israelis, to nourish the paranoia of the CIA — his Lebanese supporters liked to tell journalists trying to meet him. With fluent French, credible English and a smattering of Spanish, supplemented by a mastery of disguises, he moved quite successfully around the globe to strengthen his networks and nurture his contacts. One of them — in 1998, in Sudan — had been with a fellow hater of the West, Osama Bin Laden. While nothing precise came out of their meeting, both knew the day might well come when their Holy War against the West would give them cause to work together.

"Those jackals of the Great Satan in Washington are getting ready to launch their savage attacks on this Arabic nation," Saddam prophesied. "They are preparing to crush our villages and cities under a deluge of their bombs. In spite of their great courage, one must fear my brave soldiers will be trampled under the weight of our enemies' arms. As for me, I will eventually become a *shahid*, a martyr as you believers say, unless, of course, these cancerous cells my French doctors have recently discovered in my body act faster than the Americans do."

Mugniyeh listened to Saddam's little speech without any outward sign of emotion until his reference to cancer which jolted him. "Surely those French doctors are wrong, my brother."

Saddam shrugged in indifference. "That devil George Bush tries to convince the world that we have weapons of mass destruction, particularly nuclear weapons, to justify his invasion," Saddam growled. "Well, my brother, we do not, alas, have nuclear weapons. However, good Islamic scientists and nuclear physicists who are far smarter than the West wishes to admit, have provided me with something almost as good. They have pierced the best-kept secrets and produced for me the design for a nuclear weapon that can reduce Tel Aviv, London or New York to dust. Their design, I have been assured, is flawless. However, to make it we had to have a source of highly enriched uranium and those damned Americans frustrated all our efforts to get it."

Mugniyeh nodded knowingly. He was close enough to many of the extremist mullahs ruling Iran to be aware of the difficulties they were having in getting fissile material for their own nuclear projects.

Saddam, meanwhile, had gotten up, gone to the wall and taken down an oil painting depicting him riding a white horse and waving a sword. The painting concealed a safe in the wall whose combination Saddam now proceeded to open. He drew out a leather case, larger than an attaché case but smaller than a full-sized suitcase. He placed it onto the table between them and sat down again.

"Brother," he said in a tone so solemn he could have been reciting a couple's marriage vows, "while I do not share the extremist Islamic views you and many of your brothers cherish, I yield to no one in my hatred of America for the evil they are preparing to wreak on my people and for the evil they and their Israeli allies have already visited on our brothers in Palestine."

Saddam pushed the case across the table to Mugniyeh. "That is why I give you today this case, my brother. In it, you will find a detailed plan covering all the steps necessary to construct an atomic bomb of awesome power. All you will need to convert these plans into a real bomb is 23 kilograms of highly enriched uranium. We, of course, needed not 23 kilograms for our national program, but six or seven hundred kilos. For you, to find those 23 kilos should be easy. Perhaps your Iranian friends can help you. Surely with money and friends you can find what you need in Russia. Take these plans now as my last will and testament. With them, you and your brothers will know how to avenge my soul, *Inch Allah.*"

Awed and moved, Mugniyeh stood and bowed to his host. "For sure, *ya Sidi,* you shall be avenged."

Saddam gestured to him to return to his chair. "Do not seek mindless, bloody vengeance," he said calmly. "Like simply blowing this up in some American city. That would be useless. Employ the ultimate power these plans can give you to achieve something positive, something that will get true justice for our brothers in Palestine, something that they and the world will accept and recognize as being right and just for them."

Mugniyeh rose and yet again bowed respectfully. "Fear not," he swore "you shall be avenged. We will win justice for our brothers in your name."

2

Waziristan, Pakistan,
India, Lebanon

Some Time Later

It was the usual handful of passengers disembarking at Karachi's Quaid-e-Azzam International Airport from Tehran aboard PIA Flight 63 — a smattering of Shiite mullahs, two of them wearing the black turbans that indicated they claimed descent from the Prophet, businessmen already in lightweight suits for the fierce heat in Pakistan's cities, a few homecoming couples with children, and a solitary woman in an all-enveloping black *chador*.

The presence of police agents both in and out of uniform, reflected the fact Pakistan was a nation infested with spies and Islamic extremists, both Sunnis and Shiites. Indeed, even the nation's president had recently declined to disembark at the airport on the advice of his bodyguards. However, airport security was in this case, both rigorous and swift. The lone woman went to the baggage conveyor belt, declined the offer of a porter and when the bags came up, lifted her suitcase from the belt by herself and left through the airport's main exit where she paused for a moment.

Among the Pakistanis waiting to greet the arriving passengers was a young man in an embroidered, pillbox style hat. Seeing the woman in her *chador*, he sauntered over to her. "The Believers are fighting," he murmured.

"On the paths of Allah," came the reply. There was nothing feminine about the voice that uttered it, however. It belonged to Imad Mugniyeh to whom Saddam Hussein had delivered his plans for an atomic bomb. His arrival in Pakistan represented for Mugniyeh a defeat of considerable magnitude. He had proven unworthy of the sacred mission Saddam had confided to him. Indeed, he had failed in both his vow to the Iraqi dictator and in his determination to seek justice for his fellow Palestinians. The design which Saddam had given him remained in his suitcase, unused. In months of wandering Russia and the other states of the old Soviet Union, he had failed to find so much as a gram of highly enriched uranium – and that despite the aide of Chechen rebels and the fact he was ready to dish out vast sums of cash for the precious metal. For Mugniyeh, this visit to the fellow Islamic extremist he had met briefly in Khartoum in 1994 represented a last hope of realizing the sacred mission Saddam had confided to him.

With proper feminine deference, he allowed the young man to take his suitcase and followed him to his parked car. Their destination was a residential quarter in the heart of Karachi called the Defence Colony. Most of its inhabitants were retired Pakistani Army officers. Al Qaeda had used its contacts in the military to establish in the neighborhood a chain of safe houses and its operational headquarters for the southern parts of the country. Mugniyeh was, of course, expected at one of the safe houses.

Forty eight hours after his arrival, he was off again in a Toyota 4X4 escorted by three mujihadeen, their AK 47s carefully concealed under their seats. He had discarded his female disguise and was now dressed in the flowing robes of a northern Pakistani tribesman and a cream-colored turban. Their destination was the legendary city of Peshawar at the foot of the Khyber Pass, once the northern gateway to Britain's Indian Empire.

In the years since the Soviet invasion of Afghanistan, the city had become a focal point for Islamic extremists, drug dealers, ex Taliban evicted from their homeland, old mujihadeen warriors, their AK 47s now available to the highest bidder. It took two days of hard driving to get from Karachi to the city whose teeming bazaars had welcomed giants of history such as Alexander the Great, Marco Polo, the Moghul Emperors, Babar and Akhbar.

He was installed in another Al Qaeda safe house. While his escorts made the arrangements for his onward

journey, he wandered the city's fabled alleys and bazaar.
They teemed with Pathan warriors in green turbans and
loose-fitting salwars, Baluchistani peasants pulling camels loaded with multi-colored carpets for sale, horse-
men from the high plateaus of the Pamir in search of
tea and spices. In the 1960s those bazaars had swarmed
with hippies looking to score a hit of hash. Spot a pale
face there now, it was joked, and it probably belonged
to a CIA officer operating under cover.

Prowling those bazaars, Mugniyeh's practiced eye
spotted a staggering array of arms from U.S. made Stingers to locally produced AK47s, a full array of U.S. military equipment from first aid kits to infrared night vision goggles scavenged from the battlefields of Afghanistan. On the walls, he was fascinated to note, dozens of
posters of the man he had come to see, each promising
a 25-million-dollar reward for his capture, dead or alive.
And he noted with an approving smile the apparent indifference to the posters displayed by passing Paks.

In the 19th century, Peshawar had been made the
capital of British India's Northwest Frontier Province
and the city retained that distinction at the birth of an
independent Pakistan. It was a singularly hollow honor,
however. The city's administrative control of the province had always been more symbolic than real. The British never made any serious efforts to bring its fiercely
independent rural tribesmen under their rule. In 2004,
the writ of Islamabad's national rule simply didn't run
in the Province. The Province and the neighboring

Baluchistan Province were governed by a three-party coalition, the MMA, closer in its ideology to extremist Islam than the government in Islamabad. The Province's so called Pakistan Frontier Corps, ostensibly responsible for controlling the province and the nation's borders, was a disorganized, underpaid, rag tag militia.

The final stage of Mugniyeh's journey began at nightfall after a three days' wait in Peshawar, in another four-by-four driven by a Pathan warrior, armed with a locally made AK47. They had barely left the city when he stopped, whipped out a pair of U.S. Army infrared night vision glasses bought in the bazaar and began to scan the sky. "Americans! Americans!" he repeated over and over again peering into the night sky. Finally convinced they were safe, he resumed their journey explaining to his passenger how the Americans had recently swept in under the cover of a thick fog, forcing Osama to flee to a new hideout. In any event, he said, the leader never stayed in the same place for more than a few nights. He and his followers also used a new technique to frustrate their American enemies. They never used telephones of any sort so that the NSA's spying ears in the sky could not intercept their conversations. In the mountains and valleys of the Hindu Kush in this springtime of 2004, messengers on mule back had replaced the marvels of modern electronic communications for Osama Bin Laden.

Forty eight hours after their departure from Peshawar, Mugniyeh realized he was approaching his journey's end. A warrior who had slipped across the Afghan-Pakistani border at night, delivered the driver a package for the Al Qaeda chief. It consisted of several flasks of insulin, a packet of syringes and a flask of medicine for his ailing kidneys.

The journey reached its climax that night at a tiny mountain village called Mirim Shah on the flanks of the Hindu Kush. There, Mugniyeh and his driver escort left their four-by-four and set off on foot for a climb three kilometers long, up a steep incline to the mountain retreat of Osama Bin Laden. No grinding motor noise, no engine vibrations, no excessive emanation of body heat was going to reveal the passage of the two men to any hidden American sensors in the area.

The meeting between the two most important global leaders of Islamic terrorism took place shortly before dawn and the muezzhin's call to morning prayer. Mugniyeh was shocked by Bin Laden's physical appearance. His regard was drawn and he supported himself on a pair of canes. His left arm seemed to be bothering him. Clearly, the turbulent decade since their Khartoum meeting had taken its toll.

"May Allah bless your arrival," Bin Laden proclaimed in a voice whose vigor belied his otherwise fragile appearance. He led Mugniyeh into the interior of his provisional headquarters, a natural cave slicing deep into the mountain's core. Its ground and the lower extremes of its walls were covered with carpets, one of which was white, bearing the words 'Allah Akhbar' in large, green, Arabic letters. Books, papers, pistols, chargers, AK 47s and a computer littered the carpets. How, Mugniyeh wondered, could Osama exercise the world wide leadership of his organization, of his struggle to reinvigorate the Islamic world, in such chaos? Had he, perhaps, made a mistake? Had he come to the wrong place, to the wrong leader, in his despairing efforts to realize the sacred charge of Saddam Hussein?

Then he reassured himself. The man before him may have aged since their last meeting, might be suffering from the frailties of the body, but he was still the most dynamic, the most charismatic leader Islam had produced for generations. This was, after all, a man against whom, for the first time in history, an American President, William Clinton, had actually signed a death warrant. This was the man who had led George Bush to sign a top secret Memorandum of Notification calling for him to be captured or killed on sight. This was the man on whose secret training camp in Afghanistan the Americans had rained 60 of their satellite-guided Tomahawk Cruise missiles at the cost of 78 million dollars. And what had they achieved? Killed a few rabbits because a high-ranking admirer of Bin Laden in Pakistan's ISI, Interservices Intelligence Agency, had warned him the attack was coming.

And here he was, calm and still in firm command of his international Jihad, to restore Islam to the glory it had once known. Of course, there was an air of chaos about this cave. But he and his lieutenants had to be ready to pack up and rush to a new hiding place in minutes, didn't they? From such an unlikely hideout protected by devoted tribal leaders in the Pakistan mountains and by his inner circle of bodyguards, he had commanded bombs in Bali, Kuwait, Riyadh, and Morocco. And the Americans with all their millions in reward money? Where were they? Nowhere to be seen. No, Mugniyeh thought, he had indeed come to the right leader for help.

The two men sat down cross-legged on one of the few empty carpets where a servant brought them tea, hard wheat biscuits and a pot of *labneh* – cheese.

Mugniyeh listened attentively to Osama's welcoming discourse. Then he ceremoniously placed Saddam's briefcase on the carpet between them and began the speech he had been preparing for days.

"Just before the Americans launched their treacherous attack on Iraq, our brother Saddam Hussein invited me to Baghdad. He presented this case to me as his last will and testament. It contains the most precious gift he could bequest the Jihad, to your brave strugglers in the righteous cause of Islam. It is a plan, a complete, detailed plan drawn up by his nuclear scientists for the most powerful of weapons, the atomic bomb."

Osama solemnly nodded his head to acknowledge the importance of his visitor's words.

"Making the bomb from this design requires highly enriched uranium, which," Mugniyeh continued "our brother did not have. He might have succeeded in obtaining it had those disciples of Satan not invaded his lands. It was his most fervent hope that I might succeed where he had failed and thus, use the bomb to avenge him. It was his final gift to the struggle, his last will before his nation was crushed by the Americans and he was captured."

Mugniyeh sighed, encapsulating in that sound all the frustrations he was about to reveal. "I spent almost a year in Russia, working with our Chechen brothers, armed with abundant finances, seeking to purchase this uranium. Alas, I must confess to you that I failed."

"That is not surprising, my brother," Osama said comfortingly. "I, too, tried to get the material we needed for a nuclear bomb this way. Our brave brother Jamal al Fadl, who you may have met in Khartoum, was ready to pay a million and a half dollars on my behalf a decade ago for uranium, but the so-called sellers who told him they had it were imposters. Another of my agents was caught in a trap set by the police in Germany in 1998. I have told the Chechens, I will give them thirty million dollars for this material. What have they delivered me? Nothing."

Osama stirred from his half reclining position to take up an erect, sitting position, legs crossed in front of him on their carpet. "I am now convinced this is not the path we must follow to obtain the great arms we seek. This path leads only to criminals, to imposters, to those who seek to rob and betray us because we follow the divine path of the Jihad. Ours must be another path, an Islamic path."

He glanced at the suitcase which Mugniyeh had opened as he was talking, yet there was a surprising lack of curiosity in his regard. "You are no doubt aware, my brother, of the *fatwa* I have published. It is the sacred duty of the Moslem peoples to obtain these weapons, these arms the infidels call 'weapons of mass destruction'. It would be a sin for the Moslem peoples not to possess these arms which can prevent the Infidel from harming the Faithful. It is our obligation to prepare as much force as possible to terrorize God's enemies. Seeking to kill Jews and Americans everywhere in the world is one of the greatest duties for Moslems and the good deed most preferred by Allah, the Exalted." Osama bowed his head in a gesture of respect for the words he had just uttered, before continuing.

"The creation of Israel was a crime that has to be erased. Each and everyone who has polluted himself or herself with this crime has to pay for it, and pay for it heavily. The American people were active participants in these crimes. Hence, they can expect nothing from us except Jihad, resistance and revenge. The Lord of the Worlds gives us permission to take such revenge. After all, it was the Americans who first made and used these weapons. Why should they be immune from their horrors."

Osama now paused again and glanced skyward as if to invoke a Divine blessing on his next words. "On that Blessed Tuesday, September 11, 2001 with our courageous and splendid operation, the likes of which mankind had never witnessed before, we rubbed America's nose in the dirt and dragged its pride through the mud."

He thrust the index finger of his right hand straight up into the air, then pinched its tip at the nail between the thumb and forefinger of his left hand. "That first attack was this size," he declared indicating his fingernail. "The next attack must be this size," he vowed, pulling away his thumb and forefinger so that the full index finger of his right hand pointed skyward.

"If it kills four million Americans, it is our right to do so in response to the evil they have inflicted on Moslems." The voice with which he uttered his bloodcurdling threat was, Mugniyeh thought, calm and matter of fact, wholly devoid of emotional intensity. This was, indeed, the leader he had admired for so long, his force, his readiness for action undiminished by time. "The blood pouring out of Palestine," he continued "must be met with revenge of equal quality."

Mugniyeh nodded, just the faintest suggestion of a smile on his otherwise dour features. He was Palestine born, of course, and had been physically engaged in the struggle with Israel for 22 years. He was well aware of the fact that the plight of his fellow Palestinians had not been at the forefront of Bin Laden's concerns against the West until his fourth call to arms on October 7, 2001, when the Americans began their bombing campaign against the Taliban in Afghanistan.

The appearance of one of Osama's men interrupted the leader's discourse. He made a respectful bow, then leaned down to whisper something in Osama's ear.

"Ah!" Osama declared. "The infidel soldiers have crossed into our lands from occupied Afghanistan and are moving through Mirim Shah where you left your vehicles to come up here. Do they suspect we are here? I doubt it but, come, we must take precautions." Advancing with surprising rapidity on his canes, Osama led the way across an open draw to yet another cave cut into the wall of an adjacent mountainside. Behind him, his followers rushed to pack up his headquarter's litter, in case an emergency evacuation became necessary.

The second cave was illuminated by the light of a single candle and a large stone was rolled across its entrance to seal it off from the outside world. The aide who had alerted them to the Americans in the valley below remained with them. Once they had settled in the darkness on another pair of carpets, he drew a syringe from the folds of his cloak and proceeded to inject a ration of insulin into Osama's forearm.

"Ah," the leader said, shaking his arm "you see the conditions in which these Americans force me to live?" Then he smiled and blew out their single candle. "I care not. Pain on the path of the Jihad is the purest of pleasures, and today Jihad is obligatory for the Islamic nation which is in a state of sin, because we rush madly after the comforts of life and have discarded the Book. We let Jews and Christians tempt us with their cheap pleasures and their sordid and materialistic values."

He waved a spindly white hand in the cave's darkness.

"To return, my brother, to the great dream which brought you here. We could, of course, have made what the infidels call a dirty bomb, using cesium 137 or cobalt 60. We experimented with such things in Afghanistan before the American invasion. We had laboratories in Kabul, Jalalabad and Kandahar and Russian scientists working with us. But such weapons are not the answer to our problem. In view of America's overwhelming dominance of the conventional battlefield, we, her adversaries, are compelled to seek these weapons of mass destruction which you have thus far unsuccessfully sought. It is only when we have them that we will be able to meet the enemy on equal terms."

Osama paused, allowing an eerie silence to envelop their blackened cave. Then, his voice dropping to something like a sepulchral whisper, he resumed. "Islam is in retreat because the people are not walking in the path of the Prophet. Love of death in the cause of Allah has deserted our hearts. It is not in the path of thieves and infidels, I realized, that we will find the arms we need. Ours must be the path of Islam. We must find brave fellow Moslems who are ready to walk with us in the vanguard of the Jihad and secure these weapons, Islamic weapons. I have found three such believers. And, my brother, they have the means to help us achieve our goal. They will be here in 48 hours and you, my brother, will stay here as my honored guest to meet with them.

Together, we shall gain the arms that will give us the vengeance we seek."

It was, indeed, exactly 48 hours later that Mugniyeh was summoned back to Osama's presence in the same cave in which their first meeting had taken place. Looking at Osama, he understood instantly just how important this meeting was going to be. The Islamic leader was wearing a brand new turban, its white folds so pristine they almost glowed. His beard had been freshly trimmed and the streaks of gray which usually marked it had been carefully dyed. Even the most devout amongst us, it occurred to Mugniyeh, is not immune to the stirrings of a little masculine vanity.

The two men awaited their guests just far enough inside the entrance to Osama's secret cave, so that no prowling American Predator spy vehicle could catch a glimpse of them. Exactly on schedule, Osama's two guests arrived on mule back escorted by two Pathan warriors, members of a tribe to whose chieftain Osama paid a regular and generous protection fee. The first man to dismount was short and slim but carried himself with the erect posture of a military man. The second visitor had a rather melancholy expression, and a neatly trimmed mustache. He wore his still plentiful hair combed back from his forehead. Osama rushed to greet both men. From the warmth of their embraces,

Mugniyeh understood instantly that they were close and dear friends, that the hugs they exchanged were not ritual gestures but the manifestations of deep and genuine affection.

Osama led the pair to Mugniyeh to introduce him. The shorter man was Major General Habib Bol, the former commander of Pakistan's elite ISI, Interservices Intelligence, the secretive organization whose responsibilities included safeguarding the storehouses in which the warheads of Pakistan's nuclear force were hidden. His name, if not his face, were familiar, indeed, to the Lebanese terrorist.

What Mugniyeh did not know, of course, was that Bol was considered by the CIA to be the most dangerous man in Pakistan. And yet, for ten years, Bol had fought with courage and determination alongside the CIA's operatives, in their war against the Russians in Afghanistan. They had baptized him the "BLG" – Brave Little General – for both his size and his valor in battle.

But for Bol, his American colleagues had become the ultimate betrayers in October 1990 when, with the Red Army defeated, the U.S. Government had imposed sanctions on Pakistan for its nuclear program, a program to which the U.S. had firmly closed its eyes during the decade in which Pakistan's cooperation in fighting the Russians in Afghanistan was essential.

To one of those colleagues, Bol had become like "a woman scorned" and "as hell hath no fury like a woman scorned", so Bol's fury at his former allies had no limits.

His son, with CIA help, had been enrolled at Texas A&M and Bol promptly pulled him out. No son of his was going to be schooled in a university of the Great Satan. He quit the ISI and joined the Islamic Extremist movement, the UTN, the Umma Tameer e-Nun, the Reconstruction of the Moslem umma. Under its screen, he had organized a series of clandestine cells composed of ISI officers, including some whose responsibilities were guarding the nation's nuclear arms.

The second man was Abdul Sharif Ahmad, a brilliant nuclear physicist. Mugniyeh recognized his name instantly. Together with a colleague, Abdul Khader Khan, he was recognized as the man responsible for building Pakistan's atomic bomb, a kind of Pakistani Einstein.

Osama led them into the cave where a meager but well-intentioned welcoming banquet awaited them. Mugniyeh could not suppress a smile at how tidy, how well ordered the cave now was, compared to the chaos he'd noted on his arrival. The notebooks, cartridge clips, computer discs had all been packed away and kerosene lamps, not candles, illuminated the place. Osama, ever the good host, waited until his guests had eaten and mint tea and coffee had been served, before formally opening their discussion.

"My brothers," he said "I asked you to join me here today because I firmly believe the time has come for our Jihad to rise above the guerilla tactics we have employed in the past. Brave martyrs driving trucks filled

with high explosives into the barracks and embassies
of the Infidel, the markets of the Jews, placing bombs
in the discotheques of their decadent youths, even flying jets into the skyscrapers of the Great Satan, were
acts of courage and nobility, but we must escalate our
struggle now to a new dimension."

"Today," he continued "the Jihad must employ those
very weapons the Infidel's scientists developed to impose their rule on our universe. The Americans are
embarked on a war of extermination against the peoples
of the umma, our Islamic community. Look at what
they did to Iraq. Look at how they help the Jews en-
slave our brothers in Palestine. And what have our leaders done? Nothing!"

He sighed as if to underscore the enormity of that
failure. "The Koran ordered us to give Moslems the
strongest means of defense. Our leader's failure to do
so is an act of treason, a rebellion against the very injunction of Allah. I say let this Bush suffer the horrible
punishment of God for what he has done. We must
take revenge upon him. We must strip him of his sense
of security and stability."

Osama paused, took a sip of his coffee, a calculated, dramatic hiatus as he drew towards the climax of
his little oration. "Thanks to the inspired work of our
great brother Abdul Sharif Ahmad and his respected
colleague Dr Abdul Khader Khan, the Sword of God
is ready to be placed in our avenging hands. Ahmad and
I have spoken often of this. He believes, as do I, that

the bombs hidden in our arsenals in Kahuta are not Pakistani bombs. They are Islamic bombs. They belong to the community of the Faithful, the umma. They must become the weapons of we, the wretched weak, to use against the powerful tyrants. Is that not so, dear friend?"

Ahmad nodded solemnly.

"Osama," injected the ISI's ex Major General Habib Bol "our missiles, perfected thanks to our North Korean friends, can deliver our atomic warheads to Madras but not Washington. We do not possess the missiles or the aircraft that can threaten America."

"But," protested Osama "surely our nuclear arms can destroy their brothers in Israel, can they not?"

"Of course, they could do that," Bol agreed. "Our newest missiles can reach Israel with no problem at all."

"My brothers." It was Ahmad. "I agree with Osama when he says ours is an Islamic bomb not a Pakistani bomb. When Prime Minister Bhutto first asked me to work on it in a secret meeting in his office in December 1974, I immediately saw it as an Islamic bomb, not as did he, as a means of defending ourselves against Indian aggression. I thought 'the Americans have the bomb. The Jews have the bomb. The Chinese have the bomb. Why is it we, the Moslems, are the only people forbidden to have it?' Today, thanks in large part to my work, we now have 47 bombs in our nuclear arsenals. Certainly, we could fire six of them on Israel and feel sure at least three would reach their targets. Israel is geographically a very small nation and three bombs would destroy it, leaving us all the arms we need to defend ourselves against India."

Smiles came about as often to Osama Bin Laden's ascetic features as snow does to the tropics, but those words brought a radiant regard onto them. "There, my brothers," he said "is our answer."

"No," Ahmad replied "it is not. Israel's nuclear force is larger than ours, larger then India's, larger, even than England's. Most of their bombs are fitted onto their Jericho missiles in hardened underground silos in the Judean Hills. They will survive our attack. Our bombs may kill three million Israelis but some will have lived to fire those missiles on us. They will eradicate our nation and kill forty million of us. I built my Islamic nuclear bomb to defend our nation, not to destroy it."

A respectful silence greeted his words. No one in Pakistan had a greater right to debate how the nation's bombs should be employed than Ahmad did.

Born in Jullundur in the Punjab, he had been driven, with his parents, from India into the new nation of Pakistan in the bloody fighting that had accompanied India's Partition. Embittered at his experience, he vowed to devote his life to Islam and to bring to his new nation the best of modern weaponry, to prevent its people from ever undergoing another experience like his.

Determined to pursue a scientific career, he went to England to study metallurgy in 1972 and then to Dusseldorf to work for Urenco, a Dutch, German and British firm devoted to developing high-speed centrifuges to enrich uranium. Stung by Pakistan's humiliating defeat in 1971, when East Pakistan, aided by India, had become the independent nation of Bangladesh, Prime Minister Zulfikar Ali Bhutto had vowed to equip his nation with atomic arms to counterbalance India's superiority in conventional weapons. He had asked Ahmad and Abdul Khader Khan to join the program in the secret 1974 meeting in his office. They agreed and returned to work with Urenco in both Germany and Holland where, for a year, they advanced their knowledge of centrifuges, translated classified German documents, then abruptly left for Karachi in March 1976, taking with them an enormous storehouse of knowledge. By July, they were running a uranium enrichment program in Kahuta for the Pakistanis.

While the CIA was well aware of his efforts, the Reagan Administration chose to ignore them in return for General Zia Al Huq's cooperation in the struggle against the Soviets in Afghanistan.

By 1981, Pakistan's first centrifuges, thanks in large part to his work, were beginning to produce enriched uranium. By 1984, there were 1000 centrifuges working, and Pakistan's scientists were running "cold" computer tests for the design of an implosion bomb. When the Russians left Afghanistan in 1990 and President George H.W. Bush invoked the Glenn-Symington Amendment, placing sanctions on Pakistan because it was producing nuclear weapons, it was already too late. Pakistan, the Land of the Pure was already a nuclear nation with close to a dozen nuclear weapons comparable to the one dropped on Hiroshima.

"No one in this cave loathes the Americans more than I do," declared General Bol, the ex ISI officer, branded Pakistan's most dangerous man by the CIA, "but as a soldier I understand and accept Ahmad's position. That is not the way to use the great weapon he and his fellow scientists have put at our disposal."

"Then what is?" Osama Bin Laden asked.

"Are you are aware, my brother, of the clandestine organization I have created inside the officers' ranks of the ISI, 'Fighters for Islam', men who share our ideals and realize as do you, the need for Jihad in these terrible times?"

Osama nodded.

"When the Americans set out to destroy the Taliban, that traitor Mushareff sold our country to them for their war. At the same time, he took our nuclear devices from their storehouse in Kahuta and dispersed them to six new, secret locations. One of them is not far from here. The ISI officer in charge is one of my Fighters for Islam. So, too, is the officer in charge of the facility in Chasma where the detonation sets are kept."

Bol reflected for a moment on what he was about to say. "Perhaps I can convince the officer in charge at Tikrim Mir to let us spirit a device out of his facility, in the middle of the night. He will see that nothing in the records indicates it has gone. We will take it to a location near Chasma where we can secretly equip it with a detonation set. Surely you, with your international network and skills, can find a way to smuggle it to an appropriate target somewhere in America where we can detonate it right in the Great Satan's heart. The Americans will not know where it came from, so they will not be able to retaliate against us because they won't know who to retaliate against or where to strike."

A glimmer of understanding flickered on Osama Bin Laden's face as he glanced towards Ahmad. The scientist displayed no emotion. Ahmad, as Bin Laden knew, was a man who loved poetry and flowers, but hopefully, his hatred of the Americans was such that killing a million or so amongst them with one of his bombs would not disturb him.

He looked next across the carpet to Mugniyeh. "I am sure that amongst your followers are brave young men who crave death so that eternal life will be given unto them as martyrs. Men who, with the help of my organization and our knowledge of international customs and travel regulations, would be prepared to deliver this weapon to the land of the Great Satan."

At his words, Mugniyeh's thoughts went to the horrors of the Ain el Hilweh Palestinian refugee camp in southern Lebanon. It was, by far, the most horrible of those horrible camps, a sinkhole festering with hatred and despair, where hope was an illusion, not a promise.

"Yes, my brother, and they will be people who can speak fluent English and glide among the Americans as one of them, believers who have spent their lives studying and preparing for the opportunity God has never given them – until now. May I ask how large this device will be?"

Osama looked at Ahmad. Although very few people knew it, he, like Dr Khan, was a member of an extremist movement called Laskar-e-Tibi, Soldiers of the Cause, an organization closely allied to Osama's Al Qaeda.

"Not large at all," Ahmad said after a moment's reflection. "What I could do is go to Chasma where no one will be surprised, of course, to see me. General Bol and I will find an appropriate place where I can connect the bomb to its detonation device. I think that what we must do is marry the detonation system to a mobile telephone of which you, brother Osama, will have the number. I can set the detonator so that it will only activate the bomb in response to a telephone call to that number. That way no matter what happens, the bomb will not explode unless the secret number has been called."

"The entire device," he concluded "will weigh somewhat more than 50 kilograms — 100 pounds. I will pack it into a large wooden crate like the kind that would contain, for example, a dishwashing machine. You will be able to transport it without difficulty, on a camel's back."

Osama and Mugniyeh listened, fascinated, indicating their approval of the scheme with enthusiastic nods of their heads. The idea of moving an atomic bomb by camel's back was intriguing but before they could question it, Bol spoke up.

"Bravo," he declared. "But shipping the bomb directly

to Karachi to put in on a U.S. bound freighter would present us with a double risk. The first is that between Chasma and Karachi it might somehow be intercepted by CIA agents or Pakistani police in their pay. From that, the second risk – the Americans would then be able to determine that the bomb came from our stores and that would be a catastrophe. We must make sure that until the bomb is on a ship bound for the U.S., it stays as much as possible on Indian soil. Since the border crossings between our two nations are all officially closed, we must pass the bomb in one of the smugglers' camel caravans that regularly slip across the Rajasthan Desert. Those smugglers' pay off the police on both sides of the border and nobody ever bothers them. All we need to do is have a team of Al Qaeda men meet them in Jaisalmer."

"And after Jaisalmer?" asked Mugniyeh whose knowledge of Indian geography was limited.

"From there, my men will take over. They will be responsible for finding a way to smuggle it into the United States. If, by any ill chance, the Americans somehow manage to find it, they'll blame the Indians, not us."

"Where do you propose to explode it?" Ahmad asked Osama.

"I would like to see it placed in New York. New York is the symbol of everything we all loathe in America, their power, their greedy, grasping hands strangling us financially, their corrupt, decadent television and entertainment industry. And, after all, there are more Jews in New York than there are in Tel Aviv. You told me in Kabul that the most awesome aspect of a nuclear explosion is the heat it generates, killing people for miles around the blast, setting thousands of fires. So be it. Let us burn New York. Reduce that evil citadel to ashes with the scourge of fire."

"*Sidi* – sir." It was Mugniyeh who had found himself assigned a far greater role than he had imagined possible when he had voyaged to Osama's secret hideaway. "May I make a suggestion?"

"Of course."

"What will detonating the bomb in a great American city achieve for our cause?"

"It will tell the Americans one thing – what you have suffered until now was only the initial skirmishing. Now, the real battle has started."

"No, my brother, it will only lead the Americans to seek blind and brutal vengeance against Moslems. The hate 9/11 inspired will seem mild in comparison. I have learned one thing in the operations I have conducted, beginning with the bombing of the U.S. Marine barracks in Lebanon: To be effective, an operation must have a very precise objective. In Beirut, my ambition was to drive the Americans from Lebanon. It succeeded. When Reagan saw how many of his beloved marines had died, he fled."

"So what would you propose? That we tell the Americans they must force their Israeli allies to leave our Dar el Islam – Islamic lands — forever?"

"No. That would never work. Israel is not going to commit suicide. We must choose an objective that we can hope to achieve. Suppose we tell the Americans 'the bomb will explode in New York or Washington or Chicago in a week, if you do not force the Israelis to promise publicly before the entire world that they will leave all the illegal settlements that they have installed on the land seized from our Palestinian brothers in 1967'?"

He sat back to sample reactions to his words. "That is something we could realistically hope to achieve. All the world, even the American people themselves, see the terrible injustice those settlements represent. Everyone, except the fanatics in Israel, will support our just demand. And if six million Americans die, it will be the Israelis' fault, not ours."

Bin Laden turned to General Bol. "What do you think as a military man? And also as someone who knows so well how our nuclear arms are stored. Could we smuggle one out? Is such a plan really possible?"

Bol stretched out on his carpet and closed his eyes in thoughtful concentration. "Yes," he said, on opening them "I think it is possible. It will take some time because it must be done in total secrecy, but I know which of my Fighters for Islam I can count on to help us."

"Brilliant!" Osama said. "Our Islamic nuclear bomb will bring justice to our brothers in Palestine, at last. In a way the whole world can accept and understand. How can the Americans do anything but agree?"

★ ★ ★

Just over six weeks later, a Toyota sedan, bearing the signs of the ISI, turned off the Hyderabad-Jodhpur Highway, some 50 miles past the Pakistani village of Naya Chor, onto a hard packed dirt track paralleling the Indian Pakistani border along the parched wastes of the Rajasthan Desert. Its destination was the tiny border crossing village of Qadr, little more than a collection of ramshackle dirt and wood huts.

The driver was a lieutenant colonel in ISI uniform, a garb certain to command respect along the frontier. Beside him, in civilian clothes, was retired Major General Bol. In the back seats were Osama Bin Laden and Imad Mugniyeh. All four men were wrapped in a respectful silence, in appreciation of the enormity of the act they were about to accomplish.

Bol's plan had worked exactly as he had hoped it would. The driver of the car was a member of his clandestine network inside the ISI. He was the officer in charge of the secret Pakistani nuclear storehouse in Kabiwala, a tiny town in the Punjab.

Under the cover of night and with the aid of a fellow conspirator, he had managed to remove one of the eight atomic bombs assigned to him for safekeeping.

It had been a delicate operation. The ISI had installed a computerized security system in the arsenal so that if any of the eight bombs were tampered with, a signal would be sent to the Nuclear Command Headquarters in Islamabad. The colonel, however, had the code by which it worked and was able to put it on standby, just long enough to remove one of his bombs from its storage site. He altered its workings so that when he turned the system back on, it showed the bomb was still in place. Only a physical inspection of the arsenal would reveal that it was missing.

However, the Pakistani military had an almost blind trust in their computer systems. The physical inspections of their storage sites were a rarity and, as Bol's accomplice knew, the next one at his site was over six months away.

Bol had driven the bomb to Chasma where Abdul Sharif Ahmad had married it to a detonation system, wired, as he had promised, to a cellular phone. His system was equipped with a sophisticated American-made scanning device which was programmed to screen out any incoming wrong numbers so that the bomb could not be exploded by error. Osama and Mugniyeh, alone, would have the cell phone's number.

From his seat beside the driver, Bol indicated half a dozen camels gathered around a clump of scraggly, burned out shrubs, the best imitation of a watering hole the Rajasthan Desert had to offer.

"There they are," he said.

The driver pulled over and as he did, three men emerged from under a cloth stretched over four poles just behind the camels. "My men," Bol said. "They know this desert perfectly. They will guide you safely into India, Imad."

Bol, Mugniyeh and the driver got out, leaving Osama in the back seat, his familiar face partially screened by the car's curtains. Bol opened the trunk. The bomb was inside, carefully packed into a large wooden crate. Two of Bol's camel rustlers came over, lifted it from the trunk and carried it to one of their waiting camels, where they carefully fitted it into a rope container suspended from the animal's hump. They, of course, had no idea what the crate contained. They tossed a red and purple Afghan carpet similar to the carpets the other camels were carrying over it.

Bin Laden slipped out of the car and went over to Mugniyeh. He gave the Lebanese terrorist a warm embrace, then pressed a small envelope into his hand. "When you came to see me, it was to seek vengeance for our brother Saddam, as he had asked you to do. Now thanks to these brave Pakistani soldiers and scientists, you have here, at last, the instrument of that vengeance. My men will be waiting for you on the other side of the border. They will take you to your destination. Everything you will need to know about the rest of your onward journey is here in this envelope."

He paused and looked at the bomb under its carpet on the camel's back with a smile of satisfaction so intense, it depassed description. "The Americans, with their helicopters and spies and the traitors of Mushareff, seek desperately every day to capture and kill me. Who knows? One day they will probably succeed. But now that matters not. I care not. For we have placed in your hands the instrument of final vengeance for me and my followers as well as Saddam. If anything happens to me, I know that you and your brave followers will see to it that our plan to wreak havoc on the Americans of Bush goes forward exactly as we have planned. They will force their Israeli friends to give justice to your Palestine brothers, or they will perish by their hundreds of thousands."

He then stepped discreetly up to the bomb under its carpet on the camel's back. He laid his hand on it, almost as though he was invoking a blessing. "For the sake of Allah, may this bomb terrorize the enemies of God," he muttered in a voice pitched so low, he could feel confident none of the ISI men manning the camel caravan could understand him.

Meanwhile, an ISI officer had helped Mugniyeh into the saddle of one of the waiting camels. The leader gave a whip stroke to his animal's flank and slowly, with their centuries-old swaying motions, the ships of the desert set off, carrying the most modern of devices towards its distant destination.

Bol, Bin Laden and the colonel watched the six animals plod their way towards the horizon, transfixed into silence inspired by the act they were watching. Finally, as the last animal disappeared from sight, twisting around a towering sand dune, Bin Laden murmured a kind of invocation to provide closure to what they had done — "At last, the vengeance of the Just shall be ours."

★ ★ ★

Bin Laden's Al Qaeda henchmen transported the bomb from Jaisalmer down to the suburbs of Bombay, exactly as the extremist chieftain had ordered. Once there, Imad Mugniyeh confided it to their capable hands and climbed back into his favorite disguise, his black chador, and with the woman's passport his Iranian friends had given him, flew back to Tehran on Air India. In the Iranian capital, his associates arranged for his onward journey to Beirut. There, a mission of considerable importance awaited him — recruiting, as he had promised Bin Laden, three volunteers ready to travel to the land of the Great Satan, to receive the bomb when it arrived, secret it in an appropriate hiding place, and make sure it was ready to go off in the apocalyptic explosion for which Abdul Sharif Ahmad had programmed it.

His Hezbollah associates had arranged for him a meeting with three volunteers, all fluent English speakers in the most sordid of Palestinian refugee camps, Ain el Hilweh, just south of the Lebanese seaport of Sidon. Nothing quite so filled Imad Mugniyeh's heart with hatred as walking down the mud and garbage-filled alleys of Ain el Hilweh. For the terrorist leader, each visit to these sordid surroundings stirred two conflicting emotions: his hatred for the Israelis who had driven these wretched people from their homes half a century ago, and his shame for his fellow Lebanese whose policies had done so much to compound the miseries of their existence.

Quite literally a human rat hole, the camp claimed

the sad record of housing the densest concentration of human beings of any of the Middle East's refugee camps. Forty thousand people were crammed into an area not much larger than half a dozen football fields. It was a site without trees, without flowers, without butterflies, without birds, with the exception of a few flocks of predatory crows.

Children grew up in the camp without knowing a shrub, a green forest, an open field or even the seawater, whose shores were, nonetheless, close to its western borders — but polluted by the overflow of the camp's sewage system sluicing into the sea. The atmosphere was so polluted that rare were the families that had not lost at least one member to its toxic wastes. Tuberculosis, malaria, dysentery were prevalent and helped contribute to the inmates' low life expectancy. It was feverishly hot in the summer, and the winter rains turned its alleys into muddy lakes.

Now with his guide, Mugniyeh made his way gingerly through the mud, the stench of urine, the hordes of flies buzzing over the fresh piles of human excrement littering the alley, stark testimony to the inadequacies of the camp's sewage system 55 years after the first refugees, fleeing their homeland in 1948, had arrived.

Most refugees had to live on the meager rations distributed by UNWRA, the United Nations Work and Relief Agency, created in 1948 to care for the Palestinians who had fled their homeland, following its division by the UN to create the State of Israel. The unemployment rate was staggeringly high, primarily because the Lebanese authorities, determined not to allow the refugees to infiltrate their society, had prohibited them since 1948 from working in 72 occupations, ranging from the law and medicine to sales, clerking and accounting, without a government-issued work permit.

The generosity of the Lebanese in issuing those permits was summed up in one statistic: in 53 years, they had delivered 2,500 permits to a population numbering 364,000; hence, the camp's staggering unemployment rate.

Nothing, however, weighed more heavily on the camp's inmates than a terrible sense of despair. It had been their constant companion since the "*Nakba* – the disaster" of 1948, when hundreds of thousands of Palestinians had fled or been driven from their homeland in the aftermath of the creation of Israel. Three generations of those refugees had been born, lived and died in places like Ain el Hilweh which were a disgrace to mankind's conscience.

Out of these sinkholes of misery had come quite naturally, a fountain of hate and violence, which for years had nourished the more violent aspects of the Palestinians' struggle. While the camp was well distant from the Israeli frontier, its inmates had always provided armed Palestinian gangs with a steady stream of volunteers for the armed combat against the Jewish State. Rare were the Ain el Hilweh shanties which were not decorated with a portrait of a man in a *kaffiyeh* who had given his life in the struggle. Their places of honor had recently been supplemented by portraits of post adolescent youth, foreheads bearing a black handkerchief. Regularly, the camp's youth had signed on with Hamas, Hezbollah, the Martyrs of Al Aqsa to give up their lives infiltrating Israel, stomachs banded by the suicide bomber's belt. Thanks to the Palestinians' traditional thirst for education and learning, however, many refugees had, over the years, managed to get university and post graduate degrees. Yet, even with their diplomas in hand, there was no way to avoid the stringent Lebanese work rules. Men with Master's degrees in physics wound up digging ditches for a living. Frustrated, embittered, those men and women constituted an ideal recruitment pool for terrorist managers like Mugniyeh.

The meeting to which Mugniyeh was destined, was set in the shanty of an attractive 33-year old widow, Nahed Jihari. Her beloved husband had died during an Israeli air assault on his Hezbollah position in Southern Lebanon in 1997.

On the wall of her bedroom, beside his photo in his fedayeen's uniform, Nahed had hung the official document he had given her as his wedding present, a British Mandate certificate of ownership of three dunums of land on the seacoast below Jaffa, as well as her own diploma from the American University of Beirut. Her dark eyes accentuated by the kohl with which she surrounded them, hers was a deceptive image of fragility. She was overjoyed by the visit of the legendary

Hezbollah leader, who she had not seen since he had promised her vengeance at her husband's funeral.

Waiting for Mugniyeh as well were two men he'd asked to see. Omar Tahiri was 42, a lean, well built man, with what seemed an expression of perpetual melancholy fixed to his facial features. His father had brought him to Ain el Hilweh as a baby. He had lived his childhood and adolescence to the music of his father's constantly repeated promise that "One day we will return to Jaffa and eat the best oranges in the world."

Of course, he had never returned. The only Jaffa orange he had ever eaten was one he had bought at Marks and Spencer's in London, on a stopover to do post-graduate work at Montreal's McGill University. Ambitious and bright, Tahiri had won himself scholarships to the American University of Beirut, then McGill, where he had earned a Master's degree in architecture. Back at Ain el Hilweh, however, he was trapped by the Lebanese work permit restrictions and he had to employ his architect's degree, building latrines.

Angry and embittered, he had volunteered his services to the Hezbollah in their struggle against Israel's occupying forces in southern Lebanon. His courage and poise under fire had caught Mugniyeh's eye. The terrorist chieftain had trained him as an explosives expert, preparing charges for the use of Hezbollah's warriors assaulting Israeli positions, until a premature explosion had blown away his left hand in 1996. No one could have been happier to get the word that Mugniyeh wanted to see him, than Tahiri. Maybe, he had thought, this was the summons back to action he had so desperately longed for, since losing his left hand.

The third person waiting for Mugniyeh was the youngest of the trio, Amr Bin Khaled, a starkly handsome 26-year old, who was the darling of the camp's few unmarried women and not a few of their married sisters as well.

As a kid growing up, Khaled had become addicted to watching American TV programs from which the bright young man had gained a mastery of colloquial, American-accented English. At 18, he had agreed to sign up as a recruit with Hezbollah's fighters battling the Israelis in the south. Three years of constant combat had given him an extensive knowledge of arms and explosives, but above all, a reputation as a fighter who, despite his young age, had a remarkable ability to remain cool under pressure, and imaginative and resourceful when faced with the unexpected and unknown. His shooting down of an Israeli helicopter with a Stinger missile had proven to his leaders that he possessed, in full, the bravery and audacity Mugniyeh was looking for.

Nahed had laid out for them the best welcoming meal her meager rations would allow. The four all embraced warmly, then sat down to her food on the four spindly chairs she possessed. When they'd finished their coffee, Mugniyeh began his recruiting pitch.

"What we are going through today is beyond description," he said. "International infidelity, led by the

Great Satan, has joined against the Moslem nation to eliminate our Holy Strugglers. The time has now come for us to strike back with the most terrible of arms available to us. We will be called 'enemies of humanity' and 'terrorists' but we must ignore such things. Prophet Mohammed was called worse names, but did he abandon his struggle?"

"To accomplish this great task, we require three brave strugglers. I cannot tell you now what the mission will be. All I can say is that it will be far from here. It will require bravery, skill and determination which I know you all possess. You will receive in time the papers you will need for the task, the money it will require and the training you will need to carry it out. Will it be dangerous, you ask? Yes, it will. You may well die in executing it. But if you succeed, your names will be forever enshrined with Islam's greatest heros."

Tahiri looked at his two companions, his eyes asking a question his tongue did not have to articulate.

"For my beloved husband, for him for sure," Nahed whispered.

"Count me in," said Amr.

Tahiri turned back to Mugniyeh. "We all thank God for having chosen us for this great matter, my brother," he said with a slight, formal bow.

3

Port Elizabeth, New Jersey, New York City

A Container of Basmati Rice

"SS Jewel of India outward bound from Bombay and South Hampton requests clearance to enter port."

Lieutenant Bob Farrelly of the U.S. Coast Guard scrutinized the white splotch on his radar screen, indicating yet another ship stood poised at the entrance of the Narrows, the channel leading off the swells of the Atlantic into the Port of New York. A quick glance at the computer screen on his desk confirmed the Jewel's expected arrival on this Thursday morning, and her destination, Port Elizabeth's Marine Terminal 4.

"SS Jewel of India," Farrelly announced into the radio before him, "Your ID is X 49Y72. Heave to and await instructions while we process your clearance."

His order was a function of the new procedures set

in place after the terror attack of 9/11 to govern shipping entering New York Harbor. They were part of a national effort to prevent terrorists from smuggling arms, people or weapons of mass destruction into U.S. ports. While ships were on the water, the responsibility for enforcing those procedures lay with the Coast Guard. Once in port, it passed to Customs, the FBI, the CIA and, in the Jewel's case, the Port of New York and New Jersey Police Authority.

A score of uniformed Coast Guard officers and enlisted men and women milled around Farrelly in their headquarters perch atop Fort Wadsworth. The fort, originally built during the American Revolution to prevent British Men O'War from assaulting New York, was now the vantage point from which they could survey the flow of traffic along the Narrows. A bank of TV monitors screened for them the images of the passing shipping, shot by a dozen cameras stationed along the waterway.

Farrelly tapped into his computer's data bank for the file on the Jewel. She was the seventh ship to enter the harbor this autumn morning, bringing to New York her share of the 21,000 containers unloaded in U.S. ports every day. They represented just a fraction of the eleven million containers circulating on the globe's seaways, the product of a shipping revolution which, curiously, had begun in Port Elizabeth in 1965.

Farrelly's computer screen flashed up what was, in a sense, the Jewel's legal dossier, another of the post-9/11 procedures. That dossier recorded any legal incident in the Jewel's recent past, whether it was a pack of heroin found concealed under her deck planking, a drunken brawl involving a couple of her seaman, or any suspicion that she might have been involved in some form of illicit traffic or a violation of maritime law.

Like so many ships in international commerce, the Jewel flew a Panamanian flag of convenience. The ship's registry listed her owners as a Panamanian corporation, Interocean Commerce. That, of course, was pure fiction. Dummy companies like that were designed to protect the ships' real owners from lawsuits arising from oil spills or other maritime mishaps. The Panamanian government simply was not prepared to reveal who owned the ships that flew the nation's flags, to anyone, for any reason.

Since she displaced more than 300 tons, the Jewel's master had been obliged under the Coast Guard's new ATS, Advanced Targeting System, to furnish the U.S. port authorities a detailed manifest of the cargo she was carrying, 96 hours before her arrival in New York. It had to include a detailed listing of the destination of each of the containers she carried and a full list of the goods each contained, as furnished by their shipper.

To further strengthen their control of incoming commerce, U.S. Customs had recently initiated a program called the Container Security Initiative, to station U.S. Customs officers in foreign ports to work with the local authorities as they loaded the cargo containers. The idea was to be sure none were employed to smuggle arms, weapons of mass destruction or, as had happened recently in an Egyptian ship, a member of Al Qaeda, bearing detailed plans of U.S. airports.

Farrelly's inspection of the Jewel's dossier was swift and routine. The 20,000-ton vessel called on the ports of New York and New Orleans four or five times a year and she scrupulously followed U.S. Customs and maritime regulations. The 175 cargo containers stuffed into her cargo holds and jamming her deck carried the creations of India's thriving handicraft industries – piles of silk and embroidered shirts, blouses, pants, shoes ordered by the purchasing agents of Gap, The Banana Republic and the other clothing dynasties servicing U.S. malls. Some containers were full of furniture, carpets, dishes and glassware destined for the display shelves of stores like Macy's and Bloomingdale. Still others were packed with sacks of Basmati rice from the Punjab, tea from Darjeeling, coffee from Kerala, jars of chutney from Goa, cans of shrimp and crab from Bengal and the exotic spices of the East for which the nations of Europe had once fought their colonial wars.

Her clearance was straightforward. Farrelly tapped it onto his computer and turned his radio on. "Jewel of India," he announced "your pilot is coming on board and you are cleared to proceed to Port Elizabeth."

The Jewel's master, a 46-year-old Bengali named Hari Das Gupta, waved his pilot on board, moved his engines up to half speed and sailed for the Narrows.

Although the master didn't know it, some of the buoys along his route were now topped with detectors meant to pick up gamma-ray emissions from the passing ships, in case some one was trying to smuggle nuclear cargo into the city.

The master's attention was transfixed by the prodigious spectacle which never ceased to enthrall him, the entrance to the Port of New York. First, he smiled at the ferries wheel and parachute drop of Coney Island, homeland now to thousands of Russian immigrants. Minutes later, he was passing under the graceful spans of the Verrazano Bridge. Then, almost before he knew it, off to starboard was the sight that had thrilled so many men and women over the decades, the green-sheathed Statue of Liberty, lifting her lantern at the door to the Promised Land. Behind her, the towers of Manhattan pierced the morning mist, incandescent trunks of a forest of glass and steel, clawing up to the sky.

And, as they had for three years now, his eyes focused on the glaring gap in that majestic skyline, the place where the Twin Towers of the World Trade Center had once stood. For some curious reason, that sight had always made him think of the gap-toothed smile of his six-year-old daughter in the weeks after she had lost her two front teeth. What a sad sight it had become, lower Manhattan without those two proud towers!

Beside him, the pilot gestured to the entrance of the Kill van Kull and the Master ordered his helmsman to come to port and start his passage up the seaway along the shores of Staten Island into Newark Bay. As he did, he picked up his radio to announce his arrival to the Port Elizabeth shipping authority.

"Roger Jewel of India," the port's shipping officer acknowledged "we are assigning you berth 17 in Marine Terminal 4."

The twin maritime terminals of Port Newark and Port Elizabeth extended along Newark Bay opposite Manhattan, from the landing strips of Newark Airport, all the way to the city of Newark itself. Together, they probably represented the largest and certainly, the most modern container cargo facility in the world. Their modern docking facilities had pretty much consigned the docks of Red Hook and the Brooklyn waterfront to history. Those piers, on which the mafia's hoods had once picked their loyal long shoremen at their daily shape-ups, were largely empty now, as were the piers of the Brooklyn Marine Terminal from which two generations of GIs had sailed to fight in European wars.

The facilities of the twin ports were a mirror of what was most vibrant and modern in American maritime transport. But since 9/11, they were something else as well, a fragile frontier through which a terrorists' weapon of massive destruction might, one day, slip undetected. The problem was tremendous.

The nation's scientific centers, like California's

Lawrence Livermore Laboratory, were working hard at developing new and better technologies but, as is so often the case, the desire to get them was as strong as the flow of dollars out of Congress to pay for them was weak. At the end of 2002, the twin ports had received three of the best of the new devices, strange-looking vehicles with long metallic arms which could run alongside the walls of a container or a truck and, hopefully, detect the presence inside of a nuclear device with their powerful gamma-ray detectors. Called VACIS, Vehicle and Cargo Inspection System, those trucks cost a million dollars apiece and could also provide a somewhat primitive image on a screen, of the container's contents, in much the same way as a camera scans a passenger's checked baggage at an airport.

The arrival of those first VACIS trucks was heralded at the twin ports as a first victory in the struggle with terrorists, but it was a victory of limited dimension. In 24 hours, the VACIS trucks at Port Elizabeth could only screen a hundred containers, representing two percent – and sometimes as little as one half of one percent – of the daily container inflow.

Early the next day, the unloading process began for the Jewel, following a well-oiled routine. Hari Das Gupta, her master, watched with satisfaction as a pair of the port's enormous cranes drew up alongside his ship to unload the 97 of his 175 containers destined for the New York area.

It was a swift and efficient process. The cranes, like

a couple of immense metallic birds of prey, lowered their claws into the Jewel's cargo holds where her crewmen fastened them to a container. The container was then lifted from the ship's deck, swung over her side and lowered to the pier to which the Jewel was berthed. Each container bore four white initials, INOS, for Indian Ocean Shipping, the name of the company to which they belonged, and a band of four numbers which indicated their contents as set out on the manifest Das Gupta had provided the U.S. Coast Guard, 96 hours before his arrival.

Das Gupta watched fascinated, as a team of Customs officers scanned each side of the container with a machine that resembled a portable telephone. Their inspection of each container lasted, to the amusement of Das Gupta, several minutes. "Maybe, they think my Bengal shrimp give off atomic rays" he laughed to no one in particular. Never had he seen a Customs inspector open a container and crawl inside to personally inspect its contents. That, as Das Gupta well knew, was an awesome task. Those containers were filthy, tightly packed, often stinking, and to get a look at them, an inspector would have to slither and slide through them on his hands and knees.

Customs had to rely on the cargo manifest declaration he had provided before his arrival in New York, just as he had had to rely on the information given to him by the shipper, in compiling that manifest. Trust, Das Gupta mused, was the essence of the American system.

The unloading process of the Jewel's New York bound containers was completed by late afternoon. Shortly thereafter, a pair of officers of the U.S. Immigration and Naturalization Service came on board. Das Gupta assembled his crew men in the seaman's lounge so the INS officers could go through yet another of the post-9/11 procedures. Each crewman had to present to the officers, his passport with a valid U.S. visa and his seaman's papers. Once they were sure all were in order, they gave each sailor who wanted one, an I 95 form which would allow the sailor to go on shore while the Jewel was in port.

"No passengers?" one of the officers asked Das Gupta.

The Indian master laughed. "My rust bucket isn't the Queen Elizabeth, officer!"

A couple of hours later, three crewmen who had decided to go ashore, passed the immigration controls and boarded the bus for the short journey to the Port of Authority Bus Terminal in midtown Manhattan. The sex shops, the peep shows, the multitude of whores who had once beckoned to arriving visitors, were gone now.

Surveying the scene, the eldest of the three crewmen, Malvinder Singh, sighed to his younger pals. "You should have seen this place ten years ago. That crazy mayor" – he pronounced the name Jooley Yani – "has made visiting New York about as much fun as going to a prayer meeting."

Undaunted, the trio marched on to their destination, a Ruth Chris Steakhouse, to savor a meal the crewmen's mess of the Jewel did not offer.

After the waiter took their order for three rare double sirloin steaks, he asked them what they would like to drink.

"A Seagrams and seven," the elder seaman said.

"Make mine a double," echoed the man beside him who then turned to the last member of their trio. "Your usual ginger ale?" he asked.

"Why not?" he answered. "While they're coming, I've got to make a phone call." He got up and went to the public telephone, slipped in a quarter, took out the scrap of paper on which he'd written the number of a cell phone.

"Allo!" he said to the answering machine which responded "I'm in New York. Everything went fine. We sail on the morning tide, God willing."

For many tourists, it was the best deal New York had to offer – nine bucks for the ultra rapid, eighty-six-story elevator ride to the top of the Empire State Building. The tragic destruction of the Twin Towers of the World Trade Center had, ironically, restored the building to the position of dominance it had enjoyed for seventy years, as the tallest building in New York and, indeed, for many of those years, in the world.

Built in 1931 on Fifth Avenue between 34th and 35th streets by a pair of financiers regarded by their contemporaries as either nuts or visionaries, the 103-story skyscraper had become a potent symbol of American power and, for Americans, of their determination to ride out the vicissitudes of the Great Depression.

Embedded into the popular imagination by the cinematic image of King Kong clinging to its summit while he plucked planes from the sky or, more recently, as a lovers' trysting spot in Sleepless in Seattle, the building was as powerful a tourist attraction as New York possessed. Every day, its 74 elevators whisked 35 to 40 thousand visitors to the Observation Tower on its 86th floor.

Since 9/11, that flow of visitors had been, quite understandably, subjected to rigorous security checks by metal detectors, X-ray scanners and a flock of security guards, most of them recruited from the ranks of retiring New York Police Department officers. From the shopping areas in the buildings and the Art Deco restaurant in the basement to the summit, the building was one of the most secure edifices in the United States.

By eight forty-five on this particular morning, an excited crowd was already waiting for the Observatory's elevators to open at nine o'clock. That was hardly surprising. An electric sign promised this would be a day of "exceptional visibility", a day when, according to the old bromide, visitors, "would be able to see forever", i.e. through a circle 40 miles (60 kilometers) in diameter around the tower platform.

A guide ushered the first elevator load of visitors to the southeastern side of the platform where visits now began with a ritual contemplation of Ground Zero and a poignant moment of silence, in memory of the two murdered towers. Then the tour of the platform began, some visitors following in the wake of the guide describing the spectacle below, others conducting their visits according to their own schedule and inclinations.

Frederico Gonzales, the security officer on duty at the observation platform was fascinated, as always, by the enthusiasm with which his visitors contemplated the spectacle of the great metropolis sprawled below their lofty perch, the streets choked with honking yellow cabs and delivery vans, the towers of the lesser buildings huddled around the Empire State like a cluster of fawning vassals, in the distance, the ferryboats cutting across the water to Brooklyn and Staten Island.

Three of the tourists soon detached themselves from the group, making their way around the platform, pausing to contemplate in silence the splendid vistas spread out below them. From his lifeguard's style chair, Gonzales studied them. Judging from the color of their skin, he decided they were probably fellow Hispanics. Tourists from Central and South America almost always made it a point to visit the building. One of the three was a woman, probably in her early thirties, wearing what looked like designer eye glasses. A school teacher type, the guard thought. The second was much younger, wearing a black leather jacket and blue jeans, probably anxious to pass himself off to the girls as a native New Yorker. The last member of their trio was perhaps in his mid forties, well dressed in a dark suit and tie, with a well-trimmed beard and a dour, almost melancholy expression on his face. They hardly talked to each other, too absorbed, apparently by the spectacular sight below.

Gonzales shifted his gaze for a moment to a more satisfying sight, half a dozen young French girls in mini skirts and tight-fitting blouses making their way around the platform. When his eyes had returned to the trio of tourists he assumed to be Latinos, they had stopped by the guard rail looking out towards New Jersey. Fascinated, he watched as the elder man took a small cellophane packet from his pocket. The poor guy, Gonzales observed, had only one hand, his right. His left was a stump at his wrist. With considerable skill, he twisted the packet open with the fingers of his one hand and scattered what appeared to be dust or ashes over the guard rail. As the morning breeze swept the dust away, the three joined hands, the woman clutching the stump of the older man's left hand.

Ah! Gonzales thought. That was some sort of religious gesture — or perhaps a commemoration of the lost towers with some of the ashes of that horrible day.

Washington D.C.

A Message From the Warriors
of the Jihad

For the White House interns assigned to it, the sprawl-ing communications center in the basement of the Ex-ecutive Office Building was jokingly referred to as 'the Cyberspace Soup Kitchen.' At its heart was a bat-tery of printers hooked up to receive all the email sent to the old White House email address, www.President@WhiteHouse.Gov, as well as the new-er website address, www.Whitehouse.gov/webmail. The President, of course, had other classified email addresses for serious government business but they were known only to his cabinet members and top aides. Their emails came into an entirely different reception center in the White House itself.

The printers in the 'Soup Kitchen' clacked out in normal times, an average of 15,000 emails a day. The variety of those messages to the President defied the imagination. They ran the gamut, from a farmer in Iowa announcing he was sending a piglet to the White House as a gift, to a 'mother in Baton Rouge, Louisiana, stating she had decided to name her newborn son "George" after the President. And, of course, there were the hatred and vitriol-filled communications from the President's enemies, political and otherwise.

Now, with his re-election campaign entering its most intensive phase, the volume of the incoming emails had almost doubled. They provided the White House with a constantly evolving image of the nation's political pulse. The interns assigned to the center were trained to break them down and classify them into categories reflecting sentiment on key campaign issues such as the President's tax reduction plan, the budget deficit, high unemployment rates, health care, the lingering aftermath of the Iraqi war, the war on terrorism. Each email was identified by the state from which it had come so the President's advisors could see how his message was playing out in different parts of the country.

For example, Saturday night, the President had delivered a blistering attack on his opponent's health care proposals as 'socialized medicine in disguise' at the Auburn School of Medicine in Alabama. Predictably, it was getting a positive welcome in the Midwest, and a distinctly negative one in urban areas and the Northeast.

Anne McCormick, a 26-year-old Vassar graduate hoping to find a permanent slot in the government hierarchy, was in charge of the Cyberspace Soup Kitchen this Sunday morning. She and her fellow interns had developed a reputation as meticulous workers, an unintended refutation of the record of other White House interns of an earlier age.

She was filing a stack of emails on the Auburn speech when one of her fellow interns rushed up to her.

"Hey Anne!" she said, thrusting an email at her. "I think you better have a look at what just came in on printer four!"

"Oh Dear Lord!" Anne exclaimed, reading it. Crackpot messages were part of the daily routine in the Soup Kitchen, but this one looked serious. "We'd better get the Secret Service duty officer at the West Gate up here right away."

He was there minutes later, a fifty-ish man, slightly overweight, gasping for breath after his sprint from the gate.

"This just arrived in the President's email," Anne said, handing him the text. "Who knows? This one may be serious."

"To the servant of the Great Satan, George W. Bush," it began. "Allah, the Lord of the World says that if anyone tries to destroy our villages and cities, then we may destroy their villages and cities. You have trampled on the cities and villages of our brothers in

Iraq. With your Israeli allies, you trample daily on the villages and cities stolen from our brothers in Palestine in 1967. Therefore, we have decided to place in your great city of New York, the most terrible of weapons, an atomic bomb. We will explode it in exactly five days at noon, New York time, if you have not by then, forced your Israeli vassals to pledge before the whole world that they will abandon every square meter of those settlements they have built on the land stolen from our Palestinian brothers and sisters. Those settlements are a crime that must be erased, and those like you and your countrymen who supported that crime will pay dearly for it if it is not rectified. Furthermore, should you attempt to save your citizens by ordering the evacuation of New York, we will detonate the bomb instantly. Since you in your utter conceit will not believe us capable of this, we have left proof of what this letter threatens, in a brown suitcase in the baggage-checking facility of Pennsylvania Station in New York, under baggage check 102475/04."

It was signed "Warriors of the Jihad" and the email address from which it had come was noted as tombald@aol.com, except aol was noted as "Australia on Line."

Looking up from the text, Bill Malley, the Secret Service officer could read a hint of panic on the young faces around him.

"Listen," he said "this is almost certainly another example of the fake extortion messages we're always getting around here. Islamic whackos in Australia?" He shook his head in disbelief. "Still, not a word about this to anyone while I deal with it, OK?"

Since the missed hints and warnings of 9/11, a whole new series of protocols and procedures had been put in place to deal with national emergencies and terrorist threats, and government employees, at whatever level, ignored them at their peril. However much this email might look like a hoax, Malley knew his duty was to convey it immediately to the Permanent Counter Terrorism Control Center at CIA headquarters at Langley, Virginia.

Rather then use his cellular phone, he dashed to the secure phone in his West Wing office.

Malley glanced at the Threat Board on his office wall. It was blessedly bare. Damn, he thought, picking up his phone, that may be about to change.

The duty officer manning the desk at the Counter Terrorism Control Center at Langley this Sunday morning was a 32-year-old with ten years of agency experience, including a four-year tour of duty in Djkarta, Indonesia. Bill Bernhart would have preferred to be spending his Sunday morning playing tennis at his club at the Washington Hilton, but listening to the text Malley was already faxing him, his vision changed. Maybe this was the big one all young officers hope they will be called on to handle. The response drill for a situation such as this had been hammered into him countless times. Even before the full fax had arrived, he had punched 'Warriors of the Jihad' into his agency's terrorists data base to see if the CIA had anything on them. It did not.

He then called the duty desk man at the NSA, the National Security Agency, and relayed to him the full text of the email with all the technical information it contained, so that they could find out to whom and where in Australia the online email address was registered. Next, he alerted the agency station in Melbourne to be ready to get some one on to the owner of that email address as soon as the NSA had located it.

Then he turned his thoughts to that package in New York. The FBI was the lead domestic agency in emergencies of this sort, so he got on to the duty officer at FBI Headquarters in the Hoover Building on Pennsylvania Avenue, with a request to send a team to Penn Station.

Finally, he alerted the Emergency Response Center at the Department of Energy on Constitution Avenue. If it turned out that there was anything nuclear really involved in all this, they, under the overall direction of the Department of Homeland Security, would be responsible for dealing with it.

Even before he had completed that call, an FBI car bearing a pair of agents was racing out of FBI Headquarters in Lower Manhattan and heading uptown to Penn Station. The stunned Haitian clerk manning the station's baggage-checking facility was terrified at the sight of the agents with their gold badges and Red, White and Blue ID cards. Immigration, he thought in horror. When he learned of their real mission, he was so relieved he could have kissed them, as he led them to the suitcase belonging to tag 102745/04. As he started to reach for the suitcase, one of the agents stopped him.

"Don't touch it!" he said pulling on a pair of gloves. "We'll want to run a fingerprint check on it."

"No problem man," the attendant acknowledged "and don't you worry. No explosives be in there. We's got a police dog in here every night, sniffing them bags for bombs and such like."

The second agent was already on the phone to the Department of Energy's Emergency Response Team in Washington to report to the scientists there on what they were finding. On the strength of the baggage attendant's declaration about police dogs, the agents were authorized to take down the suitcase and open it. The FBI men were baffled by what they found inside.

"Looks like some kind of a plan or a design," the lead agent reported back to Washington. "Some computer discs. And oh, yeah. There's a chunk of metal in there, too, kind of glinty, about the size of boxer's fist. There's a note on it. It says 'this is a sample of the HEU employed in our device.' What the hell's HEU?"

"Highly enriched uranium," the desk officer in Washington replied. "Pick it up and describe it to me."

"Christ!" the FBI man said "it's a heavy fucker. Kind a dull-grayish black metal."

The two men at the Department of Energy listening

to the call looked at each other. "What do you think? Could it really be HEU?" the first said.

"Well, we can't take any chances," his superior agreed. "Listen!" he said to the lead FBI agent. "What I want you to do is get that suitcase and everything that's in it out to the Marine Air Terminal at LaGuardia as fast as you can. We're going to order up a jet from McGuire Air Force Base in Jersey to fly it out to our Lab in Livermore, California, tooty sweety as the French say."

"Damn!" the first officer observed, once they'd hung up. "This could be the big one we've all been afraid was going to come crashing down on us one of these days."

"It does," his boss agreed "but I don't think we push the panic button — at least, not yet. Let's wait until Livermore has done a preliminary read on that design and the rock." He glanced at his watch. It was almost nine o'clock. "They'll have that chunk of whatever the hell was in that suitcase under a gamma-ray spectrometer by five o'clock our time, this afternoon. That will tell us if it's HEU or not. I think we have to assume the worst, so we'd better set up a meeting of the Emergency Response Team here for five o'clock. I'll pulse all our sources to see if anyone has any reports of HEU missing anywhere in world. And I'll give Andrew Card, Bush's Chief of Staff, a heads up right now."

"How about New York? The Mayor, the Governor?"

"That will have to be the President's call. Knowing

him, he won't want to jump the gun. He'll want to wait until we have a solid assessment of just how serious this thing really is. Now get cracking. Alert the Agency, the Bureau and the NSA to what we're doing."

By five minutes to five, everything was ready in Room B26, headquarters of the Department of Energy's Emergency Response Team. Closed-circuit TV conference links had been established with the national laboratories at Livermore, Los Alamos and Sandia in New Mexico and Brookhaven out on Long Island, the CIA and the FBI, and the Chief of Staff at the White House. Two senior nuclear physicists attached to the team had been summoned into headquarters from their Sunday pursuits, as had David Graham, the head of the NEST, Nuclear Explosives Search Team. Paul Anscom, the Homeland Security Ministry official in charge of the team, was in the chair. He was in his early fifties, a man with a PhD in Physics from Carnegie Tech. He could have been making four times his government salary in the private sector but he had spent his career in Energy and Defense, mesmerized by the adrenalin shot that inevitably came from life at the center of power.

"O.K. people!" he announced, to kick off their conference, "while we're waiting for Livermore's preliminary analysis on that rock, I'd like to ask our CIA guy if you folks have got anything on these so-called Warriors of the Jihad?"

"Negative!" came the answer. "We ran that name through all our data banks and came up empty. But I don't think you should read anything into that. These Islamic extremists have a habit of making up names to cover an operation and keep us off balance. Like the guys who did the UN in Baghdad. Those so-called Armed Vanguards of Mohammed's Second Army. Or the Hezbollah, when they took out those Jewish institutions down in Buenos Aires a decade ago, using names no one had ever heard of before. Or has heard of since."

"Would that point a finger at Hezbollah?" Anscom asked.

"It could. Or it could just mean that Al Qaeda, for example, has taken a leaf from their book."

"Gentlemen!" It was the director of the Livermore National Laboratory. A man in shirtsleeves had just moved in beside the director on Livermore's TV monitor. "Dr Paul Mott's here with his preliminary report."

"That rock is indeed highly enriched uranium," the newcomer said. "My preliminary spectrographic analysis gave a reading of an enrichment to at least 90%, but I'm convinced that in the lab that figure will move up to a purity level of 92-93%."

"In other words," Anscom said "weapons-grade material."

"No doubt about that. If those people — whoever the hell they are — have 23 kilograms of the stuff, they can have a bomb alright."

"And those plans that came with it. Have your people had a chance to study them yet?" Anscom asked.

"Yes," Mott said. He had a rather full beard, its blonde hairs liberally streaked with gray, and rimless glasses. "It looks to us like a very valid working design. In other words, if a bomb has been made from that design, it will explode".

"Just a moment!" a voice interrupted. It was Andrew Card, the Chief of Staff, speaking from the White House. "It seems to me this has become a most serious development. It's probably time to inform the President, and knowing him, once he's been made aware of the situation, he will want to be involved in these discussions."

"Where is the President?" Anscom asked.

"He returned from Alabama half and hour ago. He's up in the living quarters watching a baseball game."

"Alright," Anscom agreed, "let's suspend our session for half an hour."

"Right," said the Chief of Staff "and when we resume, I'd like to transfer our meeting over here to the White House Situation Room as, in all probability, the President will want to join us."

The President, one hand clutching a mobile phone, linking him to his father in Kennebunk Port, Maine, the other holding his television remote control, was staring, mesmerized, at his TV screen when the door to his study opened.

"Excuse me for the interruption, Sir," said his Chief of Staff "but this is important."

"Important?" the President laughed "What could be more important then the Astros having the bases loaded and a three and two pitch coming up?"

"This," said the Chief of Staff, handing him the terrorists' threat note and Livermore's preliminary analysis of the materials found in the Penn Station left luggage locker.

"Damn hell!" the President gasped, reading it.

"Dad!" he said into his mobile "either our ultimate nightmare may be coming true, or we have the mother of all hoaxes on our hands. Listen to this."

Slowly, he read the text to his father. There was a moment of silence while the elder Bush digested its contents. "Well," he said trying to comfort his son "it could be, as you suggest, the ultimate extortion threat. Play it very tight until you have the absolute proof that there really is a nuclear device hidden in New York. I'm here any time you need me."

The President could not have heard more comforting words from anyone. His regular conversations with his father provided him a constant stream of sound advice and political and global insights, something he himself frequently lacked. While very little of the contents of their chats ever leaked to the public, they constituted a critically important backdrop to his presidency.

"Mr President," his Chief of Staff interrupted "I've convened a Principals Committee meeting in the

Situation Room. The same people we had for the Iraq and Afghan wars, plus our nuclear experts from Energy and Homeland Security. It's scheduled to start in twenty minutes."

"Good thinking," the President said, hanging up his phone and switching off his TV set. "That will give me a few moments to wrestle with this."

There was no one in whom the President had more confidence than his Chief of Staff, Andrew Card. He was a man he knew could be counted on to inevitably do the right thing, do it fast, and do it with a minimum of fuss. In short, the perfect Chief of Staff.

As the door closed behind his departing aide, the President leaned back in his chair and closed his eyes. "Dear Lord," he murmured "let this chalice pass from my lips. May this, I pray, turn out to be a hoax."

His instinctive turn to prayer reflected a deep and meaningful side of the President. Since the day almost two decades earlier when, on the urging of his wife Laura, he had given up the alcohol that had been his constant companion and major weakness since his days as an undergraduate at Yale's Deke — Delta Kappa Epsilon — fraternity house, his religious beliefs had become a regular source of strength and comfort. To his cynical critics, it was "Goodbye Jack Daniels, hello Jesus!" But in the President's case, his was a very genuine conversion. "I wouldn't be President today," he frequently told close friends "if I had not stopped drinking, and I could do that only with the grace of God."

And if this bizarre message the White House had just received turned out to be something besides a sick joke, he was going to need a full ration of spiritual strength and comfort in the days and hours to come. The first nine months of his presidency had been notable for their banality. Indeed, to many of his fellow Americans, he had been elected by the votes of the Justices of the Supreme Court and not by those of the American people. His foreign policy in those months had consisted mainly of a visit to Mexico, and his studied indifference of the problems of the Middle East and the Palestine leader, Yassir Arafat. To a stumbling economy, all he had had to offer was a tax cut that was going to favor the nation's wealthy.

Then, just as Pearl Harbor had defined the final term of FDR's time in office, so the assaults of 9/11 had placed an indelible stamp on his first term. He had become, in spite of himself, a wartime President, presiding over his self-proclaimed War on Terror. He, whose own military career had been anything but noteworthy, had led the nation into two wars, the first against the Taliban in Afghanistan, the second against Saddam Hussein in Iraq. It could not truly be said that either conflict was completely over yet. The most critical conflict of all, his War on Terror, was clearly anything but won.

He stood up, stretched and paced with deliberate strides towards the door. If this turned out to be a real threat, one thing was certain: the decisive crisis of his presidency was upon him.

Even in the darkest days of the Afghan and Iraqi wars this President, inevitably, opened crisis committee meetings with a smile, a word of encouragement to his subordinates, or even, on occasion, a quip inspired by the morning's headlines.

Not today. Shoulders slumped, face drawn into a taut mask, he marched to his seat at the head of the White House's Situation Room conference table, without so much as a glance at his associates waiting for him, for the most part, men and women who had been at his side in those dark hours.

For a site steeped in so much history, the Situation Room in the west wing of the White House was a remarkably banal-appearing place. It looked to many who had worked there, like the board room of a middle-sized mid-western bank. Yet, it was here that John F. Kennedy had pondered the perils of a nuclear Armageddon during the Cuban missile crisis, Lyndon Johnson had issued the orders that had sent thousands of Americans to die in Vietnam, Jimmy Carter had agonized over the failed U.S. mission to rescue Ayatollah Khomeini's American hostages, and the President himself had given the order to attack Iraq eighteen months earlier. In fact, the wood paneling surrounding the room concealed the most sophisticated, state-of-the-art communications equipment imaginable.

His first gesture as he took his seat was to bow his

head in silent prayer, a particularly heartfelt gesture this autumn Sunday. His colleagues around the table, well aware that this was how these meetings invariably began, did likewise.

"So," he announced to open their meeting "the vision that has haunted me since I took office may be upon us – weapons of mass destruction in the hands of a gang of terrorists. Anscom!" he demanded, waving a copy of the report his Chief of Staff had handed him in his study "any new developments we should know about before we start?"

The director of the Department of Energy's Emergency Response team had half walked, half run to the White House from the Department of Energy Headquarters. Paul Anscom, veteran of so many years of bureaucratic existence, was convinced physical fitness was the key to effectiveness in U.S. government service. Now, he had the rumpled appearance of a man who'd left for an important meeting without first benefiting from an inspection by his wife.

"Yes Sir," he said "our nuclear physicists have just concluded that the design we found at Penn Station is the design for an implosion bomb employing highly enriched uranium – perhaps a copy of the design that the U.N. weapons inspectors uncovered in Iraq in 1995."

"How do they know that?" the President asked.

"Two giveaways. Whoever designed this bomb – and we must admit they did a first class job – knew they probably wouldn't be able to test their design, so they employed in it more core fissile material, 23 kilos, instead of the 20 you would normally use. It was a kind of insurance that it would work. Second, the plan contains computer codes detailing how they could produce perfectly symmetrical explosions at each of their detonation points. The codes used in this design match very closely those in the Pakistan bomb developed by Abdul Khader Khan and his team, which were peddled in that Islamic nuclear market to Iran and Libya and probably, North Korea, in return for missile technology."

"Could these so-called Warriors of the Jihad be Iraqis then?"

"Mr. President!" It was Milt Anderson, the Arabic specialist head of the CIA he'd appointed to replace George Tenet. "I wouldn't jump to that conclusion. The Islamic world is crawling with extremists who hate you, hate this nation and everything it stands for."

Few people in the room knew the Arab world better than Anderson. Brought up in Lebanon, the son of a professor at the American University of Beirut, he'd learned Arabic on his nanny's knees. As an agency operations officer, he'd served in Sudan, Iraq, Bahrain. His clandestine work had been so admired by Bill Casey that he was made the agency's director of operations in the war against the Russians in Afghanistan. "We've got a whole world of potential terrorists out there to choose from."

"Damnit!" barked an angry President "I swore on the Fourth of July a year ago, I would attack any terrorist group that threatens the United States with mass murder. How can I attack these people when I don't even know who the hell they are? How about Osama Bin Laden? Could he have been behind this?"

"That has to be a real possibility, Mr. President," Anderson replied, raising the massive shoulders he'd employed playing middle line backer for the University of Oklahoma. "I find the text in that threat note very similar in tone to some of his writings. For him, Islamic nukes are the one decisive way to reverse the balance of power between Islam and the West. The Germans arrested his top lieutenant Mamdouh Mahmoud Salim in Munich in September 1998, with a suitcase full of dollars, on his way to trying to buy highly enriched uranium from the Ukraine. We have good evidence that he was ready to give the Chechens 30 million dollars to buy up the ingredients of a couple of dirty bombs."

Anderson glanced down at the top-secret notebook he brought to meetings like this. "Most worrying, we know he and his close personal friend, Abdul Sharif Ahmad, another of the fathers of the Pakistani bomb. They had at least two secret meetings with Osama in Kandahar before the Afghan War. Unfortunately, nothing ever leaked out about what went on in those meetings, but you can be sure they weren't talking about Sex in the City."

The President sighed and looked down the table to the youngest man in the room, an officer of the NSA, the National Security Agency, the organization responsible for intercepting and decoding the millions of messages flashing everyday through the boundless seas of cyberspace. "Have your people been able to pin down exactly who was behind that email address out in Australia?"

"Yes," the young man replied. "The agency got an officer out to the owner of the computer, a 13-year-old boy. In Adelaide."

"A thirteen-year-old kid!" the President exclaimed, a wide smile suddenly breaking over his face. "So this a hoax, after all!"

"I'm afraid that's not the case at all," the young man replied. He was frail, shoulders hunched, thick rimless glasses on his face, the kind of guy his pals had once dubbed a "nerd" at Cal Tech. For his post graduate work, he had become a computer hacker until his skills had brought him to the attention of law enforcement and the government had convinced him to put his talents to more legitimate ends.

"The boy was the victim of a cyberspace ploy. The real author of that message employed a whole chain of relays to disguise its origin. It's a technique known to computer hackers and well-informed terrorists and criminals who have studied ways of manipulating the Internet. They break into that kid's computer, send their message to the White House, then wipe out the memory of his hard disc so there's no trace of the message or where it came from."

"Fortunately, Australia on Line was able to find the call that came into his computer just before it crashed.

We traced it back to a schoolteacher in Dorset, England, who'd been the victim of the same manipulation as our 13-year-old in Adelaide. With the help of AOL, and Wanadoo in France, we were able to work our way back through computers in France, Poland and Germany and eventually, to an internet café in Sanaa, the capital of Yemen. The trail ended there. One of our people just visited the café. Given the time difference, it's past midnight out there. The owner says he has no idea who was using his computers at the time we estimate the original message was sent."

Listening to all this, the President was aghast. Like most men of his age, he had no idea of the complexities represented by the cyberspace age.

"So what you're telling me is we're never going to find out who the hell sent us this message?"

"I'm afraid, Sir, that's a very real possibility," the young computer whiz answered.

"One thing seems clear to me," Milt Anderson of the CIA observed. "The fact these guys went to such lengths to disguise the origins of their message indicates that whoever they are, they are motivated by a high degree of seriousness."

"Exactly the degree of seriousness I expect from you at the agency, and everyone else in this room, in finding out exactly who the people behind this threat are," the President declared in what was uncharacteristically close to an angry snarl. "You all know how faithfully I start every day by reading your President's Daily

Briefing Paper and Threat Matrix Report. Was there even a hint in there — anytime in the past week — that something like this was coming? Hell, no!"

"I have to admit you're right, Sir," Anderson acknowledged. "If this threat is for real we have got to recognize that the people behind it have, until now, played their hand like real pros."

Those words provided scant comfort for the President. Here he was, presiding over the most powerful nation in the world, the globe's only remaining superpower, a nation whose empire surpassed in a sense those of Rome and Babylon, Britain, France and Turkey combined. He had at his disposal, military power that made the power of all history's Caesars, Gengis Khans, Kings and Kaisers shrivel in comparison. Yet, what good was it if he had no foe against whom to employ it?

Terrorism, as he had noted so often, was the tool of choice of those who would attack his nation. It was their way of leveling the playing field. And, by hiding behind a cloak of anonymity as they seem to be doing here, if this is a real threat, they turn us into a helpless giant by rendering all our deterrent power useless.

The President was a man who, since his "conversion", led a remarkably disciplined life, no booze, an hour of solid exercise every day, in bed at 10:00 with his wife – no precocious interns in his administration. Yet, in times of crisis, he was a gut player, a man who relied on his instinctive reactions. Those reactions, some of his aides noted, were in a way his second religion, and something in his innermost self was whispering to him now that maybe, just maybe, this one was for real.

"So, Gentlemen and," he bowed towards his National Security Advisor "Madame, four questions. One, if this threat is genuine and not some kind of sick joke, what are the chances these terrorists, whoever the hell they are, succeeded in getting their hands on the highly enriched uranium they needed to make the bomb on this plan of theirs?

"Two, if they did, could they have smuggled it undetected into this country?

"Three, while we are trying to determine if this is a real threat or simply an extortion threat, what do we do about New York? Who do we inform up there – Mayor Bloomberg? Governor Pataki? The police? Senator Schumer? Hillary Clinton, God forbid? And four, if such a device really exists and is in New York, what kind of destruction would its detonation cause?

"You all know I believe in results, so let's attack these questions. I want answers, not speeches. Anscom, the first one's yours."

The head of the Department of Energy's Emergency Response Team sat up a little bit straighter, as bureaucrats tend to do when they address the President.

"For the past four years, Mr. President, our efforts here in this room have been focused on nuclear proliferation, preventing Axis of Evil nations like Iraq, Iran and North Korea from becoming nuclear powers. To be a nuclear power, you need not one, but at least a dozen bombs and most important, your own source of fissile material. However, to be nuclear terrorists, as these people claim to be, all you need is one bomb and someone else's fissile material."

"So," pressed an impatient President "where do they get it?"

"The first place to look is Russia and the Ukraine. We've pulsed our sources in both countries despite the time difference. Gram quantities of weapons-grade material have gone missing over the years. There have been seven cases we are aware of — attempts to smuggle material out, but always in quantities far below what would be needed for a bomb. As of last night, our contacts have no reports of a significant amount of bomb-grade material missing."

"Can we be sure of that?" the President demanded.

"No we can't," Anscom admitted. "Their nuclear watchdog agency admits that their security programs are under-funded, their security is weak and the danger of theft or terrorism is strong. You may remember, sir, Homeland Security requested $38 billion in 2003 for our cooperative US-Russia threat reduction program but we only appropriated $1 billion. We've been pushing Putin to buy into the Nunn Rudman Nuclear Threat Initiative and there has been some improvement in the situation. Just before the Chechens seized that theater in Moscow in October 2002, for example, they tried to hit an old Soviet nuclear site but the Russians shut them down completely. Frankly, Sir, nobody really knows how good our information on the Russian situation is, but our feeling is that this would be a tough nut for a bunch of Islamic extremists to crack."

Anscom paused, knowing how unwelcome his next words were going to be. "There are unfortunately sites in this country which are still not properly safeguarded and are vulnerable to insider-assisted theft. There are tons of HEU, practically unguarded, stored in 50-year-old buildings in Oak Ridge Tennessee."

"What!" the President exploded. "Why the hell aren't those sites secure?"

"The same old story, Sir," Anscom answered. "As always, this administration and our congressional allies have been long on rhetoric and short on cash to back up our words."

A grim-faced President let Anscom's remark pass. "China?" he asked.

"Our and the CIA's penetration of their nuclear program is very limited but their secrecy is so tight that it, in itself, would mitigate against their being the source. And besides, they have an ongoing struggle with their own Islamic separatists."

"North Korea?"

"Their program employs primarily plutonium, not highly enriched uranium."

"India?"

"Fundamentally the same situation."

"Pakistan?"

"That has to be a real concern, in spite of the good relations you have enjoyed with General Musharref since 9/11. You heard what Milt Anderson said about the scientists who are behind their bomb. Their Chief of Staff General Mohammed Aziz Khan is on record as saying that 'America is the Number One enemy of the Muslim world.' Some of their military and scientific leadership like to refer to their weapon as an Islamic bomb, not a Pakistani bomb, suggesting by implication that it could be employed in conflicts beyond those between India and Pakistan."

"So," a frustrated President said "the bottom line is we haven't got a clue where this damn bomb – if it really exists – came from."

"Not yet, Mr. President, but with a little luck we may get an answer before too long."

"How's that?"

"Our scientists out at Livermore are employing, right now, a series of nuclear forensic techniques on that chunk of highly enriched uranium that was left at Penn Station. There are very few large-scale uranium enrichment facilities in the world. By studying the radioactive signatures in that rock, the characteristic balance of the isotopes it contains, our people ought to be able to come up with a good idea of how and where it was created."

"How long is that going to take?"

"Hopefully, not too long."

"OK," the President acknowledged, the grimace that had clouded his face since the meeting began easing ever so slightly. "Now, if this bomb really exists, could these so-called Warriors of the Jihad have somehow managed to get it into New York?"

The Deputy Commissioner of Customs took the question. Larry Schorr was thin, frail almost, but a bushy mustache drew attention away from his physique to a round, florid face. Barely a pair of Italian designer sunglasses, a Japanese car, a French camembert cheese or a bible printed in Bangladesh, entered the nation without passing the formalities, however vague, of his service. Since 9/11 and the creation of the Homeland Security Department, Customs had become an integral part of emergency response planning.

"Mr. President," he declared "as I am sure you know, preventing the smuggling of nuclear weapons or radiological materials into this country is the highest priority of U.S. Customs. We now require a detailed cargo manifest from all ships calling on U.S. ports, 96 hours in advance of their arrival. In addition, under the program developed by Commissioner Bonner, we now have U.S. Customs officers stationed in 30 foreign seaports to work with local authorities, checking the contents of U.S. destined freighters as they are loaded."

"Oh horse shit!"

The outburst shocked the room. It came from Andy Mears, the director of the White House Office of Counter Terrorism, a thirty-year veteran of service on the National Security Council, who had been transferred to the White House at the beginning of the administration at the President's request. Theirs, however, had not been a happy marriage. Mears, a registered Democrat, liked to joke that he was the "in house liberal" but the disillusionment with the administration's policies and rhetoric that had swept over him in the last three years was no laughing matter.

"The amount of container cargo coming into this country unchecked is simply staggering. We inspect every suitcase arriving at JFK and Newark airports, but we let thousands of containers into Port Elizabeth without so much as a glance. Customs is going to try to tell you that they check two percent of those containers. The real figure is closer to 0.5 percent."

"Is Mears right?" an angry President asked.

"Mr. President," the embarrassed deputy commissioner of Customs answered "Manufacturers and merchants in this country, from General Motors to Walmart, are completely reliant on goods shipped in from abroad. If we try to pick apart every one of the 21,000 containers hitting our ports every day, we will create economic chaos. GM will have to shut down production lines. Walmart stops — and they are our largest employers, over one million people."

"But how about all this new technology we're supposed to be developing to detect nuclear devices?" the President asked.

"Mr. President." Mears just wasn't going to let go. This was a subject he'd labored on for weeks — and with few positive results. "A well-shielded nuclear device is going to slip right by even the most sophisticated screeners we have in place today. Make no mistake about that."

"I asked about the new stuff we're supposed to be developing."

Mears was well aware he was digging his political grave with his words but he pressed ahead anyway. "Nothing's being done. We spend eight billion dollars a year on a strategic defense system designed to protect us against missiles that may not even exist, and less than 600 million on port security. In this so-called War on Terrorism, our deeds have never come close to matching our words. We've just been feeding the people a bunch of Pablum when we tell them how much we're doing to protect them from the dangers of terrorism."

Anscom saw the President's face reddening in anger. He rarely lost his temper but when he did, his outbursts were legendary, and Mr. Mears was going to be looking for another job soon. Better step in and defuse things if it's not already too late, he thought.

"In fairness to our friends at Customs," he said "we've had tremendous problems coming up with detectors that can localize the emissions we really want to register. The radioactive emissions given off by highly enriched uranium are thin and weak. Homeland Security has been equipping our Customs officers with little, hand-held portable detectors. But what are the chances they could walk alongside a truck or a container and pick up an emission from a bomb inside? Practically zero."

As he was speaking, the Marine Corps major administering the room's communications facilities had raised his hand for attention, a bit like a student in a classroom, anxious to answer a question or ask for permission to go the loo.

"Gentlemen!" he announced "Livermore has re quested an immediate TV feed." A large TV screen came down from the ceiling. Within seconds, the two men who had appeared earlier on the Department of Energy's screen, the lab's director and his bearded aide, Dr. Paul Mott, confronted the White House conference.

"Dr. Mott has completed his analysis of that chunk of highly enriched uranium the FBI recovered at Penn Station" the director announced. "Paul, over to you."

"Our isotopic analysis revealed that the piece of HEU in question was enriched by a technique developed by the URENCO enrichment facility in Anselm, Holland, in the mid seventies." Mott revealed.

"Holland!" mumbled an incredulous President.

Mott who had, of course, heard his comment, addressed it directly. "Sir, at least two of the senior scientists who developed the Pakistani bomb worked at Anselm. It is widely believed that they took back to Pakistan a whole series of working blueprints for an enrichment plant when they returned in 1976. In any event, the limited studies we have been able to conduct on Pakistani enriched uranium, all indicate that they employed enrichment techniques similar to those used here. It is our conclusion, therefore, that this particular piece of enriched uranium came from the Pakistani stock-pile."

Paul Anscom intervened at his words. "Mr. President, this is a most troubling development but we mustn't allow it to rush us to premature conclusions. What exactly do we know? That these terrorists have gotten their hands on a scientifically viable design. And that they may — or may not — have had access to a source of highly enriched uranium to employ in that design. But, to marry up the two would require a level of scientific skill and sophistication, I somehow don't see these people possessing."

"Well, I'm a lot less sanguine," Milt Anderson, the CIA chief interjected. "For me, this report opens up a whole new concern. Suppose these terrorists had accomplices inside the Pakistani military and they helped them smuggle a bomb or two out of their stockpile?"

"Just how likely is that?" the President asked.

"Very damn likely, I'm afraid," Anderson answered. "I know a lot of those guys from my service with them in Afghanistan. Some of them hate our guts and are convinced we are Islam's real enemies. We estimate, Pakistan now has between 35 and 50 bombs. For security reasons, they keep the fissile cores of their bombs and their detonation devices in different sites — the bombs in Kahuta, south of Rawalapindi, and the detonators in Chasma, near Islamabad. We know very little about those sites and just how secure they really are. The Paks are paranoid about letting foreigners near them. But we have every reason to believe some of the extremists in their military are among those assigned to protect their bombs. Some of them also aided Abdul Khader Khan when he was peddling nuclear technology to Iran, Libya and God knows who else. What guarantee do we have that they wouldn't be involved in something like this? None at all."

The President glanced at his watch. "I reckon it's almost seven in the morning out in Islamabad. Musharref's an old soldier, an early riser. I'm going to put in a call to him right now. If anybody can help us in this dreadful dilemma, it's him. Thank God, he's there. Then let's adjourn for dinner and reconvene here in exactly one hour."

The President took a handful of his top aides up to the living quarters to join him for dinner. The others drifted off to a considerably less elegant meal at the White House mess. Anscom slipped into a seat by himself. As he finished his macaroni and cheese, he quietly drew his wallet out of his hip pocket. He slipped a photograph from it, contemplated it almost reverently, then bent to kiss it. It was the photo of his 19-year-old daughter, a junior at Hunter College in New York.

As the President had requested, the crisis meeting reconvened at nine p.m. sharp. "President Mushareff was most distressed and promised us his full cooperation," the President announced to open the meeting. "They are undertaking an immediate physical survey of their nuclear stockpile, bomb by bomb. Now, for the moment, let us turn our attention to New York."

"Mr. President," Anscom said "we have placed all 1000 members of our NEST, Nuclear Explosives Search Teams, on alert and have ordered an advance party to link up with the FBI in New York. In view of what was said in the threat note, we are, for the moment, setting this up as a drill."

"Good work!" the chief executive said, ready to follow up on that, when the Marine Corps major in charge of communications glided up to his elbow.

"Sir," he said "President Mushareff is on the phone in the Oval Office."

The President excused himself and left to take the call. He was back in three minutes, his face ashen, his voice hoarse with tension.

"President Mushareff has just informed me that an atomic bomb is missing from the Pakistan stockpile."

"Oh my God!" exclaimed his attractive female National Security Advisor. "Then this threat is for real!"

A horrified silence embraced the Situation Room. For the first time, its occupants found themselves forced to face the full horror, the catastrophic dimensions of a nightmare that had suddenly become a reality. Appropriately, it was the President who broke the silence, his voice now thin and drawn.

"Clearly," he said "this is as grave a crisis as any this

nation has ever faced. I suggest, we all pause a moment to ask for Supreme Guidance as we deal with it." He bowed his head, then turned to Anscom. "Paul," he asked "if these so-called Warriors of the Jihad have managed to get this bomb of theirs into New York, what will be the consequences if they detonate it?"

"Almost unimaginable carnage, Mr. President," Anscom answered. "We've been studying that question since the threat came in. Our estimate, based on the terrorists' design, is that it would produce an explosive yield of between ten and twelve kilotons, close to Hiroshima and Nagasaki."

With a gesture of his head, he beckoned to a pair of men sitting in chairs, their backs to the Situation Room wall. "Mr. President, I have asked two of our experts to address the matter for you."

One of the two men took a seat beside Anscom, placing a small blue pocket computer on the desk before him. The other set an enormous six-foot square map of New York on a stand at the head of the conference table. The pair, Jerry MacPherson and Tom Fraser had spent the better part of their professional lives studying the horrendous effects nuclear and thermonuclear bombs might have on America's cities. For them, the horrifying statistics of the unimaginable were as familiar as temperature changes are to a weatherman.

MacPherson turned on his pocket computer. Everything he might need, to answer any of the questions soon to be fired at him, was stored in it: the pressure per square inch that would break a window, burst a blood vessel, twist an iron bar out of shape; the degree of surface burns a ten kiloton bomb would cause on a human being five miles from Ground Zero; the kind and intensity of radiation that would be found 30 miles away.

"We have been asked to describe the effect of the detonation of a ten to twelve kiloton device on Manhattan Island. The situation there is, unfortunately unique," he began employing the tone of an archaeologist getting ready to describe the vestiges of a lost civilization. "There is absolutely no doubt – they would be devastating. We have assumed the bomb has been hidden somewhere in mid Manhattan." He gestured to the map on its stand and his assistant standing beside it with a pointer. "The primary effect of the explosion would be total devastation within the area of a circle, approximately two kilometers in diameter."

His aide indicated the innermost of four red circles traced on the map having Times Square as their center. "Inside that circle, the blast overpressures would run from 15 to 5 pounds per square inch. Virtually everything would come down. The heat from the blast would ignite paper and other combustible material inside the circle and there would be the real possibility it would set off a firestorm like those that gutted Hamburg, Dresden and Tokyo in World War Two."

"Staggering!" murmured the Secretary of State who had, after all, spent most of his professional military career studying such scenarios. Few images were more familiar to Colin Powell than the skyline of New York, over which he flew regularly in his helicopter, enroute to meetings at the United Nations. To think that those sparkling ramparts of glass and steel from Wall Street to the Empire State building could disappear in a second! And, as he well knew, such an image was not the demented product of some bureaucrat's brain.

"Casualties?" the President asked.

"The average residential population of Manhattan is about 50,000 people per square kilometer, but in the daytime, with incoming workers and tourists, that figure jumps by a factor of almost ten — so we would be looking at close to a million casualties just from the explosion itself."

"A million!" gasped Condoleezza Rice, the National Security Advisor, her voice almost a sob. The uncle and aunt who had brought her up after her parents' death were, this very morning, attending a congress of United Baptist missionaries in Greenwich Village, well inside the red tracings of the first circle.

"And we estimate, probably another 200-250,000 casualties outside the blast area from radiation. There won't be an empty hospital bed within a hundred miles of the city. New York, from the Battery to 50th Street, the Hudson to the East River, would become a pile of ash and rubble. Our nation's financial center will have ceased to exist. The damage will be in trillions of dollars. This nation and our way of life will have been changed forever."

The nuclear expert's words struck the men and women in the Situation Room with what might be described as the force of a verbal nuclear explosion. The President's shoulders sagged and he slumped in his chair, almost as if he had been struck with a physical blow. Tom Ridge, the director of Homeland Security, on whose department the heaviest burden was certain to fall in the hours and days ahead, kept shaking his head in stunned disbelief.

Not surprisingly, it was Andrew Card, the President's Chief of Staff, who forced the gathering out of its horrified stupor and compelled its participants to face the decisions that now had to be made.

"Mr. President," he said "I think you've got to do what John F Kennedy did when the Cuban missile crisis broke. He was campaigning in Chicago and feigned a sore throat in order to get back here to take charge of our response. I think we'd better have Dr. Shaugnessy give you some kind of intestinal disorder so we can cancel all your public appearances, to give you an excuse to isolate yourself here in the White House for the next week so that you can manage this crisis 24 hours a day.

"Right," the President agreed "set it up with Shaugnessy. No need to lie," he continued, regaining a trace of his sense of humor, "this damn business is making me sick anyway."

"Next question," Card continued "what do we about Governor Pataki, Mayor Bloomberg? And New York itself, in view of that threat of detonating that bomb if we start an evacuation?"

"Get Pataki and Bloomberg on the phone right away and tell them I've got see them down here tomorrow. Say, it's Top Secret. National Security. They'll go along with that" the President ordered.

"How about Senator Schumer? Hillary Clinton?"

"Chuck Schumer's a good guy. We can trust him, but I don't want Hillary within a mile of this. She'll blabber it all over town."

"And New York?"

"For the time being, we've got to sit on this. After all, we have five days." The President snapped.

"Suppose these damn terrorists, whoever the hell they are, decide to go public with this themselves. How are we going to look in front of those folk up there in New York, if they learn we sat on this for days without telling them to get out?"

The President emitted a painful groan. These were the moments when leadership exacted its price. "We'll have to deal with that if it happens, I guess."

"Mr. President, how do you propose to deal with Ariel Sharon and the Israelis on this?" asked Colin Powell. "When do we bring them in on what's happened?"

"Well, not now. It's the middle of the night out there," the President replied. "Can we trust them to keep their mouths shut on this? We'll have to make that decision in the morning."

"Mr. President" interjected his National Security Advisor Condi Rice. "I think you can count on Sharon.

But some of those Likudniks he's surrounded himself with? I doubt it. For them, those settlements go right to the heart of their justification for existing. It's going to pose an appalling dilemma for them."

"Yeah," said the CIA's Milt Anderson "and can you imagine the firestorm of hate and anger that's going to erupt in this country if a million Americans die for those damn settlements? Settlements every American president since LBJ" – he looked up the table towards Bush – "and most particularly, your own father, opposed?"

The President shook his head in despair. "And how the hell do we find out who these Warriors of the Jihad are? Open up some channel of communication so we can try to talk some kind of reason to them?"

"The danger is that these guys are going to be impervious to reason and logic," Anderson said "but I think Mushareff's the key here. That investigation he's running into how their bomb went missing may give us the clues we need."

"How about the Allies?" Colin Powell asked. "What do we tell them?"

"For now, nothing," the President answered.

"Not even Tony Blair? The Brits?"

The President reflected a moment. "No. For now, I want this crisis to stay right here in this room." He looked at Tom Ridge, the ex Pennsylvania governor running his Homeland Security department. "How are we going to find that damn thing and disarm it, Tom?"

"As soon as we adjourn here, I'm sending Paul Anscom to New York to open our Emergency Response Center there. I will order a full deployment of our NEST teams and the FBI's bomb squad experts to the city. Paul will meet with Police Commissioner Kelly and his Chief of Detectives later tonight, to decide how we go about searching the city without starting a panic and alerting the press. We will mobilize our Customs inspectors to start immediately scrubbing out the manifests of every ship that has entered Port Elizabeth in the last 30 days, to see if we pick up any hint of suspicious cargoes."

"Alright," the President declared. "We are, all of us here, going to be facing in the coming days and hours, the worst crisis in the history of the Republic. Activate everything we've discussed and we meet here at nine tomorrow. Try to get some rest if you can. You're all going to need it."

5

New York, Washington, D.C.

The Crisis, Day One

With his neat little gray beard, his long, ill-combed hair, his all enveloping brown smock, the man looked more like a Greek Orthodox monk on Mount Athos than a king of the international food trade. Yet Charlie Birbaki, 54, born of Turkish parents who'd come to New York for the World's Fair in 1939, was, in fact, one of the largest distributors of oriental gastronomic products on the eastern seaboard of the United States.

His catalogue was mailed out every month to 30,000 clients from Maine to northern Florida. Ensconced in the little glass booth of his Brooklyn warehouse which served as his office, he watched a steady parade of customers leaving his premises every day, their arms, or the baggage carts he provided, crammed with sacks, boxes and cartons of his delicacies: Basmati rice from

India and Pakistan, coffee from the Yemen, Sumatra, Kenya: frozen shrimp from Bangladesh, frozen Egyptian artichokes, green lemon jellies from Syria, pistachios from Turkey and Jordan, chutney from Ceylon, couscous from Tunisia and Morocco. To those products, he had recently added a line of European specialities, such as the famous cassoulet from Toulouse in France and foie gras from Perigord.

The warehouse in which he kept them stored was a cave of delights, reeking of spices and grilled almonds, divided into alleys named after the products they sheltered, in carefully arranged ceiling-to-floor stacks.

For over a decade, Charlie had brought his imported merchandise into the U.S. via containers offloaded in Port Elizabeth. They came from ports all over the East, Malaysia, Alexandria, Latakia, Istanbul, Karachi, Bombay, Singapore, all brought in via his shipping agent up in Albany. The system worked to perfection. When the containers got to INOS, the Albany shipping agent, he got a call and the next day, a truck delivered his containers straight to his Brooklyn warehouse. On this September morning, he was expecting four containers, two filled with bags of Basmati rice, one with Turkish pistachios and a fourth containing a mixed assortment of goods.

It was a rather special delivery. Four months earlier, one of his clients who loved Turkish pistachios, had come to him with a Godfather offer. Let him, he said, put a crate into his shipments of rice once a month.

He'd come and pick it up at the warehouse and give Charlie a wad of bills — $20,000 worth, to be exact.

Now Charlie was no dope. The guy who always showed up in his New York Yankees baseball cap, had to be a Turk, right? So what was Turkey's primary export? Heroin, right? So, that's what you'd figure, was going to be in those crates. Well, 20K was 20K and above all, it was 20K the IRS was never going to see. If there were assholes out there who took that shit, the hell with them. What concern was it of Charlie's?

As always, Albany's containers showed up at his warehouse right on time. He set his men to work unloading them, holding back the second basmati rice container to last. To his surprise, it was not his Turkish pal with his New York Yankees cap who showed up to make the pick up, but a couple — a woman wearing a white kerchief, driving a white van, and a rather distinguished-looking guy of about forty.

"We're here for that case you're expecting today," the woman explained. "Don't worry. Everything's in order." She smiled "and, of course, I have your envelope."

Charlie ordered his men to open the Basmati rice container and they found the crate they were looking for, packed as usual in the rear, behind stacks of burlap bags full of rice. It was a bit bigger than the usual consignment.

Again the woman smiled. "Bigger package, bigger envelope," she said pressing Charlie's money into his hands. His touch told him it was almost twice the size of his usual 20K packet. Then, as she and her partner moved towards the crate, Charlie noticed that the guy's left hand had been amputated at the wrist.

"Hey!" he shouted to two of his workmen. "Help these people put their crate into the van." They did, its weight requiring the solid efforts of both men.

A few minutes later, the woman waved a friendly hand to Charlie and he watched as her Easy Rent van headed out of his warehouse towards Flatbush Avenue.

This has got to be the seediest place in all of New York City, Paul Anscom thought, driving across the potholes and exposed cobblestones leading into the parking lot of 11 Water Street, an aging, windowless warehouse built into the base of the Brooklyn Bridge's Brooklyn Tower, adjacent to the East River.

And yet, as he well knew, those tacky surroundings enclosed the most sophisticated, hi-tech, post 9/11 counter-terrorism headquarters in the United States, and almost certainly in the world. Officially, the place was labeled the New York City OEM — Office of Emergency Management. The first OEM had been built by Mayor Rudi Giuliani on the 23rd floor of 7, The World Trade Center, a decision much critized at the time for setting such a critical site in so evident a terrorist target. And, indeed, the first OEM had been destroyed, almost at the outset of the 9/11 bombings.

The new OEM was the creation of Police Commissioner Ray Kelly. Kelly was serving an unusual second term as police commissioner. In his first term, under Mayor Dave Dinkens, he had been largely responsible for the dramatic fall in crime in New York City, although his successor had grabbed most of the credit for it. In his years out of the commissioner's office, Kelly had broadened his knowledge of the world, serving as the U.S. representative to Interpol, in Lyons, France, and as an expert in money laundering at the Treasury Department and Customs.

September 11 hit him personally as he and his wife lived in Battery Park City, and for weeks, they could not return to their home. So when mayor elect Mike Bloomberg asked him to return to the commissioner's office, he accepted immediately, vowing to make sure the catastrophe of 9/11 would never be repeated.

And indeed, Anscom told himself, stepping out of his car onto a pavement littered with old candy bar wrappers, cigarette butts and empty beer and coke cans, Kelly had put his OEM in a location, no self-respecting terrorist would want to visit. And yet, once past security, the building's doors led into the command center's heart, a huge, open space, uncluttered by pillars or dividing partitions, half the size of a U.S. football field, gleaming with futuristic electronic equipment. At its Intelligence Center, computers displayed electronic maps, regularly updated with satellite imagery of Moscow, London, Tel Aviv, Jerusalem, Riyadh, Islamabad and

Baghdad. In its Global Intelligence Room, a dozen TV monitors carried live newscasts from Al Jazeera, Al Arabiyah and other critical TV channels while a battery of Arabic, Urdu, Farsi and Pushtu speakers maintained running translations of the programs. That was Kelly's doing. At the time of 9/11, the Police Department's only Arabic speaker was an Israeli from Jerusalem.

On each side of the central aisle dividing the OEM were five working areas rung by black computer consoles. Each console had its own working desk, a set of four chairs, and was identified by the owner's initials in white tape — CG for example, for Coast Guard.

The telephones at each desk were equipped with keys which, if activated, automatically encrypted electronically their conversations. Each computer had access to a score of constantly updated data bases, the latest intelligence reports and briefing books on the world's known terrorist groups.

Those computers were also wired into a data bank built up since 2002 which provided up to date satellite photography of every square foot of the city, allowing an operator to zoom in on and identify a couple embracing on the corner of, say, 75th Street and Amsterdam Avenue, if he chose to. At the center of the cavernous room was a raised square platform, the command center itself, labeled the ASOG — the Alternative Seat of Government. A bank of computer desks similar to those elsewhere in the room, rung that platform — computer desks for the NYPD, the FBI, Homeland Security, the

NYFD, the hospital service, Customs, and a set that could be turned on, if desired, to the White House Situation Room. The desk at the center of the circle was meant for the mayor, but in this crisis, it would be Anscom's.

Kelly himself was waiting for Anscom inside the headquarters, anxious to show him the resources that would be available for the crisis confronting them. He liked to boast that "New York City was safer than it has ever been" and indeed, no city in the world, from Washington D.C. to London or Paris, could offer its citizens facilities like Kelly had provided New Yorkers. As usual, Kelly, a former Marine Corps captain, was impeccably dressed in a freshly pressed blue suit, a white handkerchief in his vest pocket, the few hairs remaining on his bald head neatly combed, and an appropriately serious expression on his face. With him were his key aides, Dave Cohen, the deputy police commissioner for Intelligence, formerly the head of the CIA's Operations Division, the deputy police commissioner for Counter Terrorism, Mike Sheehan, formerly a State Department Counter Terrorism expert, and the officer in charge of the OEM, Deputy Police Commissioner John Odermatt.

Also invited were Kevin Donovan, the director of the 1100 FBI Agents assigned to New York, and his deputy, Joe Billy, the agent in charge of the 125 agents assigned to the FBI-NYPD's Joint Terrorism Task Force, the JTTF. Anscom had briefed Kelly by phone from Washington on Sunday night. He now sat the full team down at the Alternative Seat of Government platform to provide them with a similarly complete briefing.

"Alright, Gentlemen," he said in conclusion "the problem we face is straightforward – how do we save New York from destruction?"

Commissioner Kelly, inspired by his days at Customs, had already been reflecting on the problem. "First thing we do, right now in the next hour, is assemble a team of fifty customs officers and fifty of my officers, and get them over to Port Elizabeth to scrub out the manifests of every ship that has docked there in the last 30 days. I want them to check everything, the manifests, the details of every container they offloaded, where those containers went, to who, what they contained, every damn thing imaginable. I want them to scrub out everything suspicious, every anomaly, anything that seems out of line. Forget this business of Customs checking incoming cargoes – it's just a bad joke."

"Second, and most important, I want to alert all my key people, right now. In view of the text of that threat note that came into the White House, what am I going to tell them? That there's an atomic bomb hidden somewhere on Manhattan Island?"

"Do that," growled Michael Sheehan, the deputy police commissioner for Counter Terrorism "and you run the risk of creating a panic. Your guys are only human. Some of them are going to call their wives and say 'get the kids out of school and get the hell up to your mother's house in Vermont'. The word will leak out and the evacuation of the city will start all on its own, just like it did on 9/11. Then we run the risk that these terrorists, whoever the hell they are, detonate the bomb as they've threatened to do."

"Yes," Anscom agreed "the President is very concerned about that. He's meeting this morning with Governor Pataki and Mayor Bloomberg. In view of the terrorist's threat, he wants to secure their agreement to using a cover story, 'unidentified terrorists have hidden a barrel of deadly chlorine gas somewhere in Manhattan."

"That might work as a starter," Commissioner Kelly said "but what are we going to tell the press when they see some of your technicians going around with Geiger counters? That they're looking for chlorine gas? How long do you figure that's going to hold up?"

"It's a critical problem," Anscom agreed "and one, I think, we're going to have to deal with on a day-to-day, maybe even hour-to-hour basis. For the moment, that damn threat note doesn't give us much choice."

"OK," Kelly agreed "we'll have to see how long it will fly. But remember, my guys aren't like Kenny Donovan's FBI agents. They don't come from South Dakota or Oregon or Montana. They come from Brooklyn, the Bronx and Queens. They've got their wives, their kids, their mothers, their girl friends, their dogs, their cats, their pet canaries, right here in the city. They aren't supermen. But if the mayor agrees, OK, we go with your chlorine gas story."

"Are you well wired into the Islamic community?" Anscom asked.

"Pretty well," Kelly replied "It's been a high priority for us since 9/11. A lot of things go down at the Grand Mosque up on East 96th street, built with Saudi money. In, of all places, the old Ruppert Brewery — the beer factory that built the Yankees baseball team."

"What we've got in front of us, albeit on a massive scale, is just solid police work, the kind of thing my officers do every day – pulse every informant we've got, run down whatever leads they provide us, follow up on every lead we can get from you people in Washington, at the CIA."

"We've got to mobilize immediately, the full Joint FBI NYPD Terrorism Task Force, all 250 men," the FBI's Kevin Donovan said "to back up the commissioner's efforts with whatever supplementary investigative work is needed."

"As I told the Commissioner last night, we're bringing in right now our NEST, Nuclear Explosive Search Teams, to give us the absolute top-of-the-line technological and scientific support in our hunt for this damn weapon," Anscom said. "We are also flying in, as I speak, four brand new mobile vans from the Lawrence Livermore National Lab out in California. They have built into them the very latest state-of-the-art gamma ray detectors which the lab designed for use in crises just like this one. This will be their first deployment."

"Most threats of this nature that come in don't name

a precise place," observed Dave Cohen, the former CIA officer who was now the deputy chief for Intelligence. "At least this one does, which, I guess, is something to be thankful for."

"Right," snapped Anscom. "Let's get cracking, Gentlemen, the fate of New York City and a million of its people is in your hands."

Not quite 15 kilometers east of the OEM, in a small auditorium of Our Lady of Sorrows Elementary School in Glendale, a sad and solemn little ceremony was about to get underway. Sister Mary Francis Duchelle shepherded half a dozen children onto the room's stage. The spastic uncertainty of their movements, a tongue rolling around in a half-open mouth, bore witness to the common affliction cursing their little bodies: they were all Mongoloid children.

To help them come to grips with their burden, each child had been assigned a poem to memorize and recite regularly over the summer recess. Now, as a confidence building gesture, they were to recite their poems to this select audience of parents and friends.

Sister Mary Francis stepped forward to address the gathering. "Katy O'Neill," she said "is going to open our program, reciting the opening lines of Walt Whitman's great Civil War epic, *Captain O my Captain*."

She reached into the circle of uplifted faces and took

the hand of a ten-year-old girl, her black hair tied into pigtails that fell below her shoulders. Gently, she led the child to the center of the little stage, then withdrew a few feet, leaving her alone before the assembly.

The little girl stood there a moment, terrified. Then she opened her mouth, but the only sound that emerged was a shrill "peep." She began to shake her head violently, sending her pigtails swirling about her face. She stamped her feet in fury and frustration. Then, as she had been taught to do, she took a deep breath.

In the first row of spectators, a heavy-set man in a gray suit stroked his sweating forehead. Each of the girl's gestures sent a tremor of anguish through him. He was her father, Detective Lieutenant T. F. O'Neill of the New York Police Department. He stared out at her as though, somehow, the intensity of the love radiating from his face might calm the tempest sweeping her little figure.

It did. She opened her mouth into the perfect "O" he had practised with her so often over the summer, and the words began to come tumbling out:

> O Captain O my captain our fearful trip is done.
> The ship has weathered every rack
> The prize we sought is won.
> The port is near, the bells I hear
> The people all exulting.

An enormous sense of pride swept over O'Neill as she poured out her concluding words "*My captain lies, fallen cold and dead.*"

At almost the same moment, he heard the faint jingle of a bell from inside his suit jacket. He pulled out his mobile phone and saw immediately that it was an urgent call. O'Neill was the commanding officer of the Manhattan South Detective Squad, and the number he had to call back was from the office of the Chief of Detectives. Something big is going down if he's calling me, he thought, I'd better answer this pronto.

He blew a proud kiss to his daughter and tiptoed out of the room. Although he couldn't know it, five hundred police mobiles were ringing all over the city at about the same time, in a grisly tintinabulation of the bells. "The chief wants you here at Police Plaza forthwith," an operator told him. "Forthwith" was New York police-speak for "about five minutes ago."

"And," he added "he wants you to come to the city by the Williamsburg Bridge and check out those sensing devices we put in there a year or so ago."

As he had done every day since taking office, the President had begun his day with a careful reading of the CIA's President's Eyes Only daily briefing paper. That paper, his father had advised him, would be the most important document that would cross his desk each day. Perhaps, but to his dismay, it did not contain on this Monday morning, the slightest advance on what he and his advisors had known at the conclusion of their meeting the night before.

At least, he noted, the media had not yet picked up even a hint of the crisis facing the nation. His "intestinal disorder" had attracted a minimum of comment. Probably, he mused, the press corps was delighted to learn something was giving him a belly ache.

"Alright," he snapped, taking his seat at the head of the Situation Room conference table, as his grandfather's clock chimed out 0930 "what's new?"

"Three things," his Chief of Staff Andrew Card replied "Governor Pataki and Mayor Bloomberg are on the way. Paul Anscom is ready to give you a report on the action they're taking up in New York. President Mushareff called from Islamabad fifteen minutes ago with the news that they have made progress in their investigation into their missing bomb, which he wants to convey to you."

Clearly, the President thought, Mushareff's call takes precedence. "Let's pipe the call to Mushareff onto the squawk box down here so everybody can hear what he has to say."

Mr. President," Bush began "I want to thank you for all the help you're giving us in this terrible crisis."

Mushareff acknowledged his thought and plunged into his briefing. "We have arrested the ISI officer who commanded the arsenal from which the device was stolen. He has confessed to doing it because of his membership in a secret Islamic order, the Laskar-e-Tibi, run by a former commanding general of the ISI, Hamid Bol."

At the mention of Bol's name, the eyebrows of the CIA's Anderson arched skyward in a gesture meant to say 'I told you so.'

"We are searching for Bol but he has disappeared," Mushareff continued. "We have also learned that our weapons designer Dr. Abdul Sharif Ahmad was seen in Chasma, where our detonation devices are stored, on the night the bomb disappeared."

"Do you know where he is now?" the American President asked.

"Yes. He's on vacation in Pyongyang, North Korea."

"North Korea!" Bush gasped "Who the hell goes to North Korea for a vacation?"

"Well, Kim Il Sung, their so-called Brave Little Leader, keeps a bevy of young ladies in his Presidential Palace to help him greet visitors. Perhaps, that encouraged our good scientist to drop by. In any event, he leaves tonight for Peking and tomorrow he flies back to Karachi."

The President couldn't resist a joke. "How come Clinton never went to Pyongyang? Listen, can you arrange to pick Dr. Ahmad up at the airport and sequester him some place where we can talk with him? He may be our only channel into the people who are behind this."

"Of course," Mushareff assured him. "I've already set that in motion, using only the most trusted members of my Presidential Guard."

The two leaders exchanged their mutual assurances that they would remain in close and constant contact during the crisis, before hanging up.

"Milt," the President asked his CIA head, as they did, "do you guys at the CIA still prepare these psychological studies, profiles or whatever the hell you call them, on important people?"

"No," Anderson replied "we shut that operation down some time ago."

"Well, I want your people at the agency to put together the best dossier on Ahmad you can, for me. I want everything from his sexual preferences to what he has for breakfast. His strong points, his weaknesses, his likes, his dislikes, anything that might help me establish a bond with the man. I want it on my desk tomorrow morning."

"And," he continued "just what do we know about the kind of guys who would be behind this? Alright, they're Islamic extremists. But what do we know about their psychology, their behavioral patterns, what motivates them?"

"Tough question," said Dr. Lisa Holmgren, an attractive woman in her mid forties who, for almost eight years, had been the National Security Council's nuclear terrorism expert. "We specialists in these questions have felt for sometime that the idea of using a device for extortion, as is happening here, was outdated. We'd concluded that nuclear terrorists would have one just idea – get their device into some U.S. location as quickly as possible and then detonate it. In other words, our current thinking on situations like this is that sheer vengeance would be the motivating factor, like suicide bombers blowing themselves up in vengeance in restaurants in Tel Aviv or buses in Jerusalem. We may have gotten ahead of ourselves here."

"Yes," echoed Dr. Clint Hartwell of the Homeland Security Department's Emergency Response team who had taken Paul Anscom's place at the table "we must assume, we are dealing here with people who are basically fanatics. People who are ready to die. I believe they will baby-sit their bomb, protecting it with their lives, ready to die in its explosion, ready to detonate it instantly if they're found. That is what makes this search we've embarked on, so desperately dangerous."

"The psychology of so-called suicide bombers has evolved over the years since 1982, when we first saw this phenomena among the Shiites in southern Lebanon," Dr. Holmgren added. "In the beginning, the bombers were in the hands of extremist mullahs who brainwashed them, so to speak, with the promises of paradise and those 72 virgins. But in the last five years, in Israel, that pattern has changed dramatically. What we are seeing now is sheer vengeance, hatred as the primary motivation and I suspect, a sheer intense hatred of the U.S. and what we stand for is behind this menace."

"OK," agreed the President "that is certainly going to complicate an already desperate situation. But tell me

– how does that bomb get detonated if the time comes? By radio? A phonecall? A cellular phone call? A timer?"

"Any of the above, Mr. President," answered the bespectacled intellectual representing the National Security Agency, NSA. "Unfortunately, the ways of detonating such a device are almost too numerous to list."

"Can we somehow throw a kind of electronic blanket around New York? Shut down the possibility of any radio signal or overseas phone call getting into the city?"

"That might be a possibility, Mr. President. I'd like to run it past some experts for you."

"Sure," said Lisa Holmgren "but suppose the bomb's in some apartment in Manhattan and one of the terrorists is out in Queens with the phone number. He gives the apartment a call and since it's a land-line, the call goes through. If the detonator is tied to the phone, the bomb goes."

"Can New York Verizon shut down the whole system?" the NSA expert asked.

"They do that and then they tie all our search and relief efforts into knots," Lisa rejoined. With her PhD in Nuclear Physics from the University of Michigan, these were issues she'd pondered for years.

A marine officer from the Situation Room's caretakers appeared. "Sir," he informed the President "Governor Pataki and Mayor Bloomberg are here."

"Good," declared the President. "I think, I'll receive them in the Oval Office." He turned to Colin Powell

and his National Security Advisor Condi Rice. "I'd like
you two to join me. The rest of you continue to blue
sky this damn crisis with Vice President Cheney and
see if you can't come up with some good ideas."

The two men stepping into the Oval Office had at least
one thing in common with the President who had summoned them to Washington – they were both his fellow
Republicans. That was where the similarities ended.
Michael "Mike" Bloomberg, 52, had arrived at Reagan
National Airport 45 minutes earlier, not, however, on
one of the Washington-New York shuttles, but on board
his private aircraft — a luxurious King Star Jet. And his
point of departure for the flight was not the city of
which he was the first magistrate, but Kingston, Ber-
muda, where he regularly spent his weekends in his palatial estate.

Bloomberg epitomized that special American dream,
the self-made man. Born into a modest family outside
Boston in Medford, Mass., he had put himself through
John Hopkins and Harvard Business School on scholarships. He worked his way to a partnership at Salomon
Brothers in New York in just six years; then, following
a change in management, he left to form his own financial information firm. The success of Bloomberg Inc
had made Mike a multi-billionaire, and his Bloomberg
Radio and TV shows were household words around the

globe. He had, quite literally, bought his way into the New York Mayor's Office, spending $40 million of his own money on his campaign.

Yet, he drew down only a symbolic one dollar of his salary, giving the rest to charity. Not for him the regular ethnic marches down Fifth and Madison Avenues of his fellow New Yorkers. He loathed the city's noisy political rallies, had never moved into the mayor's official residence, Gracie Mansion, preferring his own luxurious 73rd Street residence, and after these many years, still remained a closet fan of the Boston Red Sox in their baseball wars with his city's Yankees.

Governor Pataki was a farm boy, brought up on his family's farm in Peekskill, New York. Like Bloomberg, he put himself through college, Yale, and law school, Columbia, on scholarship. After a spell practising law, he became, in a sense, a professional politician, serving as mayor of his native Peekskill and ten years in the New York State legislature before running for governor. He took particular pride in the fact that under his leadership, New York had enacted the most sweeping anti-terrorist laws in the nation.

Neither man, of course, had any idea of why the President had summoned them to Washington. He swiftly disabused them of their innocence, handing each a one-page text, reproducing the terrorists' threat note and summarizing everything his government had been able to learn since it had arrived, and what steps the federal government was taking to address it.

Bloomberg was horrified. "A million or more of my fellow New Yorkers at risk!" he gasped. "This is a disaster of unparalleled magnitude!

"Damn hell! I've been trying for months to get two billion dollars out of you to reinforce the city's counter terrorism measures and all I got was a lot of platitudes! You're giving every citizen in Wyoming twenty two dollars a year for counter terrorism, Wyoming for God's sake, are terrorists threatening the cows up there? And what do you give New York? Three dollars a head. I took over a city after 9/11 which everyone wanted to help, and what did I get? Nothing, except the empty cash drawers Giuliani left me. I even had to close down some of the stations of our heroic firemen to keep the city running."

"Damn right!" echoed Pataki. "You threw away eighty seven billion dollars on your stupid war in Iraq! And your war on terror? Zilch! You never wanted to put your money where your mouth was. You let Mike and me deal with the basic function of government, defending New Yorkers, and this is what happens!"

The President was aghast at the fury of their statements. He had expected a 'rally around the flag' reaction. Still, he did his best to stifle the tide of anger rising within him. "Listen," he said "this isn't the time for arguments and recriminations. We have a crisis on our hands. How are we going to deal with it?"

"OK," said Bloomberg. "First thing. Is there really a bomb hidden somewhere in New York? Do we know that for a fact?"

"No, we don't. But we have to assume, based on that threat note and Pakistan's missing bomb that there is. To do otherwise would be madness."

"Then what are our chances of finding the bomb before the terrorists' deadline expires?" Pataki asked.

"We've mobilized all the scientific, technological, police skills we possess and have headquartered them in Mike Bloomberg's excellent Office of Emergency Management. Will they succeed in finding it? God only knows. Pray that they do," the President answered.

"What about the terrorists' threat to detonate the bomb if we go public and start an evacuation?" Bloomberg asked.

"That could be the mother of all extortion threats," Pataki declared.

"And yet, if it's not and we order an evacuation and it goes off, then we'll have the deaths of a million New Yorkers on our conscience," Bloomberg rejoined.

"And if we don't find the bomb in time and it goes off? We'll still have their deaths on our consciences," Pataki added.

"Gentlemen!" the President intervened "the government feels we must play for time here. We have to strive to keep this a secret on a day-to-day, hour-to-hour, even minute-to-minute basis. I think, both Secretary Powell and Miss Rice will agree with me on that."

His two cabinet members nodded their agreement.

"Have you talked to Sharon and the Israelis yet?" Bloomberg asked.

"Not yet. I will shortly."

"Look, I've been an ardent Zionist all my life" Bloomberg said. "But I was always against the settlement program and, quite frankly, I don't think you stand a chance in hell, in getting Sharon to back down in the face of this extortion threat."

"A million dead Americans for his settlements?"

"He's a fanatic, just like the guys who planted this bomb are. Maybe he'll agree to dissimulate, to fake some moves to disarm them. But more than that?"

"Look, Mr. President," Pataki interjected "for better or for worse, dealing with this ghastly crisis has to be the responsibility of you and the federal government. Mike and I will support you in anyway we can. Such as agreeing to try our best to keep this threat a secret for as long as we can, by using this chlorine gas cover story you propose in this paper."

"Yes," Bloomberg agreed "and I'm going to head up to New York to the OEM right now. If a million of my fellow New Yorkers are going to have to die because of this horrible act, then I'm going to have to die along with them. What else can I do?"

Normally, passengers on the Lucky Line Falcon 500 Jets out of Las Vegas, Nevada, were high rollers, gamblers at the city's casinos flying home in luxury on their winnings. David Graham, the Falcon's sole passenger this autumn morning, had never been in a casino in his life, yet he was, in a sense, the ultimate gambler. He was the director of NEST, the Nuclear Explosive Search Teams, Paul Anscom had ordered to New York to provide top-of-the-line technological support in the search for the terrorists' nuclear bomb. For the next days, Graham would be gambling that the best scientific and technological equipment available to the U.S. government would enable him and his fellow workers to find the bomb, before the terrorists could go through with their threat to explode it.

Graham glanced out the window as the jet rolled towards its landing pad at New Jersey's McGuire Air Force Base. Somewhere out there, in the base's crowded hangar decks, would be half a dozen C141s which had flown in overnight with NEST's top-secret, ultra-sophisticated equipment, packed into vans banalized as Hertz and Avis trucks.

Among them were half a dozen of NEST's most modern detection vehicles, trucks equipped with Gamma Ray Imaging Spectrometers which would allow their NEST operators to take pictures of radioactive emissions over large areas. The truck's designers, scientists at the Lawrence Livermore Lab in California, believed their new trucks would provide NEST's operators with a tenfold increase in sensitivity in detecting nuclear materials or devices.

Each was the size of a large television set and installed in the rear of one of the trucks. Manned by a

pair of NEST technicians, they would prowl through
the streets of New York, searching for the tell-tale emissions the terrorists' bomb might give off. The spectrometers were designed to first pick up the emissions given
off by a nuclear device, then allow the operators to pin
down the precise location from which the emissions
were coming.

They were the result of recent advances in micro-
electronics that had allowed Livermore's scientists to
build a gamma-ray camera which was, in a sense, a cluster of gamma sensors designed to work together, much
like a digital camera for gamma rays. The beauty of the
system was that it allowed the NEST technicians manning the device in their truck to eliminate, immediately,
a whole range of "false-positives" — emissions coming from construction materials containing elements
such as cobalt, phosphorescence rays off substances
meant to glow in the dark, or even a patient leaving a
hospital after receiving chemio-therapy.

The trucks were just the latest in a series of detection devices developed at Livermore, called "Ultra
Specs" for Ultra High Resolution Gamma Ray Spectrometers. Some of the earlier ones were small enough
to be carried by a NEST technician on his or her back
like a hiker's back pack. They worked at an incredible
one degree above absolute zero farenheit – 459 degrees
– so they could pick up traces of a single gamma ray.
They were connected directly to a computer which in-
creased the ability of the scientists using the back packs

to determine, with five times greater accuracy, just what kind of a device was giving off the emission.

Graham's NEST organization was unique in the world. No other nation possessed an organization like it. All one thousand of its members, men and women, were volunteers, most of them scientists or technical people at the nation's great laboratories, Los Alamos, Nevada, Sandia, New Mexico and Livermore in California. Like most of the others, Graham had been summoned from a Sunday night dinner in front of his TV set by an urgent call from NEST's Department of Energy's Headquarters in Washington. Every time one of those calls came, the NEST team members knew they were potentially putting their lives at risk. If the terrible weapon they were being sent to find was really there and detonated, a large number of NEST volunteers would be among its first victims.

The organization went all the way back to 1964, when a B29 bomber about to crash, jettisoned its bombs over the open fields and orchards of Palomares, Spain. Los Alamos dispatched a team of scientists armed with the best detection devices then available, to find them. They couldn't.

If we can't find a bomb in an open field or forest, reasoned the team leader Bill Chambers, a nuclear weapons designer, how the hell could we find a nuclear bomb hidden in an American city by a terrorist? With his thought, NEST was born.

Almost fifty times in the years since then, NEST

teams had been deployed in U.S. cities, in response to nuclear threats. Fortunately, none had ever materialized. In the days following 9/11, NEST teams had patrolled night and day around the White House and other key sites in Washington D.C. Twice since then, they had been summoned to U.S. cities following intelligence leads indicating terrorists might have smuggled a dirty bomb into the country.

Yet, the press never picked up a hint of their deployment. That was because secrecy and speed were the golden rules of NEST's operations — secrecy, so terrorists couldn't learn they were being hunted and perhaps, detonate their device in a moment of fright and also, of course, so as not to panic the population. Speed, because every moment could be crucial in their efforts to save thousands of lives.

An unmarked government car was waiting for Graham as his plane rolled to a stop. A veteran of over a dozen of these missions, the nuclear weapons designer could feel his stomach tightening into the angry, nauseous knot that was always there whenever he had to lead NEST into action. Graham was built like a tight end, six feet four inches tall, solidly muscled and dressed like a ranch hand, in cowboy boots, with a broad-rimmed hat, a blue and white checkered shirt and a Navajo good-luck charm hung around his neck on a rawhide cord.

As soon as he settled into the car, the driver headed up the New Jersey Turnpike towards New York. Graham closed his eyes and sighed. No one knew better than he, how desperately difficult, despite all the technology his team possessed, the job ahead was. The tightly-packed city blocks of New York were a high rise forest of glass and steel, providing an abundance of natural screening to smother those gamma-ray emissions his sophisticated equipment was designed to pick up. And if the terrorists had wrapped their bomb in lead? Then his men and women would have to be right on top of it to identify it. And the skyscrapers! Sure, he had half a dozen NEST helicopters to patrol the city rooftops, to do fly-bys of its skyscrapers. But what a nightmare job!

He sat back and tried, unsuccessfully, to sleep. An hour later, they were approaching the New Jersey entrance to the Lincoln Tunnel and there before him, across the dark waters of the Hudson was the magnificent skyline of the city he was supposed to save. A line of F Scott Fitzgerald he'd read as a schoolboy came back to him. To see Manhattan like that was to sense it "in the first wild promise of all the mystery and beauty in the world."

Well, on this autumn morning, that skyline held out no promise of beauty for him. What was waiting for him over there was perhaps a taste of hell, the ultimate challenge to these techniques he and his teammates had so carefully assembled. He would follow all their exchanges by radio, praying that he would not hear in his earphones that terrible phrase "Gamma Ray Four" which would indicate a nuclear device was indeed hidden somewhere there, in that magnificent city.

★ ★ ★

Nahed Jahiri, her white scarf still firmly knotted around her head, eased her Easy Van out of the Brooklyn Battery Tunnel onto the foot of Manhattan Island. As she steered the vehicle across Trinity Place, towards lower Broadway, the usual collection of impatient, petulant or just plain rude New Yorkers was leaning on their horns, creating a noisy symphony.

Nahed laughed. "Just like driving in Beirut or Jerusalem." Omar Tahiri sitting beside her, jerked his head towards the rear of their van. "Well, what we've got back there will shut them up soon enough."

The two terrorists, along with their colleague, Khaled, had arrived in the United States a few days ago. Shortly after they had agreed to undertake their mission, Imad Mugniyeh's trio of would-be terrorists had had their photographs taken at the Ain el Hilweh refugee camp. The photos were hand carried to Montreal by a French Algerian member of Al Qaeda, where they were delivered to a Pakistani master forger — counterfeiter, Farid al Mansour. Mansour was not affiliated with Al Qaeda. His artistry was for sale and it did not come cheap. Counterfeit Indian passports, U.S. visas, birth certificates and New Jersey driver's licenses, ostensibly issued in November 2002, when the Garden State licenses were notoriously easy to copy, had cost Mugniyeh close to $100,000 for his three terrorists.

However, they worked perfectly. The three had

flown from Paris to Montreal. From there, they had gone
by train to that quintessential tourist destination, Niagara
Falls. On a Saturday evening, they had ostensibly spent
hours gambling in the Casino Niagara, then headed off
to Buffalo on a shuttle bus full of American gamblers,
over the Peace Bridge. Their fake New Jersey driver's
licenses were all the I.D. they needed to slip into the
United States with their busload of happy gamblers.

An Al Qaeda operative from Rochester met them
at their hotel the next morning and drove them to a
motel in Yonkers, one in a chain of motels frequented
principally by illegal immigrants. Nahed did most of
the driving to get herself well accustomed to American
traffic.

Now, at 23rd Street, she turned onto Fifth Avenue
to head for the hideaway they had selected for their
atomic bomb. They had to double park in front of the
building, but in that part of midtown Manhattan, everybody did. Indeed, one of the most common criminal actions in the neighborhood was for a robber to
pop open a van's rear door and walk away with whatever was valuable inside.

Khaled, the third member of their trio, was waiting
for them in front of the nondescript building they had
chosen for their hideaway. It was four stories high, over
a century old, and its front façade was 'decorated' by a
green metallic fire escape.

To one side of the building was Mimosa's Pizza
Parlor, to the other a souvenir shop selling "I Love N.Y."

tee shirts. The neighborhood was redolent with the odor of the hot dogs roasting on the peddler's stand on the corner.

"Everything went fine," Omar assured his colleague "except this crate is heavy as hell."

"We'll slip the super fifty dollars to give us a hand with it," Khaled said." It would not be their first act of generosity towards the toothless old man. They had already slipped him six thousand dollars in cash for three months' rental of a two-room flat on the fourth floor. Needless to say, the sum went straight into the super's pocket. The building's absentee landlord, an insurance company in Texas, would never see a trace of that cash, nor was any official document like a lease or rental agreement exchanged.

Khaled and the super wrestled the heavy crate past the Korean hairdresser's shop occupying the ground floor, into the building's creaky elevator for a noisy ride up to the fourth floor which they shared with an Afghan carpet dealer. The intervening floors were filled with a multitude of small shops selling electronic goods and out the door stocks of pirated DVDs, TV cassettes and even fake Hermes handbags.

It was a simple affair, a living room, a bedroom, a bathroom and a primitive kitchen. Once the super had disappeared, the three proceeded to open their crate and remove the protective casing in which their bomb had been stored.

Working with care and precision, they set it up as

they had been instructed to do, by Mugniyeh's experts in Lebanon. Then, with the most delicate of gestures, they verified the connection of the mobile telephone, as they had been taught, to the bomb's detonator, installing along with it the relay that would divert any false numbers that somehow might come into it. When they'd finished, Tahiri stood back to admire their work, then looked out the window towards the high-rise buildings across the street.

"There won't be much left of them when this thing goes off," he said. Then, suddenly, a mother clutching her infant child appeared in a window of the building just opposite theirs. That gave a troubling image to the tragedy they were preparing. "Or them either," Tahiri mumbled.

Then he turned to Nahed. "You'd better get that van back to the rental agency," he ordered.

Across Manhattan Island, Detective Lieutenant T. F. O'Neill pulled his unmarked New York Police car up to the police command post at the Brooklyn end of the Williamsburg Bridge. He flashed his gold shield at the patrolman on duty and said "I want to get a look at that scanning device we installed here at the end of 2002."

The device was part of a top-secret program set up by the New York Police Department that year. Scanning devices similar to those employed by David

Graham's NEST teams, but much less sophisticated, had been secretly placed at all the entry points to Manhattan Island, in toll booths, on bridges and at the entries to the Lincoln, Holland and Brooklyn Battery Tunnels. The idea was to pick up any terrorist attempting to smuggle nuclear material into the city. As O'Neill was about to find out, it was one of those ideas that looks great on paper and becomes a shambles in execution.

"That goddamned thing!" the patrolman said "We turned it off months ago. It picked up every son of a bitch going over the bridge who'd come out of a hospital after having radiotherapy. We even got your Chief of Detectives one day."

"Well, I'd better get him now," O'Neill said and rang up Police Plaza on his mobile. There, he learned from the Chief of Detective's assistant that those devices had been turned off all over the city. Why? Because in their first month of use, they had turned up a staggering 70,000 false positives and the police had simply stopped using them.

"The goddamned program was a shambles" the assistant growled. "Forget about technology saving this city. Still, the PC wants them all turned back on to full power right now. And don't forget, the chief expects you down here forthwith."

O'Neill passed the message to the disconcerted patrolman and climbed back into his car. So, he thought, something big is going down, which explains why we have this 'all hands to the pumps at Police Plaza' order.

And if the chief is insisting all those scanning devices get reactivated immediately, that could well mean it involves, of all things, something nuclear.

"This is it?" the President exploded, slamming the single sheet of paper onto the Situation Room table with the palm of his hand. "This is all, your stations in Islamabad, New Delhi, Kabul, and your nuclear non-proliferation experts could come up with on this guy?"

'This guy' was Dr. Abdul Sharif Ahmad, the nuclear physicist who'd helped build Pakistan's atomic bomb. "What have you got in here we can use as a lever, to open up a dialogue with this guy? He used to stay up all night reciting Urdu poetry? He grew roses when he was a kid? How about all the Dutchmen, the Germans, the Brits he worked with in the seventies? They have any clues to his character we could work on?"

"Mr. President," said Milt Anderson of the CIA, whose officers had been working all night assembling that brief document "you may be a little harsh here. There are a couple of elements in that report which might facilitate our contact with the man."

"Which ones?"

"First, there's the fact Ahmad is a member of an Islamic Group, the Laskar-e-Tibi, Soldiers of the Cause, which we know has ties to Al Qaeda and Osama Bin Laden. So we're dealing here with an apostle of the Jihad.

Yet, there is a contradiction to that in the man's behavior. He's clean shaven, for example. No beard of the Prophet for him. He doesn't drink, however. And as far as we know, he's lived a strictly monagamous existence, always faithful to his one wife."

"Despite those trips to Pyongyang?"

"Alas, Mr. President, it seems clear they were scientific, not sexual, in nature. He seems to be a man of civilized behaviour, which may help in establishing a dialogue with him."

"Civilized? Civilized!" exploded Donald Rumsfeld, the secretary of defense. "Just how civilized can some one be, who doesn't stop proclaiming that the atomic bomb he developed is not just for Pakistan but for all the Moslem world?"

"Look, we're getting off course here," the President interjected. "The problem before us isn't deciding who Dr. Ahmad built his bomb for. It's finding out how we can convince him to help us solve this crisis. He's obviously a deeply religious man. Shouldn't we find some Islamic authority to help us open up a dialogue with him?"

"Now we're on the same page, Mr. President," Milt Anderson answered. We have with us Sheikh Omar Habibullah. He's a Pakistani who runs the Institute of Islamic Studies here, in Washington. He's ready to either help you in a conversation with Ahmad or talk directly to him, himself. Do we know yet, if Dr. Ahmad will agree to talk to us?"

Bush looked at the clock. "His flight landed in Karachi an hour and a half ago. Let's call Mushareff for an update on the situation."

A few minutes later, the Pakistani President's image appeared in a direct TV link from Karachi to the Situation Room closed-circuit TV. "Dr. Ahmad is in the next room," he informed the Americans. "He has admitted to me that the bomb missing from our inventory was taken on the orders of Hamid Bol and his group of extremists. He's also admitted that he himself activated its detonation set so wherever that bomb is, we know it's a fully functional atomic bomb. I've avoided, for the moment, any talk of bringing formal charges against him and at my request, he has agreed to speak with you, but only to explain the reasoning that led Bol and his associates to perform this terrible action."

Well, the President thought, at least he's agreed to talk. That's something to be thankful for. While the room's technicians had been setting up the TV link, a slight man in a beige djellabah and white turban had been ushered into the Situation Room. The President stood, smiled and beckoned him to a seat at the head of the table. The sheikh, the President knew, had been fully briefed on the situation by the CIA.

He turned back to his microphone. "Dr. Ahmad," he said "I want to thank you, first, for agreeing to talk to me in this hour of crisis."

If the President had imagined courtesy was going to get the conversation off on a friendly footing, Ahmad swiftly disabused him of that illusion. "Mr. President," he said "I did so because I want you, of all people, to understand why we did this. It is because your so-called War on Terrorism was never a war on terror. It was always a war on Islam."

"Dr. Ahmad!" the President interjected "you are, I know, a man of deep religious convictions, as am I. The Jesus I worship is acknowledged as a Prophet by your own Holy Book, the Koran."

"Mr. Bush," Ahmad replied "you are a pious fraud. You invaded the land of my Iraqi brothers in search of weapons of mass destruction which never existed. Your so-called Road Map for Middle East peace was a grotesque joke. You never raised a finger to stop that war criminal Ariel Sharon from slaughtering my Palestinian brothers and sisters with your Apache helicopters, your F15s, your rockets. You stood by and did nothing, while his tanks demolished their cities and their homes. Well now, Mr. Bush, an Islamic atomic bomb is hidden somewhere in your nation, and if you do not force Sharon and his Israeli henchmen to return to our Palestinian people the lands they seized in 1967, every square foot of it, then it is your countrymen who will pay for Sharon's intransigence."

The President was aghast. He wasn't going to be able to reason with this man. Probably, his best hope lay in the sheikh, to whom he nodded.

"Good day, Sir," the sheikh began "it is a privilege to address the honored teacher, the much admired intellectual benefactor of our great nation, Pakistan."

"Who are you?" Ahmad asked in a tone that indicated he had long since learned to ignore flattery.

"A fellow Pakistani like you, born in Lahore. I teach Koranic Law at the Islamic Institute here in Washington. The President has asked me to speak with you. I know from studies that you are a devoted follower of our great faith. I speak to you, therefore, in the name of tolerance and understanding, those virtues extolled and practised by our great Prophet, God rest his soul. Surely you know these terrorist fanatics who have planted one of your bombs somewhere in an American city."

"No, I don't know them personally."

"Well, surely you understand that if this bomb, which exists because of the great intelligence which Allah bestowed upon you, explodes, killing hundreds of thousands of innocent people, their deaths will blemish forever, the history of our great faith."

"Look, doctor," Ahmad replied "as I told you, I do not know personally these people you call terrorists, but I can tell you, I admire them and bless their combat. The Jihad is an act of faith. If Allah blessed me with the knowledge to build this device and then placed it in their hands, surely it is to obtain justice for our Palestinian brothers and install upon their stolen land, the blessings of divine justice. I wish for their success."

"Placed in their hands by that bastard Hamid Bol," growled the CIA's Milt Anderson, in a voice too low for his microphone and hence, his listeners in Karachi to pick up.

"My dear Dr. Ahmad," the Professor replied "I'm sure you know, as I do, the surats of our Holy Book which urge us to tolerance, mercy and forgiveness for our enemies."

"Yes," Ahmad answered "and I also know by heart, those surats which urge us to Jihad against those who spread injustice on this earth and crush the weak – 'fight, in the path of Allah, those who fight you' or 'those who are attacked are authorized to defend themselves'. The Palestine martyrs recite verses such as those, before sacrificing their lives on their Israeli targets. Theirs are acts of desperation because no one — and particularly, your American friends — is prepared to offer them hope, a future. If this bomb is menacing the lives of so many Americans, perhaps it can play a crucial role in giving to the Palestinians a future. Perhaps, it can force the enemies of Islam to make peace at last. A just peace. That is now up to your American friends and Ariel Sharon. I have no more to say, learned brother. God keep and preserve you."

The sharp 'click' of a telephone being hammered into its cradle reverberated through the Situation Room. Ahmad had cut the communication.

"Son of a bitch!" said Vice President Dick Cheney "there's going to be no reasoning with that bastard!"

A chorus of grunts and mumbles gave an approving echo to his words. For several long seconds, the room was reduced to silence, its occupants shaken by the brutality of the Pakistani scientist's refusal of a dialogue. It was finally broken by the tones of a feminine voice, that of Condoleezza Rice, the National Security Advisor. "Mr. President" she said "let's let a few minutes go by and then see if I can get Dr. Ahmad back on the line."

"Condi," said Vice President Cheney "with all due respect, that's a terrible idea. That guy is, obviously, a hard-core Islamic extremist. The last person he's going to accept to talk to is a woman."

"I'm not so sure, Dick," Condi Rice replied. "that CIA report describes him as 'civilized', right? He had that childhood upbringing under the British Raj, and those years in Germany and Holland, so 'civilized' might also mean 'courteous.' He could well be more responsive to a female voice than you think. And if he is, I might know how to establish a rapport with him."

There was no one in his government to whom Bush felt closer than his National Security Advisor. With her fluent Russian and knowledge of the Soviet Union, she had played a key role at his father's side in the critical days when the communist empire was collapsing. In his own administration, she was often the first advisor to speak to him after she'd finished her morning workout and, often, the last to talk with him in the evening.

He much admired her ability to calmly synthesize and analyze the arguments surrounding the issues before his government. And the two also shared a passion for watching baseball and football games on TV in the White House.

"Listen," he told the room "let's let Condi give it a try. What have we got to lose? Get Mushareff back on the line and see if we can't get him to reestablish contact with Ahmad."

To everyone's surprise, the Pakistani scientist agreed. "Doctor," Condi began in her warm and husky voice "I want to thank you for agreeing to talk with me. I was anxious to have the opportunity to speak with you because, I think, I am particularly well-placed to understand and sympathize with some of your concerns."

"Sympathize?" Rumsfeld mumbled with an angry glower on hearing her words.

"I have read much about you, Miss Rice," Ahmad replied "and as a fellow academic, I much admire your achievements."

"Thank you, doctor, and I, too, can appreciate the enormity of your scientific accomplishments. We share, I would venture to say, certain common elements endowed to us by history. We — and our peoples — know what it is to suffer the burdens of discrimination practised on us by the wider society surrounding us – you, as Moslems in an Indian Raj dominated by British and Hindu values, we, as Afro Americans, the descendants of slaves, in a society dominated by the values of its white majority. For both of our peoples, religious faith has been a critically important anchor, to which we have clung in our hours of trial, Islam for you, the Baptist faith for most of my brethren. For you, as for me, the pursuit of knowledge was critical in freeing us from the prejudices and hardships our societies imposed on us. We share that, just as we share the darker color of our skin, setting us apart from much of our surroundings."

"Ah yes, Miss Rice," Ahmad interjected with what seemed to the leaders gathered in the Situation Room as just the hint of a laugh "as you Americans say 'black is beautiful'."

The President glowed at his words. Condi's done it, he thought. She's made him laugh.

"Our struggle in this country," she continued "was often marked by hatred and bitterness for our white brothers and sisters."

"And," Ahmad noted "the murder and lynching of your people."

"Indeed," Condi replied "but it was the message of tolerance and wisdom, understanding and fraternity, given voice by great men like Martin Luther King that led us, doctor, to where we are today."

"King, of course. A disciple of India's Gandhi, I saw as a youth," Ahmad noted.

"Suicide bombers, however just they may feel their cause is, do not, Dr. Khan, represent the true ideals of Islam anymore than Timothy McVeigh, the Oklahoma bomber, represented those of Catholicism. Islam, the great Faith that it is, is no more represented by Osama Bin Laden than Christianity's values were represented by the excesses of the Crusaders of Pope Urban II."

"Indeed," Ahmad said "well put."

"I know doctor, that you, like I am, are a great lover of poetry."

"Quite true, Miss Rice," Ahmad replied, with what was almost a sigh.

"I have always liked that Persian epic, the *Rubaiyat* of Omar Khayam."

"Ah yes. I share your enthusiasm for that great work."

"How often do I reflect on that line *'I sing of man's brief life, separated from death by the space of a breath'.*"

"How true those words," Ahmad sighed.

"Yes," Condi continued "and surely you would wish that the harvest of your great scientific achievement will be the triumph of justice and understanding. Not hatred and bloodshed, the stifling of life's short breath in hundreds of thousands of people."

She paused to give emphasis to the plea she was now ready to utter. "Come with me, doctor, in the footsteps of Martin Luther King. They lead to the broad uplands of human understanding and reconciliation, not the hell of hatred and vengeance the explosion of your bomb will wreak. There is still time, doctor. Reflect and help us overcome this crisis embracing us all."

An almost eerie silence followed her words. "You are a powerful advocate, Miss Rice" Ahmad answered finally, his voice suddenly subdued. "I shall reflect on what you have said, overnight. God willing, we will talk tomorrow."

Once again, a click indicated that he had hung up his receiver. As it did, something happened which the somber premises of the Situation Room had not wit-

nessed since Khruschev signaled his willingness to withdraw his missiles from Cuba. The entire room burst
into applause.

Holy smoke, Detective Lieutenant T.F. O'Neill thought,
looking at the mob crowding the auditorium of the New
York Police Department at One Police Plaza, everybody's here but the men's room attendants. There were
FBI agents by the hundreds, probably every damn detective in the NYPD, Customs guys, Secret Service,
Counterfeit Squad guys, New York State Police Troop-
ers. The only thing missing from the city's police community were the girls from the Society for the Preven-
tion of Cruelty to Animals!

And the brass up on the platform, the PC, Ray Kelly;
O'Neill's boss, the Chief of Detectives; Dave Cohen,
the deputy PC for Intelligence; the Irishman who ran
the FBI, a couple of 'suits', probably spooks from Washington or Albany. All the flags were on the platform
behind them, the nation's, the city's the state's, the
NYPD's, the FBI's. You'd think they were getting ready
for a parade down Fifth Avenue.

Commissioner Kelly got up, walked to the lectern
and banged a gavel to silence the clamor of a thousand
men and women talking anxiously to each other.

"Alright people," he said "let's come to attention and
listen up." For a long moment, he stood there staring out

at the gathering, the Marine Corps officer bracing to send his troops into battle. "Ladies and Gentlemen, we have a crisis on our hands, perhaps the worst crisis this city has ever had to face."

"Worse than 9/11?" an incredulous voice from the audience asked.

Kelly ignored the speaker. "We have solid intelligence information that a group of terrorists has smuggled a barrel of chlorine gas into Manhattan Island. I don't think I need to tell you just how deadly chlorine gas is. Should those terrorists release it into our atmosphere if their demands are not met, the result could be the death of hundreds, thousands of our fellow New Yorkers."

Kelly's words sent alarm bells ringing in O'Neill's head. They wanted those gamma-ray detectors on the bridges and tunnels turned back on full blast to pick up chlorine gas?

"I'm sure you all remember from your chemical warfare training sessions, how toxic that damn stuff is. The fact that, that barrel has been hidden here in Manhattan and we're looking for it must, and I repeat, must be kept a total secret. If it got to the public, we'd risk having a panicked flight of the population like the one we saw on 9/11. I can tell you because you are all responsible, intelligent law enforcement officers."

O'Neill looked at his fellow 'responsible law enforcement officers' mesmerized by Kelly's words. Sure, he thought, pick up chlorine gas with gamma-ray detectors.

Believe in this chlorine gas barrel story and you'd believe in the tooth fairy.

"What are the terrorists after?" someone shouted from the audience.

"It's an Arab-Israeli thing," Kelly answered. "That's the State Department's concern, not ours. Ours is to get to that barrel before the terrorists blow it up. The lives of one hell of a lot of people are going to depend on our succeeding in that job. Unfortunately, we have very little intelligence of the perpetrators at this moment, but I will turn the meeting over to Deputy PC Dave Cohen, who'll give you all we've got."

"This has all the earmarks of an Ai Qaeda operation," Cohen began "so we will want to activate every source we have on Arab terrorists and activists. And we will want to look at every source we have on people who are into providing them with false IDs, driver's licenses, credit cards, whatever. This will be an 'All Hands' operation, bringing in every human resource we have available, Treasury, Customs, Narcotics, the lot. We have already mobilized the Joint FBI NYPD Anti Terrorism Task Force. Inspectors accompanied by federal officers are to begin immediately, scouring out potential targets, the Empire State Building, Madison Square Garden, Penn and Grand Central Stations. We have selected fifty senior grade detectives to leave immediately for Port Elizabeth where they will be paired with FBI officers and Customs agents, to comb through the manifests of every container unloaded there in the last 30 days.

"Unfortunately, we have no physical description of the perpetrators available, as of this moment. We do not know their number or anything of their movements, except that we know these people realize it's best to blend in as middle-class folk, do as little as possible to draw attention to themselves. They usually live well but not ostentatiously. They don't want for money. They do have a tendency to stay with their own kind, so we'll want to check out everything we have on the Arab communities, over in Brooklyn, for example. But what is called for here is good, solid, hard-headed detective work. Let's go. There'll be assignments waiting for you in your precincts. And the 50 guys selected for Port Elizabeth will find their names on the bulletin board in the hall."

"Hell!" said O'Neill, finding his name on that list. Here I am running Manhattan South which is supposed to be the most terror-prone place in the city, and I have to go junketing off to Port Elizabeth for the night!

The sense of relief that had swept over the U.S. government officials gathered in the White House Situation Room after Condi Rice's conversation with Dr. Ahmad had been brief. Now the President and his advisors faced yet another challenge, one which promised to be almost as difficult as the conversation with the Pakistani had been.

"We just can't put this off any longer, Mr. President," Colin Powell said. "You've got to get Ariel Sharon on the line. We've prepared a one-page summary of the situation in Hebrew that we can put onto the closed-circuit link by facsimile, so he'll have everything in front of him."

The President gave a worried stroke to his forehead. His conversations with the Israeli leader were never easy. This one promised to be a nightmare. "Where is he?" he asked.

"At his residence, on Balfour Street in Jerusalem, probably just finishing up his dinner," Powell said.

"Kosher cuisine," smiled the President "just like we had for him here when he came to dinner at the White House. It's not bad. Milt," he said to the head of the CIA, "you've studied this guy. Is there anything in his history or background that gives you reason to hope he might be accommodating to us in the face of this menace?"

"Absolutely nothing, Mr. President. His reputation for activism goes all the way back to '49 or '50, when he was a young officer and led his company on a punitive raid into a village in Jordan in which fedayeen were alleged to be hidden. Gratuitously killed, I think, it was 60 of the village males. He became a fully-fledged hero in the 1973 war, when his division smashed across the Suez Canal and encircled a large part of the Egyptian Army. He was a powerful advocate for action against the PLO in Lebanon because of their raids into Israel.

When the war started, he promised Begin he'd stop twenty miles inside Lebanon but, of course, he went all the way to the suburbs of Beirut. If he'd had his way, he would certainly have killed Arafat right there and then, but he was under pressure from Reagan to exercise restraint."

"And, of course, there was that business of killing all those Palestinians in a refugee camp," the President recalled.

"Sabra and Chatilla."

"Yeah, wherever. Just how guilty was he really of that, my 'man of peace'?"

A faint ripple of laughter followed the President's words.

"At the best, Mr. President, he was guilty of doing nothing to stop it." Anderson replied.

"And tell me, is he really a believing, religious man?"

"He follows, outwardly, the requirements of Jewish life. Like his kosher dinners here at the White House. Does that reflect belief or political expediency? I don't think I'm entitled to say. However, Mr. President, there is one thing on which I think we at the agency all agree – it's that famous visit he made to the Temple Mount or what the Moslems call the Haram al Sharif, in September 2000. That, we are convinced, was sheer expediency. He could have gone up there any time he wanted to, for 33 years. His aim on that visit was to blow the Oslo peace process out of the water, which he certainly succeeded in doing."

"And his thoughts on the settlements?" the President asked.

"Oh hell, Mr. President, you got the answer to that when you were trying to implement your Road Map for Middle East Peace. All you got out of him was a little lip-service. Knocked over a couple of trailer camps for the TV cameras, which were set back up the next day."

"Well," the President sighed "this conversation is going to be a bitch alright. Colin," he ordered his secretary of state "I guess, you'd better get him on the line."

Powell did the preliminaries, then passed the facsimile over the TV line to Jerusalem.

"My God!" Sharon exploded, on reading it, in the deep parade ground voice for which he was noted "this is the most outrageous, incredible effort at extortion, at blackmail, in history. As the leader of the world's only superpower, you have only one choice open to you before history, before the world. Reveal this to the world immediately, and denounce it for the horrible act of blackmail that it is."

"And put the lives of a million of my fellow Americans in New York at risk?"

"It is not you who is putting them at risk, Mr. President. It is these Islamic extremist terrorists in Pakistan who are behind this. People surely tied to Osama Bin Laden. You tell them publicly that if that bomb explodes, Pakistan's Northwest Frontier Province, Baluchistan, those areas where these acts are coming from, will disappear from the face of the earth. And you won't have to worry about finding Osama Bin Laden anymore. As you Americans say, he'll be toast."

"Ariel," the President replied — the two men had been on a first-name basis for years now — "that's an appalling suggestion. Six million Pakistanis would die in such an outrage! You have always chosen to ignore the hatred, the thirst for vengeance, your retaliatory acts against the Palestinians create. Do this, and you'll have the entire Moslem world thirsting for vengeance against you."

"Don't worry. They're the same ones who will cheer and dance in the streets if that bomb ever explodes in New York. Just like they did on 9/11."

"Look, Ariel, whether you like it or not, you and I have got to, at least, consider addressing the demands in that note. Every American President since Lyndon Johnson has opposed those settlements as an unwarranted and illegal abuse of another people's lands. My own father and his Secretary of State Jim Baker were particularly opposed to them."

"That is absolutely out of the question, George. God gave those lands to the Jewish people. We, the Jewish people, have a historic right to the whole of the land of Israel. We are going to surrender them in response to a heinous attempt at blackmail, at extortion such as this? I have made my feelings on our rights to at least some of those lands clear to you, often enough."

"Ariel, a majority of your own people are ready to dismantle those settlements. You know, as well as I do, that they cost your nation 560 million dollars a year in subsidies of one form or another — subsidies, which we Americans somehow always seem to wind up paying. We have always been your nation's best friend and closest ally. How much love do you think is going to be left for Israel in this country if that bomb explodes?"

"George, if I bend my knee before this ghastly attempt at blackmail, it will be the end of Israel. I have never, in the past, made a concession with the security of Israel. I will make none now and none in the future. That is the historic responsibility that I bear for the future and fate of the Jewish people. You tell your friend Mushareff to announce to these criminals that if they go through with this, six million Pakistanis will die – and if you don't have the guts to take them out with your weaponry, I will do it with our Jericho missiles. Forget what you have read about some pilots in our air force questioning orders. Jericho missiles don't question orders, George. This is a horrendous problem but it is one that you, and not me, will have to solve. *Shalom.*"

Once again, a stunned silence enveloped the American leaders in the Situation Room. "Dear God!" murmured the CIA's Anderson. "Pray those New York cops and the Feds can find that damn thing in time!"

Two hundred miles from the crisis meeting in the White House Situation Room, the three terrorists who had smuggled their bomb into New York, were finishing dinner. The remains of the dinner they had purchased from their nearby neighbor, Mimosa's Pizza, a "Five Cheeses Pizza", littered the living room of the terrorists' squalid midtown Manhattan flat. A camp bed, a table and three chairs, for which they had spent the afternoon shopping, consisted of the living room's furniture. The bedroom's furniture was their atomic bomb, a two-foot high device in a cylindrical form, looking a bit like an oversized barrel. Protruding from its top, was the Nokia cellular phone designed to receive an incoming detonation signal, which they had properly secured to it on their arrival.

Omar Tahiri glanced at his watch. They could now safely make their call. A London colleague had equipped them with a pair of Nokia phones purchased at a computer warehouse for 450 pounds. Each phone had an identical "chip", a SIM which was fitted into its base and which was equipped with a pre-purchased 50 minutes of calling time. The beauty of the system was that the two phones could call each other but no one else. That meant they would be rarely used and calls made on them would be extremely difficult to trace. They, of course, had one. Imad Mugniyeh had the other.

Omar used his first name when the phone answered. Mugniyeh replied by simply saying "your friend is listening."

"We are here. Everything has been set in place, as instructed." He then proceeded to give Mugniyeh the address and details of the building in which they had placed their bomb, in a verbal code which Tahiri had been given before they left.

"That is good," Mugniyeh said "I will now take over."

Both men had been careful not to use any Arabic or any revealing Islamic-style phrases. Mugniyeh was particularly anxious to keep his part of the call brief, because he knew the Americans' NSA had multiple recordings of his voice with which they could run a voice print analysis to determine if he had been one of the speakers, should they somehow decide to scrutinize the call after picking it up with one of their spy satellites.

The terrorist trio had rented rooms in a comfortable hotel not too far away. One of them would stay constantly in this flat. On the table they had purchased was an electric switch they had wired to the detonator. Should the police break down the door of their flat, the member of the trio 'baby-sitting' the bomb would have only to press that button and the bomb would explode.

Omar had volunteered to take the first shift until mid morning, allowing the others to get a reasonable night's sleep in their hotel rooms.

As they were preparing to leave, Khaled sat down beside Omar and squeezed his knee. Of the three, his experience in the struggle with their Israeli enemies was, by far, the freshest. "Listen," he said "I know how the Israelis run most of their targetted assassinations. It's with these mobile phones. The Americans developed a technique they passed on to the Mossad. If they have your mobile phone number, they can call it. You won't know that the phone's been called but it will send back an answering message. Then they call the phone from somewhere else and triangulate, and they know exactly where the phone — and presumably you — are. Boom! They hit you even if you're in a car with that mobile turned off. They can figure out what building you're in, even what room. We had to call Beirut and you can be sure that's one place their satellites are focused on. They get our number and they may be able to trace us right to this room. I suggest, I chuck this in a waste can on the way back to the hotel. We don't need it anymore, do we?"

The President pushed away his TV remote control with a weary gesture. "I'm exhausted," he announced to his wife, Laura, and his National Security Advisor Condi Rice, who'd joined the couple in the White House Living Quarters for a final review of the day's work. "I don't have the strength or the desire to watch a ball game tonight. What a day! The worst in my presidency since 9/11."

"Yes," Condi agreed "It can't get much worse than today."

"Oh yes, it can," the President sighed. "The only high point in the day was your talk with Dr. Ahmad."

"He did come around a bit, didn't he?" his National Security Advisor noted.

"Because of you, your human touch with him." Suddenly, the President sat up straight in his chair. "Of course," he said "it was that human contact between the two of you that did it. What if we could set that up live, on a person-to-person basis? Condi, suppose we could get Mushareff to agree, would you be willing to fly out to Karachi and try to reason with Dr. Ahmad, talk to him on a one-to-one basis? That just might be the way out of this damn mess."

"Mr. President, if Mushareff will agree and you so desire, of course I will. Obviously, I'm ready to do anything to ease this crisis."

"Let me handle Mushareff. I don't think he'll be a problem. He's being very helpful so far. I'll call Andy Card and have him get Air Force One at Bolling geared up to take you to Karachi. You get out there as fast as you can."

"Certainly." Condi closed her eyes for a second or two, reflecting on the task she'd just been assigned. "One thing, Mr. President. Can we ask the Press Office to put together a package of the very best, the most moving video tape we have of 9/11? Not the shots of the planes hitting the towers and the buildings collapsing. Islamic extremists just love that footage. Of the anguish, the pain, the suffering, the faces of the women and children. That's what I want."

"Of course."

★ ★ ★

Detective Lieutenant T.F. O'Neill struggled to suppress the ill humor that had been building up in him for hours. Here he was, the commanding officer of the Midtown South Detective Squad, the elite unit assigned to protect what even Police Commissioner Kelly acknowledged was the most terror-prone area of New York City, and what was he doing to stave off the menace threatening his city?

Not a damn thing he could see. He was parked in front of a computer screen in Port Elizabeth, New Jersey, methodically plodding his way through hundreds, soon to be thousands, of manifests and bills of lading of every ship and container that had called on the port in the thirty days prior to the arrival of the terrorists' threat note at the White House. That tiresome, boring task was supposed, somehow, to allow O'Neill and his fifty fellow NYPD detectives, each of them paired off with an FBI agent, to spot a suspicious cargo in which the terrorists might have somehow smuggled their deadly device into New York.

The only consolation for T.F. in this grotesque misuse of his years of experience was sitting beside him. It was the FBI agent assigned to work with him, a relative rarity among the Feds, an African American female. What's more, she was stunning. In her tight black leather skirt and blouse, with her full lips, beautifully combed hair and lithe, athletic figure, she could have done a centerfold for Playboy.

Not that he would pay her the compliment of suggesting that, of course. Not in these days of ultra-sensitive feminists, ready to misread even the slightest slip of the tongue as an unwanted sexual advance. His FBI mate — her name was Olivia Phillips — was from the Louisiana Bayou country. The Bureau had recruited her out of Tulane Law School, she'd said, and sent her to their Quantico, Virginia academy for training and a final polish.

He glanced at her peering intently at the manifest on her computer screen, then let his eyes fall to her slim legs protruding from her short, tight skirt. How times change, he thought. When he'd joined the force, Feds came in one sex — male. They all dressed alike, dark suits off the racks from Barneys, hair cut short, never any question of facial hair of any sort.

Now they came in sports shirts, wearing baseball caps turned fashionably backwards, ill shaven. Hell, he'd even seen one of them wearing an earring! And now, of course, some of them came in skirts and blouses, like this lovely creature sitting next to him.

"Spot anything, Olivia?" he asked.

"Oh sure," she said, as bored by this task as he was, "another container full of bed sheets from Singapore for Walmarts." She shrugged and clicked the button on her computer to pull up yet another manifest for her appraising — and tiring — eyes.

On their arrival, a Customs officer had assigned them to the first floor of the port's administration building. It housed a dozen gigantic offices, one for each of the port's terminals. They were given a large desk with two computers, its windows looking out across the towering cranes and warehouses of the port. Their charge was the vessels that had docked in berths fifteen to twenty of Marine Terminal Four in the last thirty days. That meant inspecting the paperwork on the cargos discharged in those berths by the 121 ships. All told, those ships had off-loaded close to 5000 containers, each of which they were supposed to study.

As it happened, however, thirty seven of those ships had been auto ferries, bringing in 32,450 new German, British, Japanese and Korean cars. The cars came pre-attached to tractor trailers which were immediately driven off to the assorted car dealerships on the eastern seaboard that had ordered them. Run those cars down to their dealers and check each one out to see if someone wanted to use it to smuggle a bomb into the country, was an impossible task.

That left T.F. and Olivia to scan the paperwork for the remaining containers. Olivia's eyes were now red with fatigue. She leaned back and rubbed them, while T.F. gave her a sympathetic look. She glanced out the window at the forest of cranes lining the terminal piers. Never had she seen a port like this one before. "Quite a place, isn't it?" she said.

T.F. laughed "On the Waterfront, it ain't, that's for sure. You should have seen the old Brooklyn Docks I knew as a kid. The mob ran everything in those days.

The morning shape-ups where they picked the long-shoremen for the day. You didn't have a cousin or uncle in a family, forget it. There'd be no work for you, pal. Now, like you see out there, it's all mechanized."

"What happened to the mob?" Olivia asked.

"Dead. Or into new things like fake credit cards. Fortunately, we've got a lot of them doing time upstate."

"Yes," she said "they taught us a lot about that at the academy in Quantico. Gotti, the Gambinos. Did you get involved in all that?"

"Oh hell, yes. A lot of those wise guys came from my precinct, downtown in Little Italy." T.F. took a deep breath. "Hey," he said "that's a nice perfume you're wearing!"

"Thanks," Olivia smiled "It's Joy by Patou." Fascinating, she was thinking. How many people would expect a New York detective to pick up on something like that? "Are you married, T.F.?" she asked.

"No," he said "I'm a widower. I lost my wife in an automobile accident six years ago."

"Oh, how sad," she commiserated "what a painful loss that must be."

"Yeah," T.F. sighed. "The holes in your life don't come any bigger than that. Well, I guess, we better get back to this exciting job they've given us."

Olivia pulled another ship's manifest up on her screen. "Hey!" she said "Here's one that at least has got a nice name – 'The Jewel of India'."

"Yeah," said T.F. "Probably carrying curry as an

easier way to poison New Yorkers than chlorine gas would be."

Twenty minutes later, Olivia laid her hand on T.F.'s wrist. "T.F.," she said "have a look at this." She pointed to her computer screen. "Here we've got two containers off-loaded from this Jewel of India on the same day, one after another. According to their bills of lading, they have identical cargoes — 250 sacks of Basmati rice, each weighing 50 kilos. The containers are identical, same model, same manufacturer. When the first one gets weighed on that scale at quayside, it weighs 31,000 kilos. Then the second one is weighed and it comes in at 31,150 kilos. Why the difference? How much do you suppose a barrel of chlorine gas weighs?"

T.F. studied her computer screen. "Yeah," he said "interesting. Of course, it could be anything, but still..."

He pulled up the Jewel's consignment sheet for the containers.

NAME OF VESSEL: The Jewel of India
SHIPPER: Maharashtra Oriental Foods, Bombay
CONTENTS: BASMATI RICE
DESCRIPTION: 250 SACKS 50 KILOS PER SACK
CONSIGNEE: Exotic Grocery Goods, Central Warehousing, Grand Ave, Albany NY
IDENTIFICATION: LOS 8477/8484

Both consignment sheets were, as Olivia had indicated, identical. So why the difference in weight? Where had those containers gone? It was pretty certain they hadn't stayed up in Albany. Those guys probably had forwarded them to a food store somewhere in the northeast. And if that store was in New York?

"Well done, Little Pal," he said. "This merits a follow up. Let's see if we can get somebody on the line up there in Albany."

A few minutes later, thanks to State Police Headquarters in Albany, they had a sleep-befuddled night watchman at Exotic Grocery on the line. He knew nothing about the containers in the warehouse yard.

"So what's the telephone number of the boss?" O'Neill asked.

"Hey man," the watchman said "It's one o'clock. He be sleeping now."

"I didn't ask you what he's doing. I want his phone number and I want it right now. Or I'll send a State Trooper out there to get it from you. And to get you too, for failure to execute a lawful order."

Three minutes later, the frightened watchman gave them the home phone number of the owner, Charles Osborne.

"Let me talk to him," Olivia suggested. "Sometimes guys will stand up a bit straighter when they hear the words FBI."

Osborne had, indeed, been sound asleep when his wife got him, steaming angry to the phone. He began to berate his callers when Olivia cut him short in her iciest voice, as she'd been trained to do at Quantico. "This is Special Agent Olivia Phillips of the Federal

Bureau of Investigation. There is a national security concern involved here and I expect your immediate cooperation."

You could almost hear Mr. Osborne swallowing his distress at her words. "Of course, I am at your disposition," he assured Olivia in the meekest of tones while T.F. looked at her admiringly.

Olivia gave him the references of the containers of Basmati rice and told him they had an urgent interest in determining where they had gone.

Osborne pondered the question. "We do a lot of Basmati rice. There's a guy in Buffalo and one in Brooklyn who get it regularly, but I don't have their addresses and numbers here."

"Can you get them for me? Urgently?" Olivia said.

"Well," said Osborne "I live down here in Pawling. It's about an hour's drive up to my warehouse. Say, another hour or so to dig through the files and get you what you want. It's a helluva chore at this time of night, but if my country needs me…"

"Yes," Olivia answered "your country needs you and is grateful for your help, Mr. Osborne."

At T.F.'s suggestion, they gave Osborne the phone number of his Manhattan South precinct to call. "If that guy's in Brooklyn, we'll want to get out there as fast as we can. What we'll do is drive back to the precinct. I have three female detectives in my squad, so there's a women's quarter there where you can catch some sleep."

He quickly explained what they were doing to the

Customs officer running the manifest search and they were released. Before long, they were heading for Manhattan through the Holland Tunnel.

"O'Neill," Olivia said "I guess you must be Irish."

"Yeah, on my father's side we go back to the potato famine and the Civil War. Lately, though, I got a French Canadian grandmother and a Lithuanian great grand mum."

"Did policing run in your family?"

"On my father's side. He and my grandfather were both on the force. How about policing in your family?"

Olivia laughed gaily. "Oh sure. When they weren't picking cotton in Massa's fields."

"Yeah," O'Neill smiled. "My grandmother loved to tell me the ONeill's were the kings of Ireland. That, and a buck will get you a beer in any pub in Dublin."

Before long, they had pulled into the precinct. O'Neill took her upstairs to the two rooms that had been set aside as living quarters for his female detectives when they had to work overnight. "It's not the Ritz," he said, as Olivia stretched out on one of the beds with a heavy sigh.

T.F. looked down on her fondly. "Well," he said "get what sleep you can. As my mother used to say, 'roses on your pillow'." He switched off the lights and tip-toed out of the room.

6

New York City, Washington D.C., Jerusalem, Karachi

The Crisis, Day Two

Dawn had long since lifted autumn's chilly veil from the skyline of New York when T.F. O'Neill's unmarked police car slid off the exit ramp of the Brooklyn Bridge onto Flatbush Avenue. Beside him, the FBI's Olivia Phillips glanced back towards the skyline of Manhattan.

"How come these bastards always pick on New York?" she wondered aloud, her curiosity activated by the three steaming cups of black coffee T.F. had served her before leaving his precinct headquarters – the best in the five boroughs, he had assured her. "Why don't they try Chicago or L. A. or even, God forbid, New Orleans?"

"Because we got it all here, babe. The money, the

people, the power. A lot of Jews living here. People hate America? First thing that comes to mind is New York, that sight you just looked at back there."

At this early hour the streets were nearly deserted and before long, they were gliding to a stop in the driveway of a red brick warehouse on which was painted the words "Birbaki Oriental Foods."

"Looks deserted," Olivia said.

"Yeah," T.F. agreed. "We may be off on a wild goose chase here. Still, a place like this ought to have a watchman. Crime may be down in New York, but it ain't down that much."

He walked to the garage door and began banging loudly on it with his fist.

"You don't shout 'police'?" Olivia asked.

"Hell no. If there's a watchman in there, let him think he's got a delivery."

After a few more imperative knocks, a sleep-befuddled African American opened the door. "Hey man," he snarled "we be closed. You want something, you come back in an hour."

T.F. 'gave him the gold' – flashed his detective's shield at the watchman. "Where's the boss?" he asked.

"He be asleep over in Green Point. You want I call him for you?"

That was the last thing T.F. wanted. He wanted to get the grocer cold, without allowing him a moment to reflect on a story if, indeed, he was a party to bringing a bomb, or much more likely, dope, into the city.

"Nope," he said "what I want is to wait in here for him to show up. And you, pal, will just wait here for him with me and my friend."

Birbaki did indeed show up 45 minutes later, stunned, as he opened the door to his little office to find his two visitors and the watchman waiting for him. Before he could give voice to his anger and amazement, Olivia stepped forward and flashed her I.D. "Special Agent Olivia Phillips, the Federal Bureau of Investigation." As she articulated those words. T.F. studied Birbaki's facial expression, hoping to see there some tell-tale hint of fright that might bespeak the man's guilt.

He then flashed in turn, his shield. "Police!" he said "We want to have a little talk with you."

"What the hell is this all about?" Birbaki gasped. "I run an honest business here. Never had any trouble with you guys."

"It's about the two containers of Basmati rice you got here 48 hours ago," T.F. said, still peering intently at Birbaki and suddenly seeing what he was looking for, an intimation of fear sweeping over the surprise on his face. Was the guy moving drugs, he wondered?

"There was something in one of those containers, my friend, that wasn't Basmati rice. I want to know what it was and where it went."

Birbaki collapsed into his office armchair, grasping his head in his hands. Scared absolutely shitless, T.F.thought, you could almost smell the fear oozing out of his glands. Time to use a different tactic with the guy.

"Moving drugs," he said. "You can figure for a guy like you, got a clean sheet and all, it's ten to fifteen years inside, depending on the judge."

"Officer, I don't know what it was," Birbaki murmured. "I really don't."

"Look!" T.F said "different guys got different ways of working. Me, I always say level with a guy, tell him where he's at. You help us, we help you, you know what I mean? I gotta know where that package that was in there with the rice went, what it looked like. Who got it. That's because I'm a downtown detective not a narc, you know what I mean?"

"OK," said a somewhat relieved Birbaki. "I'll tell you everything I know." And he did, beginning with the Turk's first request, the subsequent deliveries and the final pick up.

"Now that Turk with the New York Yankees cap," O'Neill asked. "You got a name and number for him?"

Birbaki did and got it off his rolodex. T.F passed it to Olivia with a nod who stepped out towards their car.

"OK," he said to Birbaki "let's go over all the details of that last pickup yesterday morning," he said.

"Well," Birbaki replied "the Turk always came for the stuff in a Hertz van. These two had an Easy Rent van. The woman was driving. She was wearing a kerchief on her head."

"A Moslem?" T.F. asked.

"Who's to know? It was chilly. The guy, he didn't have a left hand so my guys had to take the crate out of the container for him and load it into his van."

"Did you see it?"

"No, I was in here. My guys said it was a wooden crate, maybe three feet long and heavy as hell. Couple of hundred pounds at least. T.F. frowned. Sounded like it was too heavy to be horse and two hundred plus pounds of hash, you'd need three of those crates. Maybe it wasn't drugs, after all.

Olivia, meanwhile, had returned from the car where she'd called FBI Headquarters. "Our Turk has flown the coop," she said. "Flew back to Istanbul Thursday."

"Shit!" T.F. groaned. A crate that looks too heavy for drugs. A Turk who conveniently disappears just when we need him. And an Easy Rent van. That was where you didn't need a credit card to rent a truck. Just drop a thousand bucks' deposit on the desk beside your fake driver's license and away you go. Maybe, he thought, this bright little FBI chick here had hit on something with those manifests last night.

"Look! Mr. Birbaki," he said "I'd like you to come downtown with us and we'll just drop by Easy Rent and see if we can find out who rented that van and where it went."

A refreshing autumn breeze stirred the Aleppo pines lining the route of Ariel Sharon's three-car caravan as it sped past Saint John's Monastery of the Cross, up the incline to the Israeli Knesset and the building housing the Jewish nation's principal government offices. As usual, a gaggle of journalists and TV cameramen were waiting as Sharon's car pulled to a stop in front of the Prime Minister's Office.

Why, they shouted at him, had he convened this extraordinary meeting of his government? Sharon answered with an indifferent shrug of his shoulders, a dismissive wave of his hand, meant to indicate it was a matter of no importance, and he set off down the long corridor to his cabinet room with a purposeful stride.

No such reticence, however, softened his exposition of the crisis before their nation, in his presentation to his cabinet colleagues. First, he passed out copies of the White House's Hebrew summary of the crisis, including the full text of the terrorists' threat note. Then he reviewed the transcript of his talk with the President from the tape recording he'd made of their conversation.

The reaction of his cabinet colleagues was a mixture of horrified surprise and fury. Many of them, of course, were well to the right, politically, of the Prime Minister. The Tourism Minister, Yisrael Ephraim, was among them and he was the first to respond.

"You were absolutely right, Arik, to tell Bush we will incinerate Pakistan's Northwest Frontier Province and Baluchistan if that bomb goes off. Those places are breeding grounds for the worst Islamic extremists on the planet. Bin Laden and the followers he trained in his camps, the Taliban, the *madrassahs* fueled by Saudi money and Wahabite hate teachings. Be sure that they are behind this."

"You'll kill millions of innocent people," protested Henry Levy of the moderate Shinui Party, one of the few non-Likud members of the cabinet. "Islam and its adherents will abominate this nation and the Jewish people for generations, as a result".

"Oh horse shit!" growled Ephraim. "They already do. Besides, did you see the results of the last elections out there? They voted those Islamic crazies into office."

"Mr. Mofaz," Sharon asked his Defense Minister in the stiffly formal tone he always employed in these meetings. He prided himself in maintaining a profile distinctly different from the other leaders of the nation, like its founder David Ben Gurion who didn't own a necktie. Since leaving the army, he was inevitably well-dressed in public, in a well-pressed dark suit, freshly laundered white shirt and a necktie from the most elegant men's store in Tel Aviv. "How about those Shaheen II intermediate range missiles the Paks tested a year ago? Could they hit us in a retaliatory strike? Three well-placed nuclear hits would destroy this nation."

"Yes," Mofaz replied "they certainly could. They have a range of 1200 miles, quite enough to reach Tel Aviv. We know from the Mossad they have, at least, 50 Hiroshima-sized nuclear warheads, and they've had a year to manufacture those missiles. Certainly long enough to manufacture at least 50 of them."

"And what of our defense against a missile attack?

Could we prevent those missiles from getting through?" Sharon asked.

"I would hope so," Mofaz replied. "The Patriot missiles which we used in the Gulf War are now much improved, and more important, we have the Arrow anti missile we developed with the Americans which has been remarkably successful in all our testing. Still, nothing is certain in life. We have no absolute guarantee one or two of them won't get through."

"A dismaying prospect!" Sharon growled.

"Arik!" It was Sharon's great political rival Benyamin Netanyahu, sidelined since Israel's last election as the nation's Minister of the Economy, a task that was as challenging as it was certain to dim his political appeal to the masses. "There is no question – this is what we have all feared for years, the existential crisis in which the very life of this nation is at stake."

A mumble of approval greeted his words. "If we crumble before this threat," he continued "our Zionist will to exist is going to be fatally compromised."

"Benji, for God's sake!" Levy interrupted. "You know, as well as I do, that the majority of the people of this nation are opposed to those settlements in the first place."

"It's not the settlements that is the issue here. The issue is, is this nation going to back down before a ter rorists' extortion threat?"

"Benji, we are not being threatened. It's a million New Yorkers who are."

"But it is we who are being asked to pay the price of this blackmail. Pay it and our reason, our right to our national existence will be compromised, perhaps fatally."

"I'll tell you how we solve this crisis," barked Avigdor Beibelman. Together with his close friend, the Minister of Tourism, he was the most extremist member of the cabinet. "We go public and say 'if that bomb goes off, we will pack every Palestinian on the West Bank and Gaza into trucks and deport the lot of them to Jordan'."

"Madness!" retorted Levy. "We will become a pariah nation."

"We already are. And those terrorists will have solved the problem of Judea and Samaria for us, once and for all."

"Look!" Sharon intervened. "I must make one thing clear. I pledged my word to President Bush that I would keep this threat a secret, in view of the terms in that terrorists' note, and I hold you all honor bound to respect my pledge."

"Oh Arik!" interjected Beibelman, "The Americans will betray us. Just like Eisenhower did in 1957 after the Suez War, when he forced us out of the Sinai."

Sharon ignored him. "Since my conversation with the President, the Mossad and the Shin Bet have been working all out to help the Americans in their search for the bomb."

"What do we tell the journalists outside was the reason for our meeting?" Mofaz asked.

Sharon thought a minute. "Tell them we were discussing a new program to bolster this faltering tourist industry of ours." Even in moments of crisis, the Prime Minister was not without a sense of humour. "I think, my friends," he continued "we have reached a very clear consensus. I will have to call the President and inform him that regretfully, this government cannot, and will not, agree to dismantling the settlements, despite the horror of the threat he faces."

Unnoticed by Sharon and unheard by anyone else in the room, Beibelman had turned to his colleague and fellow extremist, the Minister of Tourism. "I have an idea," he whispered. "An idea that will blow this crisis right out of the water."

T.F. O'Neill had planted his flashing blue 'clear the streets' light with its in-built siren, on the roof of his police car as he had left the warehouse of Birbaki's Oriental Foods. Now, traffic was melting before his car as he raced up Hudson Street to its junction with lower Eighth Avenue and Bethune Street. There, at the corner was his destination, the only Manhattan garage of Easy Rent cars. It was Easy Rent's closest garage to Birbaki's warehouse. Therefore, in O'Neill's judgement, the most likely site at which the man and woman who had picked up the mysterious crate secreted in the container of Basmati rice, off-loaded from the Jewel of India, would have rented their van.

The garage owner, alerted by a call from Police Headquarters, was waiting for T.F., Olivia Phillips, his FBI partner, and Birbaki, at the garage door. As she and T.F. had agreed, Olivia flashed her government I.D. and laid the imposing phrase "Federal Bureau of Investigation" on the owner, to make him stand up a little bit straighter than he might have for a NYPD shield.

At the request of police headquarters, the owner had laid out for them in his office the rental agreements covering all the vans his agency had rented out in the last ten days. They were divided into two piles, one for male renters and a second, much smaller, for females who'd rented a van.

T.F. sat Birbaki down at the owner's desk and pointed to the smaller pile. "O.K., pal," he said "see if you can find her in there."

Each rental agreement in the piles contained a photostat of the driver's license employed by the renter with, as required by law, a photo of the renter as well as a photostat of the credit card used as a deposit, unless he or she had opted to put a thousand dollars down as a deposit. Anxious to demonstrate the degree to which he was cooperating with O'Neill and Olivia's investigation, Birbaki began to study the Easy Rent documents. At the third agreement, he paused.

"You know," he said "I told you guys she was wearing a headscarf. If I try to imagine a scarf on this woman, it could be her. He showed T.F. and Olivia a New Jersey license registered to a Sally Wonder, 1428 Carrolton

Avenue, Hackensack, New Jersey. "This woman's about the right age, thirty eight. And there's something about her eyes that rings a bell with me."

T.F. and Olivia studied the agreement Birbaki was holding out to them. T.F. plucked his cell phone from his vest pocket and called headquarters. "Listen!" he said. "Have the Hackensack police get a car out to 1428 Carrolton Avenue and see if they can get their hands on a Miss or Mrs Sally Wonder."

Birbaki, in the meantime, continued to work his way through the stack of rental agreements on the desk while Olivia pondered the one he'd selected from the pile. "Look, Mr. Chief Inspector," she said, using the title she'd playfully assigned T.F. "the timing on this agreement checks out pretty well. The van went out yesterday morning at 9:37 and was brought back here to the garage at 4:32 that afternoon."

"Remember what time they showed up at your warehouse, pal?" T.F. asked Birbaki.

"About 10:30."

"Figures," said T.F. "That's about the time it would take them to get out there from here." The chorus from "*Aida*" rang out and T.F. grabbed his cellphone.

"Shit!" he announced, listening to his caller. He turned to Olivia. "Pardon my French, but that Jersey driver's license is a fake. 1428 Carrolton Avenue is a vacant lot." He rubbed his forehead, "Until November 2002, we had a big problem with counterfeit Jersey driver's licenses. They were making them everywhere. This must be one of them."

"Well," said Olivia "at least, we now have an ID photo of the woman we can circulate."

"Yeah," said O'Neill "and you can figure she isn't a Sunday School teacher. Where's the van now?" he asked the garage owner.

"Out back. It went out last night with a young couple who were moving house."

"OK," O'Neill said "keep it there. We're going to have to ask some people to come by and take a look at it."

Olivia turned to the garage owner. "Did you get a good look at this woman?" she asked.

"I wasn't here when she checked it back in, but I have a vague recollection of her in the morning when she checked it out."

"Did she say what she wanted it for?"

"Not really. She just said she had some errands to run."

"Was she alone?"

The owner frowned, trying to recollect the moment. "No," he said "there was a guy with her. An older guy."

"Can you remember anything about him?"

"He was just a guy, you know what I mean? But, hey wait, there was one thing about him. He only had one hand. I had to light his cigarette for him because his lighter wasn't working."

"Bingo! Mr. Chief Inspector," Olivia laughed, grabbing T.F. by the forearm "these are our people alright."

By now, a car from the NYPD's Bomb Squad, another bearing technicians from the FBI's Criminal Lab, and a car carrying a pair of NEST inspectors had arrived to examine the van. By common understanding, the NEST inspectors went first with their Geiger counters. They found nothing, although they had not expected to. Unless a piece of the device itself had somehow come loose, there would be no tell-tale traces of gamma radiation still present to indicate that the van had transported an atomic device 24 hours earlier. Neither the Bomb Squad, nor the FBI's experts looking for paint scratches that might have signaled the vehicle had been in accident somewhere, found anything suspicious.

When they'd left, Olivia gave T.F.'s forearm a playful tug. "Tell me, Chief Inspector Dear, did they teach chemistry at Brooklyn College?"

"Damned if I can remember. Why?"

"I was just wondering when they started to look for chlorine gas with a Geiger Counter."

O'Neill looked at her with fresh admiration in his eyes.

"You've got a point, Little Pal," he said "I think you just hit on something the honchos down in Washington, at FBI headquarters among other places, want to keep a secret."

Olivia shrugged. Keeping secrets was part of your job when you were an FBI agent. She picked up the rental agreement. "But we've got something critical here" she said, waving it. "They brought the van back in with 22 miles on the clock. And it took just two gallons to fill up its tank so the reading must be right. How far do you figure it is from here to Charlie's warehouse?"

O'Neill went over to the big map of New York on the garage owner's wall. He pinched out the distance using the scale at the bottom of the map. "Four-and-a-half miles."

"OK," Olivia said to the owner. "Have you, by any chance, got a compass like those things you used as a kid in geometry class?"

"Yeah," he said "I think so."

Fumbling around in his desk, he found one and passed it to Olivia.

"Okay," she said "nine of those twenty two were used getting out to Charlie's and back. That leaves us 13. She set the pin of compass on the garage on his map, then set its width at what would be a distance of 13 miles. She then drew a circle on the map, using that 13-mile width as its radius. Her circle included parts of Flatbush, Brownsville in Brooklyn, Ridgewood, Maspeth and Woodside in Queens, all off Manhattan, south of 106th Street, and a chunk of New Jersey.

"My dear Chief Inspector," she announced "that barrel of radio-active chlorine gas we're looking for has got to be somewhere inside that circle."

T.F. grabbed her in his arms. "You're terrific, Little Pal! Next to you, J. Edgar Hoover was a keystone cop. Come on. We've got to get your map and the woman's photo to Police Plaza, forthwith."

For Condoleezza Rice, the National Security Advisor to the President, it had been the voyage of a lifetime. Here she was, the only passenger on Air Force One, the personal airplane of the presidents of the United States, an aircraft fitted out with the most modern technical equipment and luxurious appointments in the sky. Sure, she had been in the plane before, but together with the President, the press, and dozens of her fellow presidential advisors. On this flight from Bolling Air Force Base outside Washington D.C. to Karachi, she had been alone, spoiled crazy by the plane's superbly trained Air Force crew. At times, her experience made her think back to those quiz programs she'd known as a kid "Queen for the Day." Here she was, in the latest version of the Air Force One's.

With her sense of history, she'd kept thinking that it was on an earlier version of this plane John F. Kennedy's body had been flown back to Washington from Dallas, in which Ronald Reagan had flown to Iceland to meet Gorbachev and begin the process that would end the Cold War. It was quite a destiny for an African American girl from Birmingham, Alabama. Well, as her father had told her when she was a girl, in America, with faith and perseverance, anything can happen.

As she sensed the pilot easing off on his engines to ease the plane into its descent pattern, she glanced out the window. Sure enough, they were over land. Although she, of course, couldn't know it, on the ground below, the Pakistan military, on the orders of President Mushareff himself, was on full alert. A tight cordon had been laid down around the airfield. Mushareff was all too aware of the fact hundreds of Stingers and Russian made SAM 7s had disappeared in Iraq. What a nightmare it would be if one of them came streaking out of the sky at the President's plane as it was landing on Pakistani soil!

When the plane finally taxied to a halt, a shiny black pre-World War II Bentley, Mushareff's official presidential vehicle, drew up to its staircase. It had been a gift from the departing British to Pakistan's founder, Mohammed Ali Jinnah. Mushareff's aide-de-camp, Colonel Lutfi Gibran, got out and walked up the aircraft's stairs to officially greet Miss Rice, a small case in his hands.

After he'd showered the President's compliments and thanks on the young woman, the colonel coughed nervously and opened the case. It contained a black *chador*, the all-enveloping garment which was obligatory for women in strict Moslem countries, and a black headscarf. For her own security, the President, he explained, thought it was essential to keep her presence in Karachi a secret. Female visitors almost never came to visit his official Karachi residence dressed in anything other than strict Islamic garb. Would she, he asked, be willing to don the *chador* he held out to her?

To the colonel's immense relief, Condi let out a delicious little laugh.

Why sure, she said. It would be just like dressing up for the school play when she was a teenager. He stood by as she slipped the gown over her lithe and athletic form, then fit the scarf to her head. Carefully, as prescribed by Islamic practice, he explained to her how to ease the few errant hairs dangling down her forehead back into the scarf's folds. Then he stood back to admire the result.

"Why, Miss Rice!" he exclaimed "You could be taken for a Moghul Empress."

Thanks to the dynamic leadership of Police Commissioner Ray Kelly and the Department of Homeland Security's Ray Anscom, the New York City Office of Emergency Management under the base of the Brooklyn Bridge, was up and running, handling an emergency exactly as its founder, ex Mayor Rudi Giulani, had intended it should.

Virtually every computer console at the half-dozen command stations ringing the room was manned, a soft undertone of muttered communications provided its background music, perhaps a hundred different images were blinking on the dozens of computers in the center. No one was working harder than the agents of the FBI. Sensitive to the criticism that had struck the Bureau for its shortcomings in the run-up to 9/11, both its Washington headquarters and its New York office were determined that their behavior in this crisis would be above reproach.

Available to all, was the bureau's new Terrorist Screening Center databank, 100,000-plus names which, since the fall of 2003, had merged a dozen existing lists maintained by nine different Federal agencies, some of which had previously restricted access to their data. They included the Transportation Security Administrations 'no fly' list of suspects barred from air travel, the State Department's massive TIPOFF list against which visa applications were screened, the FBI's National Crime Information Center list and the CIA's hithertoclosed suspects file.

One team of agents was in constant computer communication with the immigration service in Washington and the Transport Security Administration screening the landing cards and visas of everyone who had entered the country in the past month, with, of course, particular attention to   people coming in from the Middle East or other suspect areas of the globe.

That massive accumulation of data had been sharply criticized by civil libertarians. It was now, in an emergency like this that, its advocates maintained, its worth would become apparent.

The OEM was, quite naturally, Mayor Mike Bloomberg's first stop as soon as he arrived in the city from Washington. The mayor was delighted to see on his arrival that not a single press or TV vehicle was anywhere near the headquarter's desolate and rather shabby location. After Kelly and Anscom had given him a tour of the building, he stopped, fascinated at the command post supervising the search operations at Port Elizabeth and Port Newark. Huge photo-murals of the thirty-eight piers, 77 miles of wharves making up the largest port facility in the U.S. and indeed, the world, surrounded the post. There was as well a poster for each of the ports' 142 docks, listing each vessel that had unloaded cargo at the dock from the Middle East or any other suspect region in the past 30 days. It contained the date the ship had called on the port and an approximate list of the cargo it had offloaded. As soon as one of the joint NYPD/FBI teams assigned the docks spotted something suspicious in the multitude of manifests being scrutinized – just as T.F. O'Neill and Olivia Phillips had the night before – the cargo was signaled to the OEM in Brooklyn. If the delivery had been scheduled for the metropolitan area, the OEM ordered the team that spotted the suspicious merchandise to track it down. If its destination was outside the metropolitan area, the FBI was ordered to get a team out to locate it.

The mayor went from post to post in the command area, offering his personal encouragement to the men and women running the search effort. A cackle of intercom communications signaled the progress of their work:

"Romeo 19 has just verified the twelve packs of sheepskin unloaded off the S.S. Grace Three from Latakia, Syria. No trace of any suspect merchandise was found."

"Scanner Four" — 'Scanner' was the code name for Customs — "Please verify the contents of two containers alledged to contain olive oil delivered yesterday to Exotic Supplies, 1148 Washington Avenue, Brooklyn. Port of origin, Beirut."

At another command post, a team of FBI agents and CIA officers were scrutinizing the personal dossiers of recent immigrants who might have had some connection to Al Qaeda or the Hezbollah. The names and addresses of those thought worth running down were radioed to FBI patrol cars to locate the individuals in question and verify their status and situation. To provide any legal backup, a brace of judges was on hand, ready to furnish documents like a search warrant the FBI teams might need.

"You're doing a great job!" Bloomberg said enthusiastically to Commissioner Kelly.

The P.C. felt obliged to temper a bit, the mayor's excitement.

"All investigations begin like this, Your Honor," he said "but then we have to get down to the nitty-gritty, pounding the sidewalks, calling on the cafes and grocery stores, looking for that one elusive clue that can lead us on. With a little bit of luck, all those efforts begin to converge on a precise point. What you need, of course, is time, and time is the one thing those terrorist bastards didn't give us much of."

"Ray, your people are doing a great job!" the Mayor assured Kelly. "Keep your chin up. You'll wind up finding that clue we need." Suddenly, however, Bloomberg's tone changed. "But listen, we can't bank on that as an ironclad certainty. We've got to, at least, prepare for an emergency evacuation of the city. How much time would we need to evacuate?"

"A minimum of 24 hours."

"These damn terrorists have given us until midday Friday. Which means if worst comes to worst, we'll have to order the evacuation Thursday, hoping that we'll at least have a few hours to save a bare minimum of people."

The problem of evacuation had haunted the mayor since the beginning of the crisis. Despite the terrorists' sinister threat to detonate the bomb if an evacuation was ordered, how could he leave hundreds of thousands of his fellow citizens to their deaths, without offering them even the slightest chance of an escape? It was an appalling moral dilemma.

"There must be a plan for evacuating the city, no?"

"Sure," Kelly said. "It's 200 pages long and was drawn up in the Cold War days when we were afraid of a thermonuclear strike. I haven't read it and most of my colleagues consider it worthless. I'll get the guy who drew it up, in here to talk to us."

A few minutes later, a Washington bureaucrat, flown in because of the crisis, joined them. Charles Morningside was 58, his cheeks reddened by a longstanding taste for vodka-tonic. He was an example of a breed of persons almost unique to Washington, a think-tank specialist whose work was subsidized by one of a score of well-meaning charitable foundations. For years, he had devoted his life to the study of evacuating urban populations in the event of a thermonuclear war. With the end of the Cold War, Morningside had had to reinvent his career in order to justify his fairly substantial think-tank income, so he had convinced the leaders of the foundation which paid him, that no concern was more critical than adopting his studies to the problem of evacuating major American cities in the face of a terrorist menace.

Kelly ushered him to the center of the command center from which they were working and said "OK, Mr. Morningside, we're all ears."

"I don't think I need to tell you," he began "that evacuating New York is a colossal enterprise. The first thing we must do is shut down all the access tunnels and bridges coming into the city. Or rather, make them all one-way. Only 27 percent of the population of Manhattan Island possess a car, which limits the potential for automotive evacuation."

How the guy loves statistics and figures, Kelly thought.

"We'll requisition buses and trucks," he said. "Fortunately, we have the subways. We'll run one-way traffic up to the outer Bronx and Queens, empty the cars, then turn them around to come back to the city for another load of people."

Driven by who? Kelly thought. The conductors will

have led the charge off the damn trains and headed for the suburbs themselves.

Morningside now placed a large poster on the easel beside him: TAKE, it read. "We will display this card fairly constantly on television, he announced. It listed those things fleeing New Yorkers were supposed to take in their evacuation: a box of Tampax, their cellular phones, a bottle of water and a spare pair of socks and underwear.

Then he replaced his card with a second reading, DO NOT TAKE. It listed three things — firearms, drugs, alcohol.

The guy's a genius, Kelly thought. He's listed the three things no Yorker is going to leave behind. And how about those thousands who won't go across the street without their pet dogs, cats or canaries?

"Mr. Morningside," the mayor intervened "I recall that during the days of Governor Rockefeller, the city had a vast, well-equipped series of air raid shelters. Couldn't they be used in an emergency of this sort?"

An embarrassed silence greeted his words. Kelly found it difficult to repress a giggle. At the height of the Cold War, the city had possessed 16,000 shelters capable of housing in an emergency, six-and-a-half million people. Millions of dollars in Federal aid had been spent, equipping them with first aid kits, bottled water, non-perishable emergency food rations, even, in some instances, Geiger counters to allow survivors to scramble out after an air raid.

"I'm afraid, Sir," Morningside answered "their current state leaves something to be desired."

"Desired?" said Kelly. "When they had that earthquake down in the Dominican Republic a few years back, we pulled those rations out and sent them to the folk down there as a goodwill gesture. What happened? Everybody who ate them got sick. What do you think of all this, Mr. Mayor?" Kelly asked.

Bloomberg mopped his brow. "Think? I've given up thinking. I've decided to try praying, instead."

The Commissioner's pocket cell phone jingled. He picked it up, listened a second, then looked at Bloomberg. "You may be better at praying than you realize, Your Honor," he said. "That was my Chief of Detectives, down at Police Plaza. We may have our first break in this case."

He opened up a computer circuit to Police Plaza, and his Chief of Detectives appeared on his screen, flanked by O'Neill and Olivia Phillips. "Commissioner!" the Chief of Detectives said. "We mustn't jump to conclusions here. What you are about to hear could conceivable be a drug case, but to me, it has all the earmarks of an important break-through in our search for this damn bomb." He turned to O'Neill. "I think, you know T.F. O'Neill who runs our Midtown Manhattan South Detective Squad. T.F., we're listening."

Carefully and methodically, T.F. ran through the investigation he and the FBI's Phillips had been running since they had uncovered the discrepancy in the weight of the containers off-loaded from the Jewel of India. He concluded by putting on the screen, the circle of those parts of New York inside the area he and Olivia had calculated, on the basis of the mileage used by the Easy Rent van that had made the pick up at Birbaki's warehouse.

"Great work!" Kelly enthused. "What's the status of that woman's photo?"

"It's being printed up and distributed, as we speak," replied the Chief of Detectives. "Sixteen thousand copies. We're getting it into the hands of every cop in the city, with orders to show it all over town — to newspaper vendors, waiters, barmen and women, every pizza parlor, fast food shop, McDonnell's Burger Kings in their area, the guys who sell falafel and hotdogs on street corners, cleaning men and ladies in all public and private lavatories."

"Good. I want it run past the checkout counters from the crummiest food store in Harlem out to the best Safeway Supermarket in Queens. Also to the guys running all the toll booths of the bridges and tunnels. What cover story are we using to describe who she's supposed to be?"

"We've pegged her the girlfriend of a couple of cop killers in Chicago."

"Good," Kelly said. "That ought to do it."

"How about the press?" Bloomberg asked. "Should we pass the photo to them?"

"That," Paul Anscom declared "is a question we will have to ask the White House."

The answer came back from Andrew Card almost immediately. Under no conditions was the photo to go to the press. The President had no doubt that there was a team of terrorist suicide bombers in the city to carry out the explosion themselves, if necessary. The publication of the photo would alert them to the fact the police were on their trail.

"He's right," Kelly said. He turned to the map on his computer screen. "That stretch of Brooklyn along Atlantic Avenue. That's a hotbed of Islamic extremist activity. It's Little Arabia down there. Hubbly bubbly shops, back street mosques, women in veils, Arabic book stores, the lot. They have a mosque, the Al Farroq Mosque, that we know raised over twenty million bucks for Al Qaeda before 9/11. It's where that blind Egyptian sheikh was hanging out. If you wanted to hide that bomb out someplace, that's the ideal spot. Let's focus some intense search efforts down there — beginning right now."

In her elaborately furnished guest suite in Karachi, Condi Rice awaited the arrival of Dr. Abdul Sharif Ahmad with a mixture of concern and curiosity. Curiosity, as to what manner of man was this Islamic Oppenheimer, a scientist who could love roses and poetry, and yet, devote his life to endowing his people with the most terrible weapon man's mind had ever devised.

Concern, of course, about her ability to strike a responsive chord in the man, to find some common area of sensitivity which might allow them to find a way out of the terrible crisis menacing New York. The black chador in which she had arrived at the Pakistani President's Karachi guest house was neatly folded away. The clean-shaven Ahmad, she knew, was not a rigid practitioner of the traditions of Islam. He was, Musharaff had explained, being kept under armed guard as a "guest" in the building, pending some resolution to the crisis caused by the theft of the Pakistani atomic bomb, an action in which he, of course, had been an accomplice.

At Condi's request, a video cassette player with a large screen had been installed in the room awaiting his arrival. To her immense relief, he was relaxed, almost friendly, when an armed guard showed him into her suite. For a few moments, they chatted over green tea and cookies. Condi congratulated Ahmad on his work which, she noted, had made him, in a sense, Pakistan's Oppenheimer. Had he, she wondered, studied the life of the father of the atomic bomb?

"Oh yes", Ahmad said. "I studied the Manhattan Project and its primary players, Oppenheimer, Groves, Teller, Szilard, at great length."

That was the opening she was looking for.

"Oppenheimer, as you probably know," she said "was in favor of employing the bomb on Japan."

Ahmad nodded his agreement.

"But when he went to Japan and saw the hell it had wrought, he was horrified. He bitterly regretted his decision to support using the bomb and that haunted and tortured him for the rest of his life."

"And fueled his opposition to the H-bomb," Khan observed.

"Indeed."

"I brought a video tape I'd like to show you, doctor," she said, firing up her cassette player. For almost thirty minutes, a parade of horrifying images filtered by children weeping and wailing, some of their little bodies mutilated, mothers embracing their dead in anguish, men weeping. The material damage of 9/11 was left aside – this was an agonizing portrayal of the human cost of the terrorists' action.

Ahmad was understandably horrified.

"These are just the scars left upon 3,000 people, doctor," Condi said. "If that atomic bomb explodes in New York, the cost it will exact in human suffering will be 350 times greater."

"Yes," Ahmad agreed, shaking his head in dismay, "but it must not go off."

"We must each of us ask that of our God – I call him Lord Jesus, you call him Allah the Greatest, but at the end of the day, it is the same Divine Entity. And that horrible toll will be the consequence of the fruits of your genius. The images they will produce will haunt you, Dr. Ahmad, for the rest of your days."

"Of that," sighed Ahmad, "there is no doubt. The

pictures on your cassette are horrifying indeed. But they are only one set of images. There is another set you, Americans, do not want to see. You never screen them for your people on CNN and Fox News. They are the images of the horrible suffering inflicted on my Palestinian brothers and sisters by your Israeli allies — of their homes being destroyed, cradling the bodies of their dead and mutilated women and children; of Israeli tanks smashing through Palestinian farms and villages. Why don't you sit yourself down in front of these images, Dr. Rice, and try to understand the years upon years of suffering that lie behind the threat you now face?"

"Dr. Ahmad," Condi replied, "I have visited Palestine, I have met with the leaders there…"

"Please! Dr. Rice, do not take me for a fool. I have my sources, some of them inside your own government. I know how little sympathy you and people like your Vice President, Secretary Rumsfeld, have for the Palestinians. You are all tools of Sharon and the Jewish lobby. In July 2000, long before 9/11, you were telling your friends, Arafat was a liar — some one the United States could not trust or work with."

"Arafat was a lying incompetent, a liability to us, to the Israelis, but above all, to his own Palestinian people."

Ahmad snorted. "And your President's Roadmap to Middle East peace! What a farce that was! All Sharon had to do was sneeze and your Mr. Bush went off and cowered in a corner."

Their conversation was breaking down into sterile

polemics, Condi saw, and if she wasn't careful, Dr. Ahmad could storm out of their meeting in a rage. Time to try another tactic, she thought, a dangerous one but one which might shake the man in front of her into a grasp of reality.

"Look, Dr. Ahmad," she said. "Just what do you think are going to be the consequences if that bomb in New York goes off, as the terrorists are threatening, on Friday? Probably to coincide with the Friday prayers in Jerusalem."

"As you yourself have said, horrifying. That is why you must convince your Israeli friends to publicly declare their readiness to remove those settlements."

"I'm not talking about New York, Dr. Ahmad. I'm talking about right here, in Pakistan."

Ahmad appeared somewhat taken aback by her words.

"Have you heard the phrase 'massive retaliation'? What do you think those men you so admire like Secretary Rumsfeld and Vice President Cheney, are going to tell President Bush to do if that bomb goes off in New York? Wipe Pakistan off the map of the world, that's what!"

She could see the shock of those words hitting home to the Pakistani scientist.

"And let me tell you something else, doctor. I know for a fact, what Ariel Sharon's reaction to the terrorists' demand was. I heard it. If that bomb goes off in New York, maybe 300,000 of the dead will be Jews. If President Bush doesn't use our nuclear arms against you, Sharon will use Israel's. Maybe thirty, forty million of the Pakistanis to whom you devoted your life will die. Is that what you would like as the harvest of your life's work?"

Ahmad was clearly shaken by her words. He slumped in his chair, grasping his head in his hands. How had they found out it was a Pakistani bomb? The whole idea was that it was to be an anonymous threat that the Americans would never know against whom to retaliate.

"Help me, Dr. Ahmad!" Condi pleaded. "Help me to spare so many innocent people, Americans and Pakistanis. Just imagine, if all those horrible images we just screened together, mutilated children, weeping mothers, the innocent dead frozen in their final agony, were Pakistani women and children."

Ahmad shook his head despairingly. "I don't know where the bomb is. I don't know who took it to your country or how they got it there. I only know one thing. I fitted a cellular phone to the detonator so that a call to that phone will detonate the bomb. I have that phone number."

"Who else has it?"

"I assume, at least two people, Osama Bin Laden and a Lebanese terrorist named Imad Mugniyeh."

"Ah yes," Miss Rice said, "I know who he is. Could you try to contact Bin Laden for us so we can try to reason with him?"

"That will not be easy – both finding him and

reasoning with him. But I will try." Ahmad scribbled on a piece of paper. "Here's the number," he said. "For God's sake! Don't tell anyone what I have done. I feel that I have just put my life in danger."

T.F. O'Neill led his FBI colleague into the 'inner sanctum' of his police precinct at 357 West 35th Street. It was the detectives' canteen, a small windowless room equipped with a coffee maker, an ancient refrigerator, a table and a few chairs. The walls were decorated with the photos of some of Manhattan South's most sought-after criminals, paint was peeling from both its walls and its ceilings, and a couple of dangling light bulbs barely provided enough light to read by. Still, O'Neill assured Olivia Phillips, she was about to savor a cup of the best *capuccino* to be found in New York City.

The FBI girl's eyes were wide with amazement. She had changed on their return from the Easy Rent garage, into a tight-fitting new Calvin Klein blouse and a pair of black slacks. This place, she thought, looked like one of those run-down police stations she'd visited in the outskirts of Mexico City during her FBI field training.

"Hey!" she laughed, "Real Third World, this place. What do you use it for? Besides making coffee, I mean?"

"This is where we have our brainstorming sessions."

"Brainstorming?" Olivia said, making no effort to conceal the touch of disbelief in her voice.

"Well, bull-shitting sessions if you like" O'Neill said, passing her a *capuccino*. "You think this is something? Wait until you see the rest of the precinct headquarters. My guys still have to use those old Underwood stand-up typewriters to type up their reports — when we have the money to repair them. Eighty seven billion dollars we pay to make war on Iraq but we can't afford to fix the typewriters in New York's busiest police precinct."

"Come on," he said "let's go see how our friend Mr. Birbaki is doing."

They had left the Brooklyn importer at the precincts' screening machine to run through all the photos the office had of criminals past, present and perhaps, future. There were well over 1000. To speed up the process, an officer entered the sex of the person sought, his or her approximate age and any identifying trait such as racial origin. The machine then filtered out the photos in the base and flashed them, one by one, on the screen.

Birbaki was scrutinizing that passing parade with no luck — it was a non-ending jumble of marijuana addicts or dealers, pickpockets, hustlers, and petty thieves.

O'Neill gazed at him sympathetically. "Well," he said "when you finish we'll call up the transvestite file. Then you'll see some really interesting pictures."

As he said that, the notes of *"Aida"* jingled on his cellular phone.

"O'Neill," he snapped.

It was the security officer of the New Yorker Hotel just over a block away. Like most private security officers in New York, he was a retired NYPD officer riding the post-9/11 security gravy train. "I got something here you got to look at pronto, T.F." he said. "Guy from Hamburg, Germany; checked in here 48 hours ago, hung his 'DO NOT DISTURB' sign on the door and disappeared. Maid called in this morning, no answer, so she did a check to see if he was okay. She found a laptop computer in there with wires hooked up to a device about the size of a VCR and what looks like an antenna wrapped up in tin foil pointing out the window."

"Holy shit!" T.F. exclaimed. "Barricade the room and don't let anyone touch anything in there. I'm on the way."

"Come on, Little Pal," he said, grabbing Olivia by the arm. "This may be what we're looking for!" As he headed for the door, he ordered his duty officer to get the NEST and the NYPD Bomb Squad to meet them at the hotel.

With its 1,500 rooms, the New Yorker Hotel was one of the largest in the city, known for its good but reasonably priced accommodations. Once, it had belonged to the Moonies set, but it had recently been taken over by the Marriott chain.

The security officer was waiting for them with a copy of the room renter's registration card and his credit card. They confirmed that the man who had rented the room was indeed a German from Hamburg. To the hotel security officer's dismay, the NYPD's bomb squad and a banalised NEST van were drawing up to the entrance. An excited crowd was the last thing he needed to promote his hotel business.

"Let's go, guys!" O'Neill ordered and the team, equipped with suitcases containing detection devices, protective clothing, a sniffer dog, and for the NEST operatives, Geiger and Gamma Ray detectors, headed for the elevator and the 24th floor.

Cautiously, the hotel security officer opened the door to 2408 with his pass key.

The sight that greeted them was worrying indeed. As the security officer had said, a laptop computer was wired to a machine the size of a VCR and, at the same time, connected to an antenna pointed at the half-open window. Several other devices which looked like some kind of computers were also wired to the central VCR-like machine.

The Bomb Squad officers let their dog sniff the device. He gave no bark indicating the potential presence of high explosives. The NEST men turned on their counters and they, too, detected no tell-tale emanations although, as one of them pointed out, what ever was in that VCR-like device could be wrapped in lead.

O'Neill sank to his knees and crawled along the carpet so he could look up at the principal device. At its base, he discovered a small metal plaque. UNIVERSAL TIME CODE GENERATOR, it read.

"That mean anything to any of you guys?" he asked.

It didn't.

He scribbled the words on a scrap of paper and handed it to Olivia. "Get this to a phone and see if your FBI services can come up with anything on this firm over the Internet."

"Could this be some kind of central timer?" he wondered.

"Yeah," said one of the Bomb Squad officers. "A centralized device capable of synchronizing the explosion of several bombs at once.

The NEST experts took the box's dimensions. At the outside, it could be a nuclear device, but if it was, it would have to be a very sophisticated one.

Suddenly, Olivia appeared at the door. "Relax guys" she said. "We got that firm in Hamburg's number off the Internet. They make watches. Their top-of-the-line product is a watch that automatically adapts to time changes as its wearer travels. Their rep here installed this machine 48 hours ago because they haven't yet been able to adapt their watches to the automatic time changes needed on the Eastern Seaboard for Eastern Standard Time. The guy is on his way here now to explain the whole business to us."

A mixture of intense relief, tainted with just a touch of disappointment, greeted her words.

T.F. smiled and gave Olivia a hug. "Hey!" he said "People are much more suspicious since 9/11, which is what they should be. There's been a tremendous increase in things we have to respond to and there's a tendency in the police to become complacent because you're constantly reacting to false alarms. But Little Pal, complacent is one thing we can't afford to be." He looked at the other officers in the room. "Any of us."

"The President of the United States!"

The men and women gathered in the White House Situation Room jumped to their feet at those words barked out by the Marine Corps Sergeant Major in charge of their security detail, in his best parade ground voice. Quite in contrast to the members of his Crisis Committee gathered in the room, George W. Bush appeared alert and charged with energy. His close associates, of course, knew that he liked to take an ice-cold midday shower as a way of giving himself a hygienic shot of energy. Today, however, he had another reason to explain his force and the smile lighting up his face.

"Ladies and Gentlemen!" he announced "Condi Rice has just called me over the secure phone on Air Force One on her departure from Karachi. Her visit to Pakistan has been a complete success. After some initial reservations, Dr. Ahmad wound up by being swayed by the arguments she presented to him." With a warm smile sweeping his face, the President took a slip of paper from his pocket and smoothed it out on the table before him.

"After an hour of sometimes difficult conversation,

Condi was able to convince him not to tarnish his enormous prestige as a scholar and scientist by supporting a nuclear holocaust that could cause the deaths of hundreds of thousands of innocent victims. Above all, it seems that he was impressed by the thinly veiled menace of nuclear reprisals against his own Pakistani people."

"Be careful, Mr. President!" called a voice from the end of the table. Milt Anderson, the director of the CIA, wanted to warn the chief executive against adopting an overly optimistic interpretation of the position taken by the Pakistani scientist. "Dr. Ahmad is a very dangerous man. Believe me and my years of experience with people like him. If he put this bomb into the hands of the terrorists of Osama Bin Laden, it's because of his profound conviction that in doing so, he was serving the higher interests of Islam. It's not some shocking pictures of the suffering caused by 9/11, or even the specter of what reprisals could do to his own countrymen, that is going to lead a man like that to change his mind after a few hours of conversation. Mr. President, let me urge you to use extreme caution in assessing the actions of this man."

The President offered Anderson, not a reproach for his criticism, but instead, a warm smile. He picked up the piece of paper from his desk.

"Ladies and Gentlemen, I think we can consider this terrible crisis resolved, well short of the disaster that was threatening us. Dr. Ahmad has, indeed, accepted

to help us save New York from disaster. He told Condi
that he, personally, had attached a cell phone purchased
in the markets of Islamabad to the detonation set of
the bomb. A call to that cell phone will set off the bomb.
This slip of paper bears the number of that phone –
42639754. Only two other people possess it — Osama
Bin Laden and, in all probability, the Hezbollah terrorist Imad Mugniyeh. It is that number they intend to call
Friday — in just three days — if the ultimatum on the
Israeli settlements on the West Bank has not been met."

The sense of relief sweeping the Situation Room
was almost palpable. The President turned to the bespectacled computer whiz who represented the NSA at
the table. "Moro!" he commanded "Get this number to
the director of the NSA immediately, with my personal
order to see that this number on Manhattan Island is
isolated from all incoming communications from anywhere in the world. Make sure that nothing, no call
whatsoever, can reach this number. I want the director's
assurance in ten minutes that this has been done."

With a visible sense of delight, he turned to the
gathering. "I want a full-scale review of this crisis to see
what lessons we can learn from it for the future."

The group was deep in a discussion of that topic
when the nerdy young genius of the NSA reappeared.

"Mr. President," he said "I am afraid that piece of
paper and the number on it is worthless. There is absolutely no way that the NSA or any other organization in
this country can prevent a telephone call from abroad,

or anywhere else, from reaching the number on that cell phone attached to the bomb!"

At the Office of Emergency Management in Brooklyn, the air of near chaotic activity that had characterized the earlier part of the day had now been replaced by a slightly calmer air of determined, if frantic, efforts. The work of T.F. O'Neill and his FBI colleague Olivia Phillips in pinning down the area in which the bomb had, in all probability, been placed had allowed Police Commissioner Kelly to focus his search efforts on an area — however vast — that at least did not encompass all Manhattan's five boroughs. Assuming O'Neill and Olivia's calculations were correct, the bomb was, in all probability on Manhattan Island, from 106th Street to the tip of the island, or in the southern stretches of Brooklyn and Queens.

As he was organizing his search, a team of FBI agents had swarmed into the Easy Rent garage to try, in a sense, to get the van the presumed terrorists had rented to "talk" — to come up with some indication of where its renters had taken it after making their pick up at Charlie Birbaki's warehouse.

Hundreds of pieces of the van, stripped and broken down, covered the garage floor. The van had had 37 known minor accidents, scrapes, shocks, the location of which had been circled in red on its surface.

Every trace of paint in every bump or scrape on the car had been subjected to spectrographic analysis. Every rental contract on the van for the previous two weeks had been studied, the renters located and their itineraries reconstituted in as much detail as possible. The young couple who'd rented the car the evening before had been located and brought to Police Plaza to see if they had found or noticed anything in the van, a discarded pack of matches, a soiled paper napkin from a restaurant, a newspaper, anything that might help determine where the vehicle had been.

Experts had carefully vacuumed out the treads of the tires to see if they contained any tell-tale traces that might indicate where the vehicle had been. The floor matting had been analyzed to see if the shoes of either the woman renter or her male companion had left any trace of some material that might help to further focus the investigation. Since it was known that certain parts of the Brooklyn Bridge had received a coat of paint the day before, the Feds scrutinized every square inch of the vehicle's surface to see if a speck of paint might indicate that it had passed under the painted bridge site.

From their stand point, the nuclear experts of NEST had run their Geiger and Gamma Ray detectors over every piece of the disassembled vehicle, in the hope that some sub-microscopic trace of radiation might somehow remain on one of them.

That enormous investigation failed to turn up any

further bit of evidence that would help Commissioner Kelly tighten the area in which he had to search for the terrorists' bomb. O'Neill's and Olivia's circle encompassed, however, some of what his department already considered as prime targets for a terrorist's assault in the city — the Empire State and Chrysler Buildings, Madison Square Garden, Rockefeller Center, Penn and Grand Central Stations, the Times Square area, areas which terrorists might thirst to destroy. For Kelly, the leaders of the FBI, the hundreds of their agents and detectives already hard at work, it was an appalling challenge.

The PC, wisely, had decided to leave the setting of priorities in each of the areas encompassed in what was now being called "T.F.'s Circle", to the precinct commanders responsible for each area. After all, their officers patrolled those streets and neighborhoods daily and no one knew better than they did, the kind of activity the facades of some of the seemingly innocent-looking buildings might conceal.

In the noise and tumult of the Emergency Operations Center, Mayor Mike Bloomberg was horrified to suddenly realize that the direct secure phone line to the President's Oval Office phone was blinking away unanswered. He grabbed it.

"Mr. President," he said "excuse us. We're so overwhelmed here, we failed to catch your incoming signal."

He gestured for silence at the center of the command module and transferred his call to the speakers around the command desk. "As you know, Mr. President, we feel we have at least been able to narrow down the area in which the terrorists' bomb could have been placed and are organizing a thorough and rapid search effort."

Still under the shock of learning that the most technologically advanced nation in the world was incapable of preventing a telephone call from somewhere overseas from reaching a cell phone somewhere on Manhattan Island, the President wanted to exhort his New York forces to redouble their efforts to resolve this crisis in what seemed to be the only means possible — finding and disarming the terrorists' bomb.

"Michael," he said "the hope which I was grasping, that knowing what the number of the cell phone on the bomb is, we could stop an incoming call from reaching it has, alas, evaporated. Our experts at the NSA say that this is technically impossible."

"Well, Mr. President, that's not entirely correct," a voice at the command center desk observed. It belonged to David Graham, the head of the NEST search teams. "If we can surround that cellular phone with a Farraday Cage, that will prevent any incoming signal from reaching it."

"A what?" asked the President.

"Farraday Cage. It's fundamentally a copper shield which prevents any electromagnetic signal from passing through it to the phone."

"Oh great!" exclaimed the President "but we still have to find the damned bomb, don't we? In other words, we're still stuck here on square one."

"And," noted Commissioner Kelly "the fact remains, the search for this device is as delicate as it is dangerous. We just have to assume that these terrorists, whoever they are, are babysitting their bomb. They will be holed up right there beside it, ready to detonate it themselves if they pick up any indication that we are about to close in on them. The closer we come to success in finding them and their bomb, the more dangerous and critical our task becomes."

The President groaned out his agreement. He glanced at his watch. Condi would be landing soon. At least, they might be able to relax for a few moments to watch an inning or two of the baseball playoffs.

Hand in hand, they walked along 38th Street towards Sixth Avenue, laughing at the absurdities of the film they had just watched, a crude effort to recapture the magic of the Matrix movies they had so much enjoyed. Jimmy Burke, a post graduate student studying to become a computer programmer for Dell Computers, squeezed the hand of his live-in German girlfriend, Ingrid. "When you and I have kids, they'll still be trying to remake those flicks. With no more luck than they had tonight."

In his right hand, he clutched a crumpled up package of Oreo cookies which they had bought to slake their hunger as they'd left the theater. Halfway down the block, they passed under a street-light, below which had been set, conveniently enough, a green New York City trash can.

"Hey!" Burke exulted. "Here comes the opening shot of the Knicks new season. Watch! Hook shot!" he laughed, arching the crumpled cookie wrapper over his head towards the trash can.

It flew through the lamplight, struck the rim of the trash can — and tumbled to the sidewalk.

"Good shot!" laughed Ingrid. "Now we know why the Knicks can never make the playoffs." Well-brought up young lady that she was, she bent down, picked the cookie wrapper from the sidewalk and leaned over to drop it into the trash can.

"Look!" she said. "What's this?"

She reached into the trash can and pulled out a shiny new Nokia mobile phone resting on a copy of the Village Voice. Jimmy studied it, then flipped open its rear.

"Hey!" he said "battery's gone. We'll buy a new one tomorrow and who's to know? Maybe we found ourselves a phone with a few minutes on it we can use to call your mother."

7

Washington, D.C.,
New York City, Jerusalem

The Crisis, Day Three

At precisely eight a.m., his hair still wet from his ice-cold morning wake-up shower, the President stepped into the Oval Office. Andrew Card, his Chief of Staff, was waiting for him to begin the day with a regular little ritual. He set before the president the ten-page President's Daily Brief in its blue, three-ring loose-leaf folder. Prepared overnight by the CIA, it was a digest of the latest information concerning world events and, in particular at this critical moment, the terrorist crisis facing his nation. He read through it swiftly. It contained nothing new or noteworthy. "OK," he ordered Card "show the others in."

Vice President Cheney, Secretary of State Powell, Secretary of Defense Rumsfeld, the CIA's Milt Anderson, his National Security Advisor Condoleezza Rice, filed into the office. If there was going to be any information of note to set off Day Four of this crisis, the President knew, it was sitting opposite him in the person of Condi Rice.

Fourteen thousand miles flown at over 30,000 feet, a clock full of time changes in less than three days, had not diminished, in anyway, the cool demeanor of his National Security Advisor. In her black tee shirt, its neckline delineated by a string of pearls, the gabardine pants suit in which she so often appeared on television, she looked more like the Dean of a graduate school at a good university than the most powerful woman in the U.S. Government.

"Condi didn't hesitate to fly out to meet the devil to find a way out of this crisis" the President said, to open his Crisis Committee meeting. "As you all know, she managed to convince Dr. Ahmad to give her the telephone number of the cellular phone hooked up to the bomb the terrorists have hidden in New York.

"Alas, despite the billions of dollars we've invested in the NSA over the years, they are incapable of preventing a telephone call from getting through to that number. However, that in no way diminishes the enormity of Condi's achievement, nor the hope that other positive results may grow out of her trip. Condi, let me turn this meeting over to you."

Her voice quiet and composed, Condi gave her colleagues a detailed account of her meeting with the scientist who'd placed an atomic bomb in the hands of a group of terrorists. Certainly, she acknowledged, President Mushareff's pressure had helped soften Ahmad's position. So, too, had the knowledge of the terrible retaliation that would befall Pakistan if that bomb exploded in New York.

"Dr. Ahmad," she said "has, I am sure, some way of entering into contact with the terrorists who are behind this. At my request, he promised he would employ it to try to open up a line of communication for us, to them."

"Bravo, Condi," said the President. "The idea of getting to them in the hope we may reason with them may be nothing more than the faintest glimmer of hope, but at least, it's that. And it is also the only glimmer of hope I can see in front of us, this morning."

"Indeed," his National Security Advisor said "and if Dr. Ahmad should indicate they are ready to at least speak with us, I'm ready to fly back to Pakistan on your orders, immediately."

As she was speaking, Milt Anderson, the CIA Director, had plugged the speaker of his cell phone into his earlobe. He held up his hand to get the group's attention.

"I have some devastating news!" he said. "Our Islamabad Station has just informed Langley that Dr. Ahmad was killed in an automobile crash near Waziristan in the Northwest Frontier Province. And the circumstances surrounding the crash are highly suspicious."

"Murdered!" Condi gasped.

"So much for our morning's glimmer of hope!" groaned the President.

A heavy silence followed his words. The Chief of Staff Andrew Card broke it. "We'd better get Paul Anscom up in New York onto our closed-circuit hookup and find out what's going on up there — if anything."

Seconds later, Anscom's face appeared on their TV screens. "We continue our all-out efforts to find the terrorists' device," he said. "We have full mobilization of the FBI, the NYPD, the New York State police and all their supporting services. We've shown the photo of that woman to thousands of people. Our search of suspicious cargoes off-loaded at Port Elizabeth and Port Newark is almost complete. NEST has all their helicopters in service over the city and their latest trucks from Livermore are in action. Unfortunately, I must tell you that all that that effort has produced, thus far, has been a dozen false alarms.

Bush glanced at his watch. "Barely 48 hours left before the terrorists' deadline expires," he said "and we are still at square one. No one to negotiate with, no lead to the bomb. We've got to do something. But what, Goddamned it, what?"

Nahed Jihari gave a discreet glance over her shoulder to be sure no one was watching her, before she moved to the public phone at the corner of Fifth Avenue and 32nd Street. Although the Palestinian woman could not know it, of course, the photo taken from her fake New Jersey driver's license was, at that very moment, being circulated all across the city. She dropped a quarter into the phone and dialed the number Imad Mugniyeh had given her before she left Beirut. She had no idea who she was calling, or why. All she had, in addition to the number, was the password Mugniyeh had given her, the same word he himself had used to meet Osama Bin Laden's aides on his arrival in Karachi airport in his woman's disguise.

The phone rang for some time before a man's voice anwered.

"*Seif* – sword," Nahed said.

"*Al Islam* - of Islam," the man replied.

"You may begin your operation," she said and hung up.

The man, his face pock-marked by smallpox, was a member of an Al Qaeda sleeper cell planted in New York before 9/11. Chuckling with delight, he hurried towards a Lebanese grocery store on Brooklyn's Atlantic Avenue, in the heart of the area on which Police Commissioner Kelly had ordered tight surveillance.

Two of his fellow cell members were waiting for him in the grocery's back room. "Our operation is on," he smiled and went to an old stove in the corner of the room. From it he took a lead box. It was divided into two halves. One contained, perhaps, three dozen rings about the size of a wedding band, to which were fixed small circular containers. The other had an equal number of tablets no larger than an aspirin.

Carefully, they fixed a tablet into each of the containers, then went into the yard behind the grocery. Three cages awaited them, filled with cackling pigeons. They were the most ordinary of gray New York pigeons, the kind that haunt almost every corner of the city. To the paw of each bird, they attached a ring with its little tablet.

"Release a bird every fifteen minutes," the leader ordered his acolytes. He looked at the squawking pigeons. "Fly away, little birdies. Don't let the cats catch you. You've got work to do for the Cause."

T.F. O'Neill's Manhattan South Detective Squad enjoyed the dubious distinction of covering the most important number of prime terrorist targets in New York City. They included Penn and Grand Central Stations, Madison Square Garden, the Empire State and Chrysler Buildings. Its population was also a puzzling anomaly. Officially, according to the 2000 census, it contained only 16,179 permanent residents. Yet, at midday on any day of the week, it encompassed well over a million people, shoppers, tourists, office workers, who poured in daily by car, train, subway and bus.

Olivia Phillips watched, as he poured her out another

cup of New York's finest *capuccino*. If we don't find that damn barrel pretty fast, she thought, he may start serving up New York's finest radio-active *capuccino*. How much longer, she wondered, is this bullshit story of a barrel of chlorine gas going to hold up? She, by now, had no doubts about what was really in the barrel they were looking for. She knew and understood the panic, just the use of the word "nuclear" could provoke. The mere thought that such a device might be in the barrel caused her own stomach to start fluttering.

O'Neill, meanwhile, had begun to whack the map of his precinct on his canteen wall with a rubber-tipped pointer. "Look guys!" he said "We're getting flak from headquarters about this goddamned barrel of chlorine gas. Where is it? This may sound like a bullshit project to some of you, but headquarters wants this damn thing found, and found fast.

"I'm constantly thinking of past experience. Experience, as you all know, is a critical part of police work. Think about some of these scumbags we've uncovered in the past three years, who rent apartments to store their stolen goods or all the CDs and DVDs they're so busy counterfeiting. Where were they working out off? Times Square? Alphabet City, down on the lower East Side? Hell no. That's what the media still thinks. Times Square is gentrified now. You want to rent an apartment or a store up there? You sign a lease, pal. Same thing's true down in Alphabet City. The drugs, the petty crime, is way down now. The place is flooded with young people, foreign restaurants, discos.

"No. This is the area we've got to focus on here, 29th Street to 45th Street between Fifth and Eight Avenues. About all you got there is commercial properties like they have in the Fashion Improvement District. You got dozens of supers or owners in that area who are ready to rent on a short-term, one-, three-, five-months, cash-in-advance, no-questions-asked basis. Lease? ID? Forget it. As long as the money's on the table, who the hell cares who you are or what business you're in? The super is just going to stuff the dough into his pocket, and as long as you don't make waves, he's not going to pay any attention to your comings or goings. Those places don't have any security to get curious about who the hell you are. As long as you put the dough on the table, you're home free."

"Right," echoed O'Neill's senior detective, a pickpocketing expert with 26 years on the force. "The other thing we got to do is scrub out the fleabag hotels in that area. Like the Culver on 43rd Street. It's owned by a couple of Pakistanis and stuffed with short-term illegals. Go in there and half the towels say "Property of Kings County Hospital." I was parked over there a couple of weeks ago and some kid comes running out to play, crying 'Hey, yesterday we were in Canada, today we're in America!' Got three illegal families, thanks to that eight-year-old."

O'Neill knew that the Empire State and Chrysler buildings, as well as a score of midtown skyscrapers, had already been scoured out, floor-by-floor and room-by-room by teams of the Joint Terrorism Task Force backed up discreetly by NEST. They were clean. The professional basketball and ice hockey seasons had yet to start, so there were no events of importance scheduled for Madison Square Garden. By a fortunate fluke of scheduling, both the Yankees and the Mets were playing their baseball games on the road this week, so the P.C. and the mayor had not been faced with the drama of canceling games at Yankee or Shea Stadiums and thus, alerting the media to the crisis threatening the city.

Time, O'Neill well knew, was running out. In addition to the critical area he had signaled to his detectives, there were, of course, other areas of concern — the gold stores at the Federal Reserve downtown and the financial center in general, and the old Jewish neighborhoods on the lower East Side. Those were areas, however, where the kind of terrorists they were looking for would stand out. It was really unlikely that they would try to hide themselves or their weapon there.

No, O'Neill was convinced that if the terrorists and their weapon were in Manhattan South, they would certainly be in the area he had outlined, a nightmare jumble of commercial properties of every ilk. That was where they would have to focus all their efforts. It was a nightmare task, one that would be almost impossible to execute in the little time they had to do it.

"OK guys!" he ordered. "Divide up that 29th to 45th Street area between your teams and get to work right now. If ever there was a time to honor that grand old NYPD slogan 'GOA GKD' – 'Get off your ass and go knock on doors' — it's now."

For New York's Mayor, Mike Bloomberg, it was the most appalling moral dilemma he had ever been called on to face. He had briefly taken leave of the emergency headquarters in Brooklyn to pick up his helicopter at City Hall and make an aerial survey of the city with Commissioner Kelly and that paragon of bureaucratic orthodoxy, Charles Morningside, the emergency evacuation expert.

But before boarding his chopper on the roof of City Hall, he first had a meeting in his mayor's office with one of the two human beings closest to his heart. Emma Bloomberg, 23, was the elder of his two daughters. She had the same pale blue eyes tinted light brown as her father, an elegant neck and features as fine as those in the portraits of Modigliani. A graduate, like her father, of the Harvard Business School, she had turned down a number of challenging jobs in the financial world to come and work at her father's side in City Hall. If the NYPD failed to find that damned bomb before the terrorists' deadline expired, she was condemned, as was he, to die along with hundreds of thousands of their fellow New Yorkers. He had chosen of his own free will to stay in the city and perish with his fellow citizens. Didn't that give him moral license to save his daughter? But how? Could he share with her this terrible secret of which, because of his exalted position, he was aware? All night, he had tossed and turned in his bed, agonizing over the answer to that questions. Somehow, he had to find a way to get her out of the city without violating the terrible trust that had been laid upon his shoulders.

"Emma darling," he said, as she entered his office and gave him an affectionate embrace "you look very tired. Worn. Are you burning the candle at both ends, staying out all night partying?"

The young woman looked at him with wondering eyes. She was, in fact, feeling particularly fresh and well-rested this morning. She'd snapped her lights and TV off at eleven o'clock the night before. Never had her father made comments like these on her appearance.

"My little girl, why don't you get out of town for a few days?" her father suggested. "Go down to your mother's in Florida, get some sunshine, do some deep sea diving which you love."

"Mother's house?" Emma said, surprised. She knew just how much her father disapproved of her mother's swinging lifestyle.

Emma got up. She circled around behind her father's desk so that she could rest her hands on his head.

"Daddy," she asked "what's going on? Why are you so anxious to get me out of New York?" She took out a Kleenex to wipe the beads of sweat glistening at his temples. Then suddenly and slowly she asked "Is it starting again? That 9/11 business?"

A long silence answered her query. "Emma darling," her father said "there are things I can't say without violating a trust. But it would be a load off my mind if I knew you were going away for a few days."

Sure, Emma thought, that's it. It's some terrorist thing. Her younger sister, Georgina, was well away from the city, out at the end of Long Island, participating in a horse show.

"And you, Daddy? What are you going to do?"

"I have no choice. My place is here in the midst of my fellow New Yorkers."

"And in that case, my place is here, too. As long as you stay, Daddy, I stay right here beside you."

By now, more than a hundred NEST vans, representing a full deployment of the nuclear search organization's resources, were prowling the streets of Manhattan, Queens and Brooklyn. They bore the insignia of truck rental firms like Hertz or Avis to conceal their real nature and, indeed, from the street there was nothing that would indicate they were anything other than normal rental vans. In fact, they were rolling laboratories, each equipped with the most modern detection devices known to nuclear science, all linked to the ordinary-appearing antennas attached to their rooftops.

Those detectors were designed to pick up the slightest emanation of gamma rays or neutrons given off by plutonium or highly enriched uranium. Most important, their computer databases allowed them to weed out, instantly, the dozens of false positives that could circulate in any large metropolitan area.

In addition, a dozen NEST helicopters, also disguised with the names of imaginary firms, were over flying the city hoping to pick up any tell-tale emanations coming from the rooftops below.

The whole operation was being run by the NEST Director David Graham from the headquarters he'd installed at the Office of Emergency Management in Brooklyn. He was, he well knew as he puffed on cigarette after cigarette, looking for the proverbial nuclear needle in a haystack but the equipment at his disposal was so modern, so technologically perfected that he was confident of his team's ability to pick up some trace of the terrorist's bomb. As for the hundreds of police and FBI officers doing their part in the search, the key element for him, as for them, was time.

Suddenly, the microphone beside his desk cackled. "Mr. Graham, one of your choppers is picking up radiation."

Graham grabbed the mike linking him to the helicopter in question. "What are you getting?" he asked the chopper's technicians.

"Ninety millirads."

Graham whistled. That was a helluva hit, particularly since, in all probability, the emanation had had to pass through a number of floors.

"Where are you?"

"We're over a public housing project at 11th Avenue and 28th Street, just a block away from the Hudson River". With two of the policemen who'd been assigned to him, Graham quickly spotted the location on his map.

"OK," he ordered "get out of there so you don't alert anybody that you're picking something up. I'll send in half a dozen vans to search the area.

He beckoned to the New York police officer assigned to him as a driver and ran out to the OEM parking lot and his unmarked police car.

"Listen!" he said to the driver. "That's public housing down there so get on your radio and have City Hall get me a full set of the plans and building specs and meet me with them when we arrive."

Twenty minutes later, as they pulled up to the first of the four public housing buildings in the project, Graham recognized the woman getting out of the first of his vans to reach the scene. Gladys Simpson was a senior Gamma Ray specialist at the Livermore National Laboratory in California. She was married with two young children and had a doctorate in nuclear physics from Cal Tech. She was well-tanned from, Graham was sure, her favorite past time out of the lab, climbing the slopes of the Sierra Morenas with her husband.

She, of course, had been filled in on the chopper's reading. Glancing up at the 15-story building, she let out a low whistle. "Must have come from one of the top five or six stories," she observed.

"Yeah," Graham agreed. The complex, he knew from the plans he'd been given, contained 800 flats and probably 5,000 inhabitants. Search that without drawing a crowd was going to be a difficult job, indeed. "We'll do the top six floors in each building." It was highly unlikely that the source of the radiation picked up by his chopper was in a lower story.

Gladys, meanwhile, had slung her portable detector on her back, looking, they all hoped, like a young person with a back pack. Graham thought she looked a little tense.

"You nervous?" he asked.

"Yes," she said in a half whisper.

"Don't worry," he assured her. "We'll find the bomb. Our very first!"

"Bomb?" she said. "Who's worried about the bomb? I'm afraid some creep with a knife is going to try to jump me up there." NEST officers, traditionally, were not armed.

Graham gestured to one of the FBI agents in civilian clothes. "He'll go with you!" he said, and the Californian woman set off to begin exploring the top floors of the building he'd assigned her. He then organized similar teams to search out the top six floors of the three other buildings.

Gladys, quite naturally, was the first to finish. Her detector had picked up absolutely nothing, not even something as banal as the emanation given off by an alarm clock whose hands were coated with a radioactive substance to allow it to glow in the dark. Before long, the other three teams were reporting back to him. They, too, had found absolutely nothing.

Graham was dumbfounded. Chopper picks up a shower of radiation and now they find not even a millirad!

"Get that chopper back down here!" he ordered. A few minutes later, he heard the whump-whump of its rotors approaching. "Get over the precise spot where you picked up those emanations. And at the same altitude, and tell me what you're getting."

"Jesus, David!" the technician aboard the chopper called down. "I can't believe it! Now I'm getting nothing, absolutely nothing."

"You sure your detector is working properly?" Graham asked.

"Absolutely. I had it calibrated before we left Los Alamos."

Graham shook his head in disbelief. "Listen," he said to Gladys "go up there on the roof and have a look around."

"Yipes!" she said a minute later "the elevator's not working."

"So what?" Graham said. "Climb up there. You're a mountain climber, aren't you?"

A few minutes later, the young woman emerged onto the roof. Below her was the dark expanse of the Hudson and at her feet, the asphalt-covered roof speckled with pigeon droppings. Her detector was silent.

"David," she said "there's absolutely nothing up here, except a lovely view and a lot of pigeon shit!"

Omar Tahiri waved his hand in disgust at the tawdry hotel room in which he and his colleague Amr Bin Khaled awaited the denouement of their plan to detonate an atomic bomb in the heart of New York. "We left our luxurious refugee camp in Lebanon to come and live here in this shit hole? Where they don't even know how to make the beds or change the sheets?"

"Well," Khaled acknowledged "the Waldorf Astoria it's not. But don't worry. Just think about all those lovely green fields and flowing fountains that will be waiting for us when we enter the gates of Paradise as martyrs."

"Oh sure!" Omar laughed "and all those beautiful virgins waiting to pleasure us for all eternity. You don't really believe in all that do you? As far as I'm concerned, I'd just like some clean sheets and towels in this lousy hotel room."

"I believe in the Cause," Khaled said. "I believe in our goal of restoring our land to our Palestinian people."

Omar gestured to their TV set, fixed as it had been for hours to New York One, the city's non-stop news channel. "It's not going to work, Khaled," he said. "There hasn't been a thing in the news. Not about a crisis in the Middle East, not about settlements, not about a heightened terrorist alert here in New York.

Nothing, but how the President is supposed to be confined to bed in the White House with some kind of stomach trouble."

"That's probably just a cover story to hide what's really going on," Khaled said, glancing at his watch. "We've still got almost 48 hours before the deadline we gave them expires. Plenty of time for Sharon to announce to the world that he's going to start withdrawing his settlements from the West Bank."

"He's not going to do it, Khaled," Omar replied. The third member of their trio, Nahed Jihari, was actually 'babysitting' their bomb in the nearby flat in which they'd hidden it. "We all know the Israelis. They'll never give in to a threat like this. Mugniyeh was dreaming when he cooked up this scheme."

Omar stood up and walked to the window looking down on 38th Street. As he did, an image crowded into his mind — that of the woman clutching her baby, in the window of the building across the street from the apartment in which they'd hidden the bomb. Down below his perch, thousands of shoppers and passers-by jammed the street. Somewhere he'd read that at times, five hundred people waited for some of the traffic lights in this neighborhood to change to cross the street. That bomb goes off and they'll all die, he thought, along with that mother and her baby. Was this really the way to win back their lost homeland? On a sea of corpses? These last days spent in New York, sharing the daily lives of these people so distant from the Palestinian problem, had begun to modify his vision of their drama. Was killing hundreds of thousands of men, women and children really the way to win back their land? It was a question disturbing him with growing urgency.

Khaled came over to join him by the window. He, too, stared at the throngs in the street below. "You're probably right, Omar. Sharon and his gang won't do it. He smacked his right fist into the palm of his left hand. "And those poor, dumb bastards down there are going to pay the price for a monster's intransigence. Because, I promise you, if the Israelis haven't caved in by the time the deadline expires, that bomb is going to go off. I'll see to that. If Mugniyeh, for some damn reason, doesn't manage to get a call through to the bomb, I'll be right there beside it. I'll set it off myself with that button we installed on it when we got here."

Omar studied his accomplice. Yes, he thought, Khaled will do it. There is nothing in that man's heart, but hate. He glanced again down at the crowds thronging 38th Street. If somehow this terrible gamble went wrong, as everything seemed to indicate it was going to, was he going to let Khaled exterminate that mass of innocent people? Or must he somehow find a way to disconnect the wire that linked the button on their living room table to the bomb's detonator?

For Avigdor Beibelman, the extremist member of the

Likud Party who had whispered to a cabinet colleague that he "had an idea to blow this terrorist crisis right out of the water", the time had come to start putting that idea into action. To do it, he had come to the Israeli settlement of Kedumim, implanted not far from the Palestinian city of Nablus, the capital, in a sense, of Palestinian nationalist aspirations.

Seven hundred settler families lived in Kedumim, most of them in small houses and bungalows built in three circling rows around the hilltop on which they had first planted their flag a decade ago. The site was surrounded by a rocky landscape sheltering centuries-old olive groves. They belonged to the residents of four small Palestinian communities clustered around the settlement. Some of those families had been cultivating their trees for generations, although Kedumim's rabbi maintained that they were, in fact, stealing Jewish property, since God had given the land on which the trees were growing to the Jewish people, two milleniums ago.

Almost a hundred of Kedumim's families were still living in trailers and vans, waiting for a chance to acquire the land on which to build a permanent home. That was exactly the chance Beibelman now proposed to offer them.

At the request of Kedumim's mayor Yaacov Weiss, the heads of most of those families had gathered to meet Beibelman in the community hall of the settlement's synagogue. "My Brethren," he began "I cannot go into full detail for you from this platform without violating a sacred trust, but what I can tell you is that our sacred right to settle our Jewish communities here in Yesha — he used the Hebrew word for what was more frequently referred to as the West Bank or Judea and Samaria – may soon be imperilled."

A gasp of dismay greeted his words.

"Yes," he continued "but thanks to brave people like you, I know we will resist this effort to curtail our God-given rights from whatever source it may come, our enemies, our beloved leaders. Even our closest and dearest friends. This is our homeland. Our rights to it are not subjected to or conditioned by any so-called peace plan or road map or international consensus. They were deeded to us by God and here we shall stay for generations to come, in witness to the eternal covenant between God and his Chosen People."

The entire assembly leapt to its feet and burst out cheering as one. Beibelman beamed with pleasure. That was exactly the reaction he anticipated and wanted. "Devoted Zionists as you all are, you deserve a piece of our historic homeland for yourselves and your families. Well, I am here to tell you the time has come for you to have your land – not next week, not next month, not next year, but now – right now!"

He pointed to a huge aerial photograph of Kedumim and the Palestinian areas surrounding it, which he had placed on an easel before the assembly. With his forefinger, he circled out a large swathe of land adjoining the outer fringes of Kedumim. It encompassed dozens of olive groves.

"This is your land!" he shouted. "Tomorrow, with your vans and your trailers, you will march forth and claim it, all of it, in the name of Zion and your sacred right to settle Yesha."

Those words could not have struck a more responsive chord among his audience. Most of the men and women before him had been clamoring, for months, for support to do what he had just told them to do — and he was not some pro-settler extremist. He was a member in good standing of the Sharon government. Again, they all leapt to their feet, shouting, clapping and yelling their agreement.

"By sunset tomorrow, you will have firmly placed scores, even hundreds of vans and trailers on that land to let the world know that you, the sons and daughters of Zion, have exercised your historic rights to your homeland."

And, Beibelman thought happily, I will make sure the media is there to record their brave actions and let the world know as well that whatever blackmail may be attempted against us, our people will never abandon a square inch of our sacred homeland.

Moved and saddened in almost equal measure by his daughter Emma's determination to remain at his side, New York's mayor Mike Bloomberg clambered into his helicopter on the roof of City Hall for an aerial inspection of his threatened city. Police Commissioner Ray Kelly was with him, as was Charles Morningside, the Washington bureaucrat who specialized in the problems of evacuating urban centers.

As the chopper's rotors thrust the little craft into the bright blue autumn sky, Bloomberg felt his heartbeat quicken. In seconds, New York was there at his feet, glistening in the fall sunshine, vibrant and so alive, you could almost feel the dynamism of the city rising up to their helicopter. Was it possible that all that power and strength down there could be wiped off the face of the earth in seconds? Alas, he knew it was. He had, in the last 48 hours, studied a photo gallery of the remains of Hiroshima and Nagasaki which left no doubt in the mayor's mind, of the horrors of the threat they were facing.

The cackle of their evacuation expert's voice intruded on his apocalyptic vision.

"Would it be possible, somehow, to order an evacuation of the city without giving the citizenry an explanation for it?" he asked.

"Are you crazy?" Kelly replied. "You can't do anything in this city without telling the people why you're doing it. Nine eleven didn't change anything, my friend. New York is still New York and New Yorkers are still New Yorkers."

Moments later, they were flying over the southern tip of Manhattan. They could see kids playing touch football at Battery Park. "Could we attempt an evacuation by motor vehicle, run the tunnels and bridges one way and do what you've done on occasion, insist on a minimum of five passengers in a car? Of course, the police would have to impose draconian measures to keep order. They'd have to be ready to employ force to prevent people from cutting into the evacuation lines."

"Sure," scoffed Kelly "they'd have to be ready to take pot shots at nine out of ten people."

The helicopter swung north, paralleling the Hudson River and the city's northeastern flank. "Of course," Morningside droned on "it will be easier here. The Lincoln Tunnel has six traffic lanes we can turn one way."

Mike Bloomberg had stopped listening to Morningside's litany of statistics acquired during those sterile years in Washington, pouring over computer printouts, maps, statistics, in the pursuit of solutions to unsolvable problems.

"Ray," he said "it's just impossible to evacuate this city in any kind of a hurry, isn't it?"

"No way, Your Honor, no way!"

"And all those Rockefeller air raid shelters? Nothing we can do with them?"

"Since the end of the Cold War, they've become anachronisms. Relics left over from a bygone era." Kelly laughed. "Hey," he said, pointing to the left "just down there you've got the New York State Office building. They had the Rolls Royce of air raid shelters. Why don't we drop down and have a look?"

The pilot set their chopper down beside the building

and the three men walked inside. At the far end of the lobby, just beyond the elevator bank was one of the old yellow and black air raid shelter signs, faded and partially obscured by an AIDS awareness poster. Kelly looked around and spotted an African American janitor. "We want to have a look at that air raid shelter," he announced.

The janitor looked at him, stunned. "Man," he said "ain't nobody been down there for years!' Kelly insisted and the janitor took him to a wall-board covered with keys. "Key gotta be on here somewhere." For fully five minutes, he studied the keys with no visible result. "Let me call another guy been here longer than me."

A few minutes later, a scrawny, white-haired gentlemen in a Mets baseball cap turned backwards, and a tee shirt covered with religious slogans like "The Redeemer is coming" and "Let Christ's way be your way" arrived. He, too, spent a good five minutes studying the mass of keys before selecting two "probables". One of them opened a door giving on to a darkened stair well. Guided by a flashlight, they made their way down a creaking wooden staircase, ducking under heating pipes wrapped in cobwebs. When they reached the cellar, Bloomberg heard a series of scraping noises from the interior.

"What's that?" he asked.

"Rats!" said their guide.

He turned his flashlight on an ancient Civil Defense poster. PROCEDURE TO FOLLOW IN THE EVENT OF A THERMONUCLEAR ATTACK, it read. Below that admonition were six steps New Yorkers were advised to follow in such an event. They included such helpful suggestions as loosening neckties and unbuttoning restrictive clothing. The sixth and final admonition was "Immediately, upon seeing the brilliant flash of a nuclear explosion, bend over and place your head firmly between your legs."

Beneath, some jokester years ago had written "And kiss your ass goodbye."

The floor of the shelter was littered with junk dumped there over the years. Barely visible were a dozen jerricans that had once been filled with water. On the pile of rubble were the remains of the First Aid kits that had once been installed in the shelter.

"Junkies," Kelly said. "They learned there was morphine in those kits and came down here years ago to score a hit. Seen enough, Your Honor?" he asked.

"Enough to know how useless these places are. Let's get back to our chopper."

As they started to scramble their way back up the creaking staircase, their guide took three pamphlets from a sack thrown over his shoulder and handed one to each of them. Bloomberg studied his. "Jesus saves," it said "bring your problems to him." The mayor couldn't help laughing. "Hey," he said "maybe he's got something there."

They were buckling themselves back into the helicopter when Bloomberg's mobile phone beeped. It was the White House.

Seconds later, the President was on the line. "Michael," he said "this is not a secure line so I must be brief. We need you here as fast as possible. Get over to McGuire Air Force Base urgently. There's an Air Force jet on standby there waiting to fly you down here."

The Operation "Sword of Islam" launched by Nahed Jihari with her early morning phone call was beginning to pay dividends. The pigeons, with their rings of radioactive material, were now in full flight all over the city and David Graham, the chief of the NEST was going crazy. Three times in the hour or so since he'd been back at his office installed in the Office of Emergency Operations, his helicopters over flying New York had reported picking up important radioactive emanations. Yet, those emanations had all mysteriously disappeared as soon as the vans Graham had ordered to the sites to search the surrounding areas had arrived.

What the hell is going on, he asked himself, pacing the floor of his improvised headquarters. Suddenly, his angry meditation was interrupted by a call from another of his chopper pilots.

"This is Plume Three," the voice called. "I'm over 23rd Street near the corner of Madison Avenue and I'm picking up something."

Graham asked him to reconfirm his position and as

the pilot started to reply, he exploded. "God damn it! The radiation has disappeared!"

Graham swore in fury at this frustrating chase of emanations disappearing like ghosts.

"Hey, wait a minute, David," the pilot called. "I've picked them up again. They didn't disappear. Their location just shifted. Now they're moving up Sixth Avenue."

"Son of a bitch!" Graham growled. "Have those guys gone and stuffed their bomb in a truck? Are they moving around the city?"

He contacted his FBI liaison and the two men ordered two dozens disguised vehicles into the area in the hope that if the bomb was in a truck they could pick it up and follow it. The chopper, in the meantime, was following the movement of the emanations, up Sixth Avenue, then into Central Park where they veered west.

"The emanations have stopped, David!" the pilot shouted.

"Where are you?"

"Near the intersection of Broadway and Columbus Avenue."

Graham ordered his mobile teams to converge on the area. As the first one arrived on the scene, Graham recognized the voice of Gladys Simpson.

"Hey!" she said. "I'm getting radiation."

"Where are you?"

"Opposite Lincoln Center." Gladys got out of her red Avis van, her portable Gamma Ray detector slung

over her shoulders, and contemplated the vast esplanade of Lincoln Center, rung with its opera house, con-
cert hall and theater. Her detector gave her a steady reading of 34 millirads but there wasn't a car or truck in
sight. In front of her, there was only the monumental
black marble fountain that was the centerpiece of the
esplanade, surrounded by the usual noonday crowd of
students chewing on hotdogs bought from sidewalk
vendors, shop-girls on their lunch hour, tourists, and a
few housewives walking their pets.

Where, in God's name, are those emanations coming from, she asked herself. As she did, Graham arrived
in a yellow Hertz van. He, too, got the same reading on
his detector as his colleague was getting on hers.

He grabbed a cigarette and studied the scene before him. Was it possible that somehow a truck had
gotten to the esplanade before Gladys had arrived and
had had the time to run a device into one of the buildings around the esplanade? That seemed impossible to
Graham. Had they been shadowing some guy who had
just had a massive dose of chemiotherapy for a cancer?
Still, he wasn't going to take chances. He ordered the
follow up teams reaching the esplanade to search all the
buildings surrounding it.

"I think it's coming from that area around the fountain," one of his NEST team inspectors observed. The
two men started to walk slowly towards the lunch-time
crowd when suddenly, the emanations shifted to the
left. An elderly woman in a tattered black coat had just

broken off from the lunchers and was moving towards the edge of the esplanade. Graham moved over to her. She had two spots of rouge on her cheeks, wishful souvenir makeup of her bygone days. In one hand, she clutched a plastic shopping bag from Macy's. Graham had barely had time to identify himself and show her his government I.D. when she sobbed: "I'm sorry, officer. I didn't know it was forbidden."

Forbidden, Graham asked himself, what in hell is she talking about? But his millirad reading had just leapt up.

"The times are so hard. I have only my Social Security to live on. I didn't think I was doing anything wrong. I just wanted to bring him back to my flat to try and cook him for my dinner."

"What is it you wanted to bring home, Madame?" Graham asked.

She opened her Macy's bag. Graham peered in and saw a gray lump. He reached in and pulled out the body of a still-warm gray pigeon. Suddenly his millirad reading leapt to over 400. On the dead bird's leg, he spotted a ring containing a tablet that was clearly the source of his emanations. Suddenly, it was crystal clear to Graham, all the false readings, the disappearing traces of radiation. It all had come from pigeons, pigeons booby-trapped to drive him and his men crazy. Not only were these terrorists fanatics, they were diabolically clever was well!

The sense of despair enshrouding the White House Oval Office was so palpable, so real, Mike Bloomberg felt he could almost reach out and touch it. The President gestured him to a chair beside his National Security Advisor Condi Rice. Also gathered around the President's desk were Colin Powell, Vice President Cheney, the secretary of defense, Milt Andersen of the CIA and Andrew Card, the President's Chief of Staff.

"Mike," the President said, in the tone of voice he might employ to announce the death of a dear friend "We're up against a stonewall." He tapped his wristwatch. "The terrorists' deadline is going to expire in less than 48 hours and we're nowhere in our efforts to defuse this crisis. We thought we were going to be able to open up a line of communication to the people who are behind this. We failed. You know how hard the police, the FBI and our other agencies are working up in New York to find where that bomb is, where the terrorists who brought it here are. What have we found?" The President threw up his hands in despair. "Nothing. We haven't got a clue."

"Mr. President," Bloomberg noted, "I've got to tell you I spent the morning over flying the city in a helicopter, and evacuating New York in the little time we have left – even if we chose to ignore their 'don't evacuate threat' – is simply out of the question."

Bush gave a sad shrug of his shoulders to acknowledge the accuracy of Bloomberg's observation. "It's our feeling here, Mike, that you represent a potentially

important card we should now play. You know Ariel
Sharon personally from your work with the United Jewish Appeal and the cultural activities you've sponsored
in Israel, your charitable actions on behalf of the state.
As the mayor of New York, you represent the people
whose lives are threatened by this menace. You are, perhaps, in a unique position to influence Sharon's thinking, to convince him to work with me to adopt in public, a position on those settlements that we can at least
hope will allow us to defuse this damn crisis. Will you
please call him on my behalf and try to get him to modify
his position?"

Bloomberg looked at the President with respect and
understanding. "Of course I will, Mr. President, but I
harbor no illusions about the chances of my success.
The terrorists behind this threat to New York are almost certainly uncompromising fanatics. Theirs is the
same mad mentality that was behind the people who
did 9/11, the people who bombed discos in Bali, syna-
gogues and banks in Istanbul. They are beyond the reach
of reason. And I know Sharon well enough to know
how inflexible he can be when he feels the security of
Israel is at risk. But nonetheless, I will try, Mr. President, I will try."

Moments later, the mayor had Sharon on the line,
at the Israeli's Balfour Street residence in Jerusalem. It
was a comfortable but far from opulent dwelling. No
priceless paintings decorated its walls. Its principal arti-
fact was a segment of the Dead Sea Scrolls presented

to the residence by their discoverer Yigal Yadin. Sharon had, of course, placed Israel's Defense Forces on high alert but given his nation's ongoing security concerns, that move had not stirred any particular attention. Furthermore, neither the Israeli nor the American media had picked up any indication that a crisis was at hand.

In the circumstances, the mayor's call hardly came as a surprise to the Israeli Prime Minister, and Sharon settled into a comfortable armchair by his TV set for what he knew was going to be a painful conversation. By mutual agreement, their conversation was played out by speaker phones to the American leaders assembled in the Oval Office. After a ritual exchange of greetings, their conversation began exactly as Sharon had thought it would.

"Arik," Bloomberg said, employing Sharon's familiarized first name "I speak to you as the mayor of the largest Jewish city in the world. But it is not just on behalf of our three million fellow Jews living in the city over which I preside, that I am calling you. It is on behalf of every one of my fellow New Yorkers, Jews, Christians, Moslems, Hindus, Buddhists, non-believers, Whites, African Americans, Chinese, Hispanics. Everyone. Why are they menaced, Arik? Because this city symbolizes the power, the values of our nation, of the freedom and democratic values we represent to the world. And you must remember, Arik, that to some of those fanatics, this city represents the citadel of Jewish power in the world. That is why the lives of a million or more innocent men, women and children are threatened. Because there is no doubt, Arik, that if that bomb goes off, a million people will die.

"I spent much of this morning flying over the city in a helicopter. Trying to evacuate the city in some kind of an emergency rush to ignore the terrible conditions the terrorists have submitted, is a physical impossibility. Clearly, it is my moral obligation to stay in the city with my fellow citizens and share whatever their fate is going to be. This morning, one of the two beings most precious to me, my elder daughter Emma, was in my office. How could I violate my trust and give her a warning to get out of town when the circumstances prevent me from giving a similar warning to my fellow New Yorkers? So, if that explosion takes place, she will, in all probability, perish by my side. You're a father, Arik. Surely, you can understand that this is the most terrible drama a father can face."

The mayor paused, feeling the tears smarting his eyes as he contemplated the horror his words had just captured.

"You, Arik, are in a special position. You can defuse this horrible crisis and save perhaps, the lives of a million people by making clear, publicly, your readiness to withdraw the settlers in the Occupied Territories, settlers who are on land that, whether we like it or not, has not belonged to the Jewish people for 2,000 years. Settlements, a majority of your own countrymen have always opposed; settlements, some of which you, yourself, have contemplated publicly evacuating..."

"My dear Michael!" Sharon interrupted "as I told your President, the issue here is not the settlements. What you are asking me and my fellow Israelis to do is to surrender to the blackmail of a band of fanatics. Since 9/11, your President has not ceased trumpeting his determination never to yield to the menace of terrorism. Yet, what are you asking us to do? Exactly what he has sworn never to do – yield to terrorism."

"Arik, please!" Bloomberg rejoined "Israel has no legitimate claim to those lands in the Occupied Territories and it never has…"

"How can you say such a thing, Michael? You had a religious upbringing as any good Jew. You know, as well as I do, that God gave those lands to Moses and the Jewish people for all eternity."

"Arik, we cannot order the world of the 21st century, of the thermonuclear age, on the basis of a forty-centuries-old religious myth. If you wish to invoke the principles of our faith, think of the Torah's command that if the life of a single being is in jeopardy, then the entire community must come to his aid. The lives of a million people are menaced, Arik, and you can help save them!"

In Jerusalem, Sharon stood up and began to pace his living room, clutching his detachable phone in his fist. "We are being asked to abandon the fundamentals of our national sovereignty in response to a criminal action which jeopardizes the very foundations of peace and international order."

The Israeli Prime Minister took a deep breath. "I will tell you what the solution to this terrible crisis has to be, Michael, the only possible solution. Your President has to go on national television now, right now, and tell your countrymen and the world, all the details of the terrorists' threat to New York. He must then make it clear that if those mad fanatics detonate that bomb, then those extremists territories in Pakistan from which these Islamic murderers have been coming will cease to exist. Disappear."

"Killing an additional forty million people who will be as innocent as the million New Yorkers who will die? What kind of a solution is that?"

"The only one mad men like the people behind this can understand, Michael. However painful the consequences may be Michael, we are not going to remove those settlements in response to criminal blackmail. For a real and lasting peace with our Palestinian neighbors, perhaps, but not for this. I'm sorry. I will pray for both you and your daughter. *Shalom*."

With that, Sharon hung up.

Bloomberg grasped his head in his hands and shook his dead in despair. Condi Rice, looking at him and thinking of what he had said about his daughter, took out a Kleenex to wipe a tear from her eye.

Milt Andersen of the CIA broke the stunned silence enveloping the room. "Mr. President," he said "you cannot allow a million Americans to be slaughtered because Sharon will not rectify the consequences of a policy that has no basis in justice or historical fact. If Sharon and the Israelis won't remove those settlers, Mr. President, then you are going to have to do it."

"How the hell am I supposed to do that, Milt?"

"I don't know. Get the chiefs of staff to come in here and brief you on the possibilities."

The President leaned back in his chair. "I'm afraid Milt has a point," he said to Rumsfeld and Powell. "Get the chiefs in here ready to brief – right now!"

"Ah!" smiled Olivia Phillips "another cup of New York's finest *capuccino* from one of New York's finest!"

T.F. O'Neill placed a steaming cup of coffee on the desk of his FBI teammate at his Manhattan South Headquarters. "Listen, Little Pal!" he said. "I've got to dash over to Brooklyn on a personal matter but I'll be back in an hour. You go on studying those Sixty Ones" — a "Sixty One" was New York Police Department terminology for a criminal report — "to see if you spot some more locations we should check out when I get back."

Twenty minutes later, O'Neill drove his unmarked police car up to the entrance of Our Lady of Sorrows Institution for Handicapped Children in Glendale, a pleasant suburb of Brooklyn. Sister Mary Francis Duchelle greeted him at the entrance.

"Nothing serious happening, I hope, inspector," she said.

"No, no, Sister, not at all. I just have to take my daughter Katy out of school for two or three days to take her up to my parents in Connecticut."

"Oh dear," the good nun sighed "I'm afraid, that's quite against regulations. I'll have to take it up with Mother Superior."

"Well, you see, Sister," O'Neill insisted "my wife's sister is arriving from her home in California for a brief visit. She's never seen Katy and we are very anxious that she meet her." He glanced at his watch. "I'm very busy, Sister. Could you be kind enough to get my daughter for me?"

"Couldn't you come back this evening after I've had a chance to talk to Mother Superior?"

"I'm afraid not, Sister. As I said, I have to deal with several pressing matters."

"Very well," the nun sighed. "Just wait here for a few minutes while I go get Katy and pack her overnight bag." She guided O'Neill to the large bay window which gave onto the school's playground. It was a playground like that of any other school, a merry-go-round, a seesaw, a slide, building blocks. As he always did looking at it, O'Neill felt tears stinging his eyes. Those eyes searched the kids in the playground for his daughter Katy. He saw Sister Mary Francis cross the schoolyard, pick out Katy and, taking her by the hand, lead her to the dormitory.

O'Neill's heart tightened at the sight of all those innocent little children, some with the gestures of the handicapped, or slightly distorted faces. What about them, he thought, almost ready to burst into tears. I'm able to save my precious little daughter but what about them?

Five minutes later, Sister Mary Francis arrived at the entrance, with Katy clutching her little valise.

Inspector O'Neill and his car had disappeared.

In view of the urgency of the situation, the secretaries of Defense and State were able to get their briefers into the Situation Room ready to address the President in barely an hour. It was just before 14:30 Washington time when the lead briefer, Lieutenant General Malcolm Touhy, the commanding general of the U.S. Marine Corps, advanced to the speaker's stand.

"Ladies and gentlemen!" he began "I want to stress that the proposals that I am about to put forward have the support of my colleagues at the State Department. They represent a jointly evolved State and Defense strategy for addressing this crisis and the President's request."

Wow, half the occupants of the room thought, without saying it out loud, that's a new departure for this administration!

"Our proposal is to mount a two-pronged assault in the hope that by carrying out the first, we will create a political situation in which the Government of Israel will feel obliged to undertake the second of its own accord. However, I propose to brief you on how we would execute both assaults, should that become necessary."

He turned to a large map of Israel mounted on an easel beside his speaker's stand. "Our Sixth Fleet is fully deployed in the eastern Mediterranean right now, less than five hours' sailing time from the Israeli seacoast. It contains two aircraft carrier battle groups, those surrounding the George Washington and the Abraham Lincoln, two of our largest and most modern carriers. It is our conviction that even given the acknowledged combat skills of the Israel Air Force, those two carriers are capable of providing, if necessary, air cover for the first of our two assaults. However, if necessary, we can also call on additional air strength from our U.S. Air Force combat squadrons stationed at Incirlik Air Force Base in Turkey, all of whose pilots have had recent combat experience in Iraq.

"Because of the tensions in the area, the fleet carries not one, but two reinforced Marine Corps combat battalions, over eight thousand men in all. We propose to land both battalions here" — he thumped the map with his rubber-tipped pointer — "just south of Netzarim, the largest Israeli settlement in the Gaza Strip. The seacoast there is shallow and will provide an excellent landing environment for our amphibious craft. The marine battalions will be equipped with armored personnel carriers, Humvees and Abrams tanks, and they will head south to occupy the settlements of Alai Sinai and Nisanet and take over the border crossing at Erez which commands the access to the West Bank."

"And what about those 15,000 Israeli army troops stationed there to defend the Gaza settlers from the Palestinians? Do you suppose they are just going to sit there on their hands and watch all this happening?" Condi Rice asked.

General Touhy turned to the civilian seated at his left. "As I said, this is part of a joint Defense State Department proposal. I'll let State's Under Secretary of State for Middle Eastern Affairs here answer your question, madame."

The State Department official stood up. "Shortly before our marine battalions board their landing craft," he said "under the terms of our proposal, the President will address the nation and by an international radio hook up, the entire world. He will reveal in full detail the threats the terrorists have made to New York City and the fact that Sharon's intransigence has forced us to take this action ourselves in order to save the lives of hundreds of thousands of New Yorkers. The timing of his speech and our subsequent action will be calculated to take place three hours before the terrorists' deadline expires on Friday, just over 36 hours from now. He will indicate that if necessary, we will continue the Gaza operation on the West Bank, and it is our hope that the speech and the Gaza action will lead the terrorists to give up their threat to New York and inform us of the bomb's whereabouts. However, as no one knows better than you, Miss Rice, we have no line of communication open to the people behind this threat, to New York, and no guarantee, therefore, that they will respond to the President's gesture as we hope they will."

"And what about the settlers?" Condi Rice pressed. "They are all armed. Suppose they open fire?"

"These men are marines, Miss Rice. They will return any fire directed at them in quantity and quality."

"And do you really imagine the IDF isn't going to fire its field artillery pieces at your landing craft as they come ashore?"

"If they do, the fleet's warship will open up with their on-board cannon to suppress their fire."

"In other words, for all effects and purposes, we will be entering into war with Israel," she pressed.

The diplomat grimaced. "We hope that it will not come to that and that ultimately reason will prevail."

"That," Condi snapped "strikes me as an example of wishful thinking at its worst."

"And," the President's Chief of Staff Andrew Card muttered to himself, "I know one thing that will prevail — the Democrats in the coming election. We won't get a single Jewish vote if we go through with this idea."

"Oh yeah?" said the CIA's Anderson "And how many votes do you think we're going to get for effective leadership if we let that bomb kill a million New Yorkers?"

The President shook his head in despair and dismay. "So what's the second part of your proposal?" he asked.

General Touhy moved back to the speaker's stand,

tall and straight, every inch a marine general. "If our forceful evacuation of the Israeli settlers in Gaza has not resolved the situation, then we will stage the 101st Airborne and the First Armored Division from their current assignments in Iraq into the West Bank to complete the settlement evacuation, with the exception of the huge settlements like Ariel north of Ramallah which everyone seems to agree must become a part of Israel, with Palestinians receiving as compensation an equal amount of territory from inside Israel's 1967 boundaries."

The President stood up, indicating the briefing, as far as he was concerned, was over. "This whole thing is madness," he said. "The world has gone crazy, utterly crazy. Barely 36 hours to go and we're nowhere near finding that bomb. What, in God's name, are we going to do? Take a chance on ignoring the terms of the terrorists' ultimatum and order a 'run as fast as you can' evacuation tomorrow? Let's adjourn for a spell. Condi, Rumny and Colin, I want to talk with you upstairs in my living room."

Barely five minutes after the meeting had adjourned, the telephone rang in the office of the Chief of Station of the MOSSAD, Israel's Intelligence Agency in central Washington. Daniel Olmert, the station chief recognized the caller's voice before he had even had to give him his code name. He was a high-ranking official of the U.S. Defense Department.

"Turn your recorder on!" he ordered. In a series of short concise sentences, he passed the Israeli spy chief a succinct account of the meeting which had just transpired in the White House. The U.S. has few secrets from the Israeli government. Within minutes, an encrypted copy of the report was on its way to Jerusalem.

The United States government possesses no facility more secret than the Menwith Hill Station of the U.S. Army's Intelligence and Security Command, set in the Yorkshire Hills, 170 miles north of Central London. Despite the term "Army" in its 53-year-old designation, Menwith Hill is, in fact, an outpost of the super-secret NSA – National Security Agency – whose mission is to suck every form of communication from the satellite transmission of telephone calls, faxes, cellular phone calls, pornography, the encrypted wire transfers of billions of dollars from the soup of cyberspace onto the NSA's massive computer data banks.

So restricted is Menwith Hill that no member of the British Parliament has ever been allowed to visit it. The base is built on U.S. soil sold under the terms of a still-secret protocol signed by Harry Truman and Winston Churchill in 1951. No aspect of its ultra-secret work is more secret than the work performed in its SBI —

Sensitive Background Information — storage depot. Among other things, that depot houses all the information pulled from the skies by another super-secret NSA installation, the "Big Ear" in Bad Ebling, Germany. That installation is responsible for intercepting all electronic communications going into and out of that most sensitive of areas, the Middle East.

The call made by the three terrorists in New York to Beirut to inform Imad Mugniyeh that their bomb had arrived and been installed in a hiding place was recorded on its computers, but because it contained no sensitive "red alert" words and was not made to a Lebanese phone number on the NSA's watch list, it had, by itself, excited no particular attention.

One thing, however, had set the call apart from the masses of calls stored on the computer. That was the fact that the call from New York had been made by a cellular phone which did not have a registered carrier service and owner. As a result, the NSA duty officer logging the call into the computer had flagged it with a red alert of its own, so that in the event another call should be made from the same Nokia cellular phone, 423756281, that call would be immediately signaled to the NSA duty officer at Menwith Hill.

Shortly after seven p.m. London time on Wednesday night, the red alert flashed on the Menwith Hill's duty officer's desk. A quick investigation revealed that the Nokia phone had just been used again, this time to call a number in Bremen, Germany. A swift check of the German phone directories revealed that the call had gone to a Frau Hildegard Helbling at 23 Wilhelmstrasse in Bremen.

The officer got onto the phone immediately to the CIA Berlin Station, with orders to get someone to the Bremen address to find who in New York had made the call from the identity-less Nokia cell phone.

"Hey," the Berlin desk man said "the chief ain't going to like that. We have to go accompanied by an officer from the BfV, the Office for the Protection of the Constitution, the Bundesamt fur Verfassungsshutz, and since Iraq, our relations with those guys are pisspoor."

"I don't give a damn if they're in love with you," the NSA officer in England snapped. "This carries top White House priority. Get someone into that woman's house in Bremen, pronto!"

Barely half an hour later, Frau Helbling was surprised when a pair of middle-aged gentlemen rang her doorbell. She was immediately cooperative. Of course, she knew who had called her from New York. It was her daughter Ingrid who lived with her boyfriend, a young man named Jimmy Burke, on 37th Street near Sixth Avenue.

His face puffed with stress and fatigue, his nervous fingertips beating a tatoo on the tabletop, Ariel Sharon opened the emergency session of his council of ministers. He had called it within minutes of receiving the secret MOSSAD cable from Washington revealing that the U.S. Government intended to land the marines in the Gaza Strip.

"I am sorry, I had to summon you all from your evening's preoccupations," he said "but I have no doubt we are facing one of – if not the worst – crisis in our nation's history." With that he turned to the Israeli Defense Forces' chief of military intelligence, Nahum Milcham.

Milcham read out to the ministers the text of the secret Washington cable. "There can be no doubt of the Americans' intentions," declared the colonel who had crossed the Suez Canal with Sharon's armored column in the 1973 war. "Our aerial observers surveying the U.S. Sixth Fleet noted half an hour ago that they have altered course and are now heading towards our shores."

His words provoked a reaction of stupor, anger and horror around the ministerial table.

"We must immediately inform the international press about what is happening!" thundered Jacob Levine, the Minister of Construction. "That will nail the Americans in place. Bush will have no choice but to turn his arms on Pakistan."

"Are you crazy?" shouted the Deputy Prime Minister Shlomo Avriel. "If the Americans learn New York is about to be wiped out by an atomic bomb because of our settlements, you won't find a single American who's opposed to taking military action against us. Hell, the Prime Minister himself has already invoked the idea of dismantling the Gaza settlements, hasn't he?"

Ehud Levy, the senior representative in the cabinet of the moderate Shinui Party tried to impose his voice on the tumult in the council chamber. "Isn't it possible that just for once, this nation of ours can recognize its mistakes? Why don't we take those settlements out our selves? All they do is immobilize our army and cost us vast sums of tax dollars and international goodwill." He turned to the Chief of Staff of the Israeli Defense Forces, a giant balding under his beret. "Will the IDF get those settlers out of there for us?" he asked.

That was not a question General Benny Dan was anxious to answer. "Our men are there to protect the settlers, not uproot them – with force. To use fire on them could thrust our nation into a civil war. And besides, you all heard the text of that Mossad communication. Uprooting the Gaza settlements is just the first step in the Americans' scheme."

Benyamin Netanyahu, seated, where he always like to be, under the portrait of the founder of the Zionist movement Theodor Herzl, intervened. "Look, as I have said from the outset of this crisis, this surrender – surrender to Islamic terrorists, is the one thing that we cannot do and survive as a nation."

"Benji is right," Sharon agreed. "When I was forced to lead the evacuation of our Sinai colonies because of our peace treaty with Egypt, I swore that never again would I force our army, the Tsahal, to employ force to drive Jews from the land of Eretz Israel. I made that vow then and I intend to keep it today."

Suddenly, the voice of Rabbi Avigdor Beibelman broke into the debate. No one around the table was aware that the extremist minister had already developed a scheme to flout the terrorists' demands publicly and openly. "Arik," he asked the Prime Minister "landing the marines on our shore line is nothing short of an act of war. Surely, in that event it must be your intention to order our troops to open fire on the Americans?"

His question was so profoundly disturbing that for a few seconds there was no sound in the room except for labored breathing of its occupants.

"Your question is one of the most difficult a prime minister can be called on to face," Sharon replied. "To order your troops to fire on the troops of your nation's friends and allies is a horrible act. I know of only one such instance in history, when in the beginning of the Second World War, Winston Churchill ordered the Royal Navy to fire on the French Fleet at Mers el Kebir after France's surrender, so that its ships would not fall into German hands. That order haunted him for the rest of his life. That is why I think, that as far as our answer to your question is concerned, it must come in a collective vote of the government. Will those who are in favor of our using force to repulse the Americans if they attempt to land on our national soil, raise their hands?"

Sharon looked on solemnly, counting the hands of his ministers as they replied to his injunction, then he, too, slowly raised his hands to indicate his support for the motion. He called for those opposed and abstentions. When the tally was completed, he turned to the government's secretary. "Please get President Bush on the phone urgently!" he requested.

In barely a minute, he had the President on the line from his living quarters at the White House where he was still conferring with Condi Rice, Donald Rumsfeld and Colin Powell.

"Mr. President," Sharon began his tone as sober as that of an undertaker "I am obliged to inform you that the Government of Israel, after a long and painful discussion, has just voted by 29 votes to seven with three abstentions, to order the armed forces of our nation to employ armed force to repulse your U.S. Marines, should they attempt to land on our shores. It is a cruel and terrible decision, probably the most painful decision a government of Israel has ever been called on to make. I hope, Mr. President, that you and your advisors will measure, as we have, the extreme gravity of the situation and that you will, as a consequence, decide to cancel your projected invasion of Gaza. However grave are the dangers this despicable terrorist action poses to your fellow Americans, you must understand, dear friend, that history will never forgive you for ordering American and Jewish soldiers to shed their blood on the Holy Land of Moses and Jesus Christ. I pray, Mr. President, that God will grant you wisdom and enlightenment in this tragic hour."

"Arik," the President replied, "we, too, have been engaged in an excruciatingly painful debate here in my living quarters. However terrible the consequences, we cannot accept the deaths of hundreds of thousands of our fellow Americans because your government will not evacuate territories to which you have no right under history, international law or contemporary geopolitics. We are agreed, Sir, that if this crisis has not been resolved by nine a.m. Washington time Friday, I shall have no choice but to address the nation and the world, reveal the full dimension and horror of the crisis before us and order the marines to land in Gaza. I pray that it does not come to that."

There was a heavy silence at the other end of the line.

"As do I," said Sharon in a half whisper. "*Shalom*, George."

"Amen, Arik," the President answered.

8

Washington D.C., New York City, Jerusalem, Waziristan

The Crisis, Day Four

"This is CNN seven a.m. Eastern Standard Time Thursday. Here are the stories we are following this morning: President Bush remains confined to the White House living quarters with the intestinal upset that has kept him off the campaign trail since Sunday. French President Jacques Chirac and British Prime Minister Tony Blair resume their conversations at noon in London on England's joining the Euro — and this just in, from Jerusalem — as many as 300 Israeli settlers are planning a march from their settlement in Kedumin near the Palestinian city of Nablus to set up new, illegal homes on the outskirts of the Palestinian city. More on that and our other stories on our morning report…"

The occupants of room 312 of the Madison Hotel on 38th Street near Sixth Avenue banged their feet onto their bedroom floor in a joint gesture of fury and disgust.

"I told you, Khaled," swore Omar Tahiri "that bastard Sharon isn't going to evacuate those Israeli settlers. Never! Not even the idea of turning a million New Yorkers into dust is going to make him change his mind. Mugniyeh's idea was a crazy dream. It was never going to work."

Khaled listened to his companion, his teeth clenched, his eyes burning with anger and hatred, a fervid desire to punish, to destroy, to kill even at the expense of his own life, as an act of vengeance for his oppressed peoples.

"Listen, my brother," Omar continued "as I told you, we can't build our homeland on the corpses of thousands of innocent people. You saw the people walking in the streets down there — Chinese, Hispanics, Italians, Blacks, the lot. Our enemies aren't down there. They're the Israelis back in Palestine, destroying our homes, stealing our land, chopping down our olive trees. Blowing off that bomb isn't going to change that. It's only going to make the whole world hate us. No one will support our claim to a homeland anymore. It would be madness to detonate that bomb."

"Well, whether you like it or not, it's going off."

"Oh no, it's not. I'll stop you from such madness."

"You'll what? Traitor! Why did you accept this mission if it was to desert and give up at the first occasion?"

Khaled swung out, using the side of his hand like an axe with which he whacked Omar's cheeks.

Omar staggered under the blow, falling against a chair and toppling onto the floor between their beds. Khaled pounced on him and grabbed his throat in the vice-like grip of his two hands.

Omar was choking. His mouth open, gasping for air, he managed to roll onto his side and with his good hand, pulled out of his vest pocket the small 6.35 revolver the Canadian who had furnished them their false papers had given him, on their arrival in Montreal. He clutched it in a trembling hand as Khaled thrust his head against the floor. He pulled the trigger but his shot missed and lodged in the ceiling overhead.

Enraged, Khaled throttled his companion, both his hands knotting the older man's neck just below his Adam's Apple. A spasm shook Omar. His mouth opened in a desperate effort to gasp air but he got none. Khaled continued to throttle him. A splash of spittle burst from Omar's mouth and he fell back, unconscious. Khaled continued his strangling action for a long moment. When he released his grip, Omar's head fell backward. He was dead.

"That bomb is going off, Omar!" Khaled vowed. "I swear that to you. I will set it off myself if I have to. You lost, traitor!"

He pulled on his leather jacket, combed his hair, grabbed the revolver from his dead friend's hand, and rushed out of the room.

★ ★ ★

It was Police Commissioner Ray Kelly's idea. Precisely at eight o'clock, every available detective, every FBI agent assigned to duty in the crisis shaking New York City was ordered to watch a closed-circuit TV conference at a police precinct in the nearest available precinct house, anywhere in New York's five boroughs. It was an unprecedented order, something that had never happened before in New York Police Department history, but there was no doubt in Kelly's mind that the gravity of the situation, as the hours ran swiftly down to the terrorists' deadline, demanded it.

T.F. O'Neill sat at the head of his officers of the Manhattan South Detective Squad. He was inordinately proud of those men and women. Budget cuts had reduced their number from forty to twenty five but they were still running an arrest rate of over 25%, one of the best in the city. He grasped a cup of New York's finest *capuccino* in his hand and stared at the TV screen, waiting for the PC's image to appear. His mind, however, was not on the screen but on the playground of Our Lady of Sorrows school in Glendale and the adorable little girl he had felt morally obliged to leave in the confines of that school yesterday. Would she survive the catastrophe threatening the city? Less important, would he?

There was a commotion at the door of the squad room. A dozen FBI agents assigned to work with his officers had just arrived, his 'partner' Olivia Phillips among them. He gestured to Olivia, indicating the chair next to his that he had kept vacant, waiting for her arrival.

The Bureau had put her up in the nearby New Yorker Hotel for the crisis. She, he guessed, must have been up since seven despite the fact they had been working past midnight. She was immaculate, her makeup, every hair in her bouffant hair-style in place. Her lithe figure was sheathed in a tight-fitting Calvin Klein pants suit. What a woman, O'Neill thought. She probably could have found some pretext to get back to her native New Orleans but here she was, where duty called, ready to die for New York City. Well, if we both get out of this mess...

The lights flashing on the TV set interrupted his thought Kelly's face appeared. "Ladies and Gentlemen," he began "I'm going to be brief because time is of the essence. I must reveal to you something we have felt we had to keep secret until now. Those terrorists who smuggled their barrel of chlorine gas into New York City have given us an ultimatum. If our national government does not respond to their demands by noon New York time tomorrow, they will unleash the deadly contents of that barrel on the city. That will cause immense pain and suffering to the neighborhood in which it has been hidden. Therefore, for each and everyone of us, there must be no rest, no down time, no diversions, however important, from the critical task before us, until we have found that barrel. I count on all of you to get out there right now, to leave no stone unturned until success is ours. Now get going!"

O'Neill stood up. "You all heard the PC," he said.

"Get to work on those targets you were assigned yesterday in that critical area I sketched out for you!"

Olivia's cell phone had in the meantime, rung. She
listened intently to her call, then beckoned to O'Neill.
"It was FBI Headquarters," she whispered. "The CIA
has come up with the name and address of the guy that
made that call to Beirut on the unregistered cell phone.
Name's Burke. Supposedly works for Dell computers
and lives in our area, 38th Street near Sixth. They want
us to get down there right away and check him out. See
if he really is who he says he is."

Three sharp knocks, a pause, two more knocks, another pause and a final knock — that was the code they
had established for entering the hideaway where they
had secreted their atomic bomb. Nahed edged open the
door and Khaled slipped in. From the look of anxiety
and concern on his face, the young woman instantly
realized something was wrong.

Khaled went to the wooden case in which the bomb
had been shipped from Bombay, now an improvised
half chair, half table, and grasped his head in his hands.

"I have killed Omar," he murmured. "He wanted
to betray our mission. He wanted to prevent me from
detonating the bomb."

Nahed gasped in shock.

"Turn on the radio!" Khaled told her. "CNN said

hundreds of Israeli settlers are getting ready to seize some more of our sacred homeland near Nablus. The Warriors of the Jihad have lost this phase of our struggle, but I am going to avenge them, come what may."

He got back on his feet, grasped Nahed by her shoulders and fixed his gaze on hers. "Nahed," he whispered "your presence here is no longer necessary. Omar is dead but I am going to stay right here in this room until the deadline expires at noon tomorrow. If the call doesn't come through to detonate our bomb, then I will detonate it myself by pushing that button," he gestured with his head to the device they had attached to their bomb, following Mugniyeh's instructions. "The enemies of our people will receive the punishment they deserve."

"Go up the street and buy me enough food and water so I can live in here without going outside until noon tomorrow. You have your Canadian passport." He took a wad of bills from his pocket and passed them to her. "Take this and head to Canada. Palestine needs you, still."

Nahed slipped on her jacket and blonde wig. In five minutes, she was back with a bundle of groceries and Evian water. Tears in her eyes, she tenderly caressed Khaled's cheeks. She wanted to say something but the words would not escape her mouth. Finally, in a half whisper she said: "May Allah welcome you to paradise as the hero and martyr you are."

She embraced her fellow terrorist, eased open the door and hurried down the stairs. The Pakistani super was cleaning the entry hall but she brushed past him like a ghost, slid out the door and disappeared into the crowd of early morning shoppers in the street.

★ ★ ★

"It was right in here," Jimmy Burke said, pointing out the green New York City trash can near the corner of 38th Street and 6th Avenue to T.F. O'Neill and Olivia Phillips.

"Yes," his German girl friend Ingrid confirmed, "it was lying on top of a copy of the Village Voice."

"I picked it up," Jimmy added. "It had no battery so I thought 'hey, maybe if I stick a battery in there, it will have some time left on it I can use'."

He had already handed the phone to Olivia. "That call I made to Ingrid's mother was the only time I used it, so if there are any other calls on there," — he shrugged — "they might be what you guys are looking for."

"Do you remember what time it was when you found it?" Olivia asked.

"Well, we went to see the Matrix at the Rivoli over on Sixth and 35th. The six o'clock show. We were walking home after the show, so it must have been eight or just after."

"Bingo, dear Chief Inspector," Olivia said to O'Neill. "The NSA placed the Beirut call at 7:04, so those guys must have been somewhere no more than one hour's walk from here."

"Right in the area we're concentrating on," he agreed. "I don't think we need to detain Mr. Burke and his lady friend anymore. They seem clean to me alright."

"Indeed. Let me pass this out to the Bureau supervisor at the Office of Emergency Management."

"Roger that," O'Neill agreed "then let's get back to the precinct and focus our search efforts on this neighborhood around here. Listen, on the way, there's one quick stop I'd like to make."

The President charged into the Situation Room of the White House with all the furious energy of a brave bull bursting into the bullring. So angry was he, he forgot the usual moment of prayerful silence with which he made it a practice to open these gatherings. Eyes flashing in anger, he waved to them a document bound in a blue binder, his daily CIA briefing.

"Ladies and Gentlemen," he said "with Milt Andersen's agreement, I've ordered a copy of this morning briefing paper prepared for each of you. The latest report from Jerusalem informs me that over 300 Israeli settlers from the settlement of Kedumim are about to set out to establish themselves, together with their vans and mobile homes, on some thirty dunums of Palestinian farmland near the city of Nablus. Their leader is Rabbi Avigdor Beibelman, the leader of the radical National Religious Party, whose proclaimed goal is to drive the Palestinians now on the West Bank into Jordan. He has invited both the Israeli and the international press to cover the event. CNN is already announcing it. It is impossible to see this as anything other than an outrageous provocation, an irrevocable act designed to wipe out any hope of a peaceful resolution to the threat facing New York.

"Son of a bitch!" an angry voice muttered from the end of the room "and so, now we lose New York for those 300 settlers!"

"Can't Sharon stop them?" the deputy secretary of defense asked.

"Perhaps," the CIA's Andersen answered "but there is no indication he intends to."

As was so often the case, it was the quiet but firm voice of Condoleezza Rice that came forward with an idea.

"Mr. President," she said "I think that you should get onto the phone to Sharon immediately."

The President nodded his agreement. "I think Condi's right. Try and get Sharon on the phone for us!" he ordered the marine officer running the room's administration.

After two agonizing minutes, the voice of the Israeli Prime Minister came up on the loudspeaker phones ringing the table.

"I'm listening, George," Sharon began, dispensing with the usual courtesy remarks which normally opened their calls. "I hope you are calling to inform me that your police have found that terrorists' bomb in New York."

"No, Arik," the President announced, making a determined effort to control his anger. "I am calling to tell you that this minister of yours, Rabbi Avigdor Beibelman, is trying to sign the death warrant of a million of my fellow Americans in New York with this mad plan of his to settle 300 Israelis on Palestinian land, in defiance of the terrorists' threat. I expect you to immediately order the Israeli Army to stop his action with force."

"Mr. President, that is out of the question. You are already threatening to land your marines in Gaza to forcibly evacuate our people from their homes there. Do that and you will leave me no choice but to order my armed forces to oppose them. And now you ask me to use force against my fellow Israelis who are only going out to occupy the land God gave them 400 years ago. The Israeli Army's mission is to protect the lives and belongings of our people, not to fire on them as they are exercising their historic rights. If I give the army the order to stop them at the same time as I order them to oppose the landing of your marines, do you know what will happen? I will have a civil war on my hands, a civil war that could very well lead to the destruction of my nation. Pray God your police can find that bomb in New York before it is too late, Mr. President, but do not ask me to sacrifice my nation if they fail to do so. *Shalom*."

There was a sharp click. Sharon had hung up.

"What in hell are we going to do?" Bush asked rhetorically. "What the hell can we do? General," he asked the Chairman of the Joint Chiefs of Staff, "how much advance notice does the Sixth Fleet require to get the marines ashore in Gaza?"

"They will need to get the order eight hours before you want the marines to start hitting the beach in Gaza."

The President acknowledged that with a nod and turned to his bespectacled NSA advisor. "Your guys still haven't come up with a way to prevent an international call from getting through to the cell phone attached to that bomb in New York?"

"No, Sir."

"Then," the President said, his voice constricting into something close to a sob, "what choice do we have? If we haven't found that bomb by midnight, twelve hours before their deadline expires, I will have to give the order to land the marines at eight tomorrow morning Eastern Standard Time. That will be just after lunch time out there, four hours before time runs out on the ultimatum. At the same time, I will have to go on a national and international TV hook up to tell the nation and the world what we are about to do and why we are doing it. I'll ask Mike Bloomberg to stand by and as soon as I have finished, I'll put him on to order an immediate evacuation of the city."

"Even at the risk of those terrorists detonating the bomb when they hear that word 'evacuation'?" Condi Rice asked.

"I will make it very clear in my speech that our actions are just the first phase in an internationally supervised evacuation of the Israeli settlements in Palestinian post-1967 territory. We will, all of us, have to pray that this will be enough to stay the hands of those madmen threatening to destroy New York and kill thousands of our fellow Americans."

He looked with tear-filled eyes at the people around the table. "Does anyone have a better idea? Can anyone think of another way of extracting us from this God awful mess?"

A rueful silence greeted his words.

"Then so be it," he said. "Pray God, this will be enough to satisfy these fanatics, to save New York, to put an end to this damnable crisis. Meeting adjourned," he concluded, in a voice that was barely a whisper.

Olivia Phillips looked up at the great Gothic spans of Saint Patrick's Cathedral and smiled. So this was the quick stop her Chief Inspector Dear had to make on the way back to Manhattan South. Well, she thought, following him into the shadowy interior of the world-famous basilica, when you see how little luck we're having finding this damn bomb, we need help any where we can find it.

O'Neill dipped his fingertips into the Holy Water fount at the entrance, made the Sign of the Cross, and started down the main aisle. He knew it well. He had walked back down its long expanse with his bride beside him after their wedding ceremony, and walked up it twice behind the coffins of both his mother and father. Not for nothing was Saint Patrick's the bastion of the Irish Catholic American community.

At the approach to the high altar, he turned towards the candle glowing in the red sacristy light, genuflected, again made the Sign of the Cross, then turned towards the bank of glowing candles in their small red candelabra on the side altar. He slipped a bill into the repository, withdrew a candle, lit one of the lights and knelt at the prie-dieu facing them. Oh Lord, he prayed, spare that small child I left entrusted to your care and help us in this, our hour of need and pain.

Olivia watched, fascinated at these rites, so distant from the spartan practices of her own southern Baptist upbringing.

"Hey," she said when they got back to the sidewalk "they didn't teach us any of that stuff down south but you're right — we can use help anywhere we can get it in the next few hours."

They had almost reached his car when O'Neill's cell phone rang. It was the desk sergeant at Manhattan South.

"Hey chief," he said "we got a homicide down at the Madison Hotel on 38th Street."

"Well," O'Neill said "homicides may normally be a top priority but with what we have on our plate today, they're in second place."

"This one won't be, chief," the desk sergeant said. "The dead guy ain't got no left hand."

Within minutes, O'Neill and Olivia were at the door of the Madison Hotel. His detective assigned to the case was waiting for him, together with two uniformed patrolmen and the hotel proprietor.

"OK," O'Neill snapped "so what have we got?"

"Guy's up in 312. Looks he was strangled. There's a round lodged in the roof but no one in the building heard a gunshot. Maid found him when she came to clean the room."

"I immediately called 911," the proprietor, anxious to display his law-abiding nature, assured them.

"Let's have a look," O'Neill said, heading for the elevator.

"You know," Olivia murmured as they got in. "I've never seen a cadaver."

"Not to worry, Little Pal," O'Neill assured her "some of these bad guys look better dead than alive."

The police officer standing guard at the door let them into 312. It consisted of a small sitting room and a bedroom with twin beds. Omar's body, mouth agape was sprawled on the floor between the beds.

"Get me a Kodak Instamatic of this guy's face right away," O'Neill ordered.

There was, he saw, a woman's brassiere and panties

on one of the beds. "You had a couple living in here?" he asked the proprietor.

"Three of them rented the suite, inspector," the proprietor said.

"And two of them slept together on one of your crummy little beds?"

The proprietor ignored his observation. "The three of them were never here together. Sometimes the woman spent the night here with one or the other of the guys. Once, maybe, the two guys were here for the night. Where they went or what they did the rest of the time, I don't know. We don't try to keep close track of their comings and goings. You know, what's their business is their business, not ours."

"Sure," O'Neill said, taking out the ID photo from the woman's Easy Rent driver's license. "Was this, by any chance, the woman?"

The hotel owner put on his glasses and studied the photo. "Yeah, I think so," he said. "Although she didn't always wear a scarf."

"What did they give you for ID when they checked in?"

"Canadian passports. We have the details downstairs in the office."

O'Neill looked at Olivia. "Probably every bit as good as that driver's license from Jersey. How did they pay? Credit card?"

No, they gave us cash a week in advance."

"Figures. Let's look around."

The two began to study the little sitting room, the ashtrays and the wastebaskets, the drawers of the closet and bureau. "Hey!" Olivia said. "Look at this!"

Delicately, so as not to leave her fingerprints, she pulled a soiled carton from the sitting room wastebasket. "MIMOSA PIZZA", it read. 314 Fifth Avenue. "Must have been our friend over there's last supper," she said.

O'Neill looked at it. "Yeah," he said. "I know the place. It's over by 32nd Street. Just six blocks from here. Let's go check it out."

He turned to the detective from his precinct. "Give this place a thorough going over. Dust for fingerprints, the lot. I'll be in touch."

As they got down to the front door, they could hear the wail of sirens in the distance. "What's that?" he asked the patrolman on the door.

"I think someone called the bomb squad to have a look," he replied.

"Tell them to turn their honker off and park their bus around the corner. We don't want to draw a crowd. And certainly not the press. Come on Little Pal. We'll walk to our Pizza Parlor."

Within minutes, they were walking into the front door of Mimosa Pizza, its air redolent with the smell of baking pizzas. The proprietor rushed up to greet them and became particularly welcoming when O'Neill flashed his shield. They took out the woman's license photo and the Instamatic print of Omar.

"Santa Maria!" the proprietor exclaimed, looking at Omar's photo. "What happen to him?"

"Had a little trouble getting his breath," O'Neill said. "Recognize either of these two?"

"Yeah. The lady, she come in a few times. Always ask for the pizza with five cheeses for three people."

"Never had it delivered?"

"No. I think she live right near here."

"Thanks, pal," O'Neill smiled. "Appreciate your help."

The pair walked out and up to the corner of Fifth and 32nd Street. O'Neill paused and stared down 32nd through the tangle of delivery trucks FEDEX, UPS, World Wide Delivery Service, Seoul Pom Inc., jamming the street near the corner of Fifth. "You know something, Little Pal? This place rings a bell in my memory. We had a little problem here two years ago at 316 Fifth. The entrance is just down there." He indicated the building next door on 32nd street.

"What happened?" Olivia asked.

"Super's a Pakistani. Real venal bastard. He'll rent anything to anybody for cash, no ID, no papers, nothing. So these two African guys come in, rent two rooms from him and fill them up with counterfeit CDs and DVDs. They're doing a booming business selling their stuff up and down the street here when some of the African American brothers see what's going on and figure they ought to have a share of the traffic. Dumb Africans don't agree and the brothers come in with their

.38s to make them see the folly of their ways. One of the Africans goes out the window and his pal dies of a gunshot wound. Twenty thousand counterfeit DVDs we find in there."

"So, you figure this might be our guys' hideout?"

"Why not? Look what's just up the street, Little Pal. The Empire State Building. With the Towers gone, could they have a more tempting target than that?" O'Neill gestured towards the building entrance. OFFICE FOR RENT, read a big sign. Next to it, in Korean and English, was a sign reading 'Korean Hairstylist.'

"Look!" O'Neill suggested "let's go in there like boy and girl friend so no one picks up on us. You can get your hair combed out at the salon. While you're doing that, I'll slip out and have a word with my friend, the super."

"Let's do it," Olivia agreed, taking T.F.'s hand in a properly girlfriend-like gesture.

Once they'd settled inside, T.F. pretended to leaf through a magazine, then announced "I'm going to go out in the street for a smoke."

Nothing could have seemed more natural, given the city's smoking laws. Once outside, he spun back in and into the super's little cubby hole. The super looked up, recognition dawning on his face as O'Neill flashed his badge.

"Hey, man," he mumbled, "I be clean. No fake CDs here today."

"Screw CDs!" O'Neill said, pulling out his photos

of Nahed and Omar. "It's these two people interest me. You seen them? Rent to them?"

The super began to mumble in an incomprehensible manner.

"Look! my friend," O'Neill said, "I'm not the housing police, you know what I mean? I just want to know one thing. Did you rent to these guys?"

"Yeah. And they had a friend, a younger guy. I think he be up there now. They take the little office next to the Afghan Carpet dealer on the fourth floor. You remember him? The woman, she walked out a couple of hours ago."

"What do they do?"

The super shrugged. "Man, I don't know. They come, they go, they don't make no trouble, what do I care?

"They get mail?"

"Never. But when they come in about a week ago, they have a package, big one, heavy son-of-a-bitch. I have to help them get it to the elevator because that guy with his mouth open in your picture, he only have one hand."

"Listen, friend. I'll be back in a few moments with some pals. In the meantime, you don't tell no one, I was here. No one. And especially not that guy up on the fourth floor. I'm going upstairs to talk to my friend who has that Afghan carpet shop opposite their flat."

The Afghan, who'd been particularly helpful to O'Neill during his investigation into the counterfeit

DVDs, recognized him immediately. "Hey, inspector!" he said. "Come in, have a cup of Afghan coffee!"

"I'm afraid, I haven't got time for that, my friend, but just between us, what have you observed about the comings and goings of your new neighbors across the hall?"

"Nothing, man. Since they arrived with their big package, they stay locked up in there almost all the time, night and day."

"Any idea where they're from?"

The Afghan shrugged his shoulders. "No. They not friendly. They never say nothing when they come out. Always use the stairs, not the elevator. But I think probably, they be Arabs."

"Why do you say that?"

"Me, I'm Moslem. OK? I only go to the mosque now once in a while, for Ramadan, the Aid el Kebir. Our Koran is in Arabic. Me, I don't speak Arabic but I recognize it when I hear it. Arabic they were speaking."

"Thanks for your help, friend. Don't say anything to anybody about my interest in those people, OK?"

O'Neill went back downstairs to the Korean Hairdresser's salon. Olivia was almost finished. He indicated with a gesture that they should get going.

"Listen, Little Pal," he said, once they stepped out into the street. "I think we're on to something big here. We've got to get to a secure telephone, as fast as possible."

"Your car?"

"Not secure. Press can sometimes pick up those calls. We'll have to go back to the precinct."

Ten minutes later, they had Commissioner Kelly, Paul Anscom, NEST's David Graham and the Chief of Detectives on a secure video phone tie to the Office of Emergency Management in Brooklyn. "Commissioner," O'Neill said, "we know now, where that package that was secreted into a container of Basmati rice we were assigned, Agent Phillips and I, to run down, is. It's in a fourth floor apartment at 316 Fifth which is really on 32nd Street."

He then described how the flat had been rented for cash with no ID. "Most important, chief, that guy with no left hand we described in our earlier report, was found DOA this morning in his hotel room. Strangled."

"OK," Kelly said "but how can we be sure it's a bomb in there, and not drugs?"

O'Neill gave the suggestion of a laugh. "Or the kind of chlorine gas you go looking for with Geiger counters, right? But I have a witness who says they were speaking Arabic."

"Arabs smuggle drugs," Kelly observed.

"Listen," said the Chief of Detectives, "that's an ideal place for the kind of bomb we're looking for. The Empire State's around the corner and that building's sitting on top of two subway lines and the Long Island Railroad tracks. To say nothing of the city's main gas and electric cables."

"Commissioner," Anscom added, "I think your

Inspector O'Neill and Agent Phillips have done some great work. I think there is every chance this is the break we have been so desperately looking for."

"OK," Kelly agreed. "Let's get a team of our emergency service people in there ASAP, bust down that door, grab the guy that's in there and find out what the hell is in the package. Find out if we're out of the woods here or whether the search still has to go on."

"NO!" The words were screamed over the OEM's hook up to the White House Situation Room by Lisa Holmgren, the National Security Agency's nuclear terrorism expert. "For God's sake, don't do that! If there really is a nuclear device in there, that guy will detonate it as soon as he hears the word 'police'. You've got go in there on tiptoe, disarm him and then render that bomb safe, once he's out of the way."

Kelly reflected a moment.

"Yes," he said, "that lady's right. Speed and silence have got to be our watchwords. We've got to go quietly, quietly so that guy doesn't figure we're onto him. No squad cars with sirens howling, O'Neill, you're there on the spot. I'm putting you in charge. Any officers you call on to come and help, you put them in civilian clothes. I'll send you the Special Operations Division team from Fort Totten. Find an underground garage near that building that they can use, so no one can spot their vehicle."

"And I'll send you a NEST van right away," Graham said. If the device in the flat did turn out to be nuclear, NEST would be in charge of operations.

"Maybe there's a window across the street, from which we can get a shot into that flat with one of our high-resolution, low-light, infra-red cameras," the Chief of Detectives suggested.

"Right," O'Neill agreed, "and there's an Afghan carpet dealer that shares that fourth floor with them. I'm sure he'll let us use his flat as our HQ."

"OK," Kelly said, "get going right now. But remember: silence is golden."

Kelly's first gesture was to call Captain Jack Walton, commander of the Police Department's Special Operations Division, or TARU, Technical Assistance Research Unit as it was also known, in Fort Totten, Brooklyn. His orders to Walton were simple: get his men with all their secret, ultra-sophisticated eavesdropping devices over to 32nd Street, as fast as possible. Their job: to find out who and what was inside that fourth floor apartment at 316 Fifth Avenue, and to do it without letting anyone suspect what they were up to.

The secrecy shrouding the operation was no surprise to Walton. His officers usually worked in civilian clothes, moving around the city in unmarked cars.

"How much time have we got?" Walton asked.

"None," Kelly laughed, "but under no circumstances are you to go busting in there without my express orders to do so."

Afghan carpet dealer, Walton thought, reflecting on the mission briefing Kelly had given him. Among his many contacts was a Broadway costume design and supply house which provided the city's theaters with costumes for their productions. In view of the urgency of Kelly's request, Walton decided to give the job to his Emergency Services "A" team, the elite of the NYPD. He would send them to 316 Fifth dressed as Middle Easterners coming to do business with the carpet dealer. Yeah, he thought, and I'll get my hands on half a dozen carpets. The team can roll their secret equipment up in the carpets and tote them into that Afghan's shop without arousing any suspicions

He got O'Neill on his cell phone and instructed him to find an underground garage in a nearby building where his team could park their truck with its NYPD markings, without drawing the attention of curious pedestrians.

T.F. was in the fourth floor apartment of the building across the street from 316 Fifth, with a NYPD cameraman employing a low-light, high-intensity, infra-red camera to photograph the two-room flat opposite, in which Khaled was babysitting the terrorists' bomb.

They could see his figure in the front room, his back to the door, sitting on what seemed to be the remains of a big crate, hunched over what was, probably, a radio to which he was apparently listening. The door to the second room was open. There was a bulky object of some sort inside the door but the light was not sufficient to allow the cameraman to get a good image of it.

"OK," O'Neill said, "focus on the crate. See if you can make out any markings or lettering on it."

The cameraman scrutinized the crate as best as he could. "It's been busted apart," he told O'Neill. "Take a look. I think, you can just make out there below the guy's knee, the end of what was a word, those letters there 'ods'."

O'Neill studied the image in the camera. Sure, he thought. "Oriental Foods." Has to be Birbaki's case.

"Listen," he ordered the cameraman, "you stay here and keep that zoom focused on the guy over there. If he gets up to leave the flat, buzz this beeper number." It belonged to an armed patrolman T.F. had secretly placed in the Afghan's shop, across the hall from Khaled in his flat. "If he opens the door of that flat, he'll nail him."

With that, he went back down to 32nd street to wait for the NEST van to arrive. The driver of the van with its AVIS markings pulled up two doors down from the entrance to 316 Fifth. Gladys Simpson sat beside him.

"We've got some sophisticated stuff in here," she told O'Neill. "It should be close to the scene."

"Not to worry," O'Neill assured her. "Park right here." He glanced down the street. "What the hell, everybody else does. Besides, if some guy gives you a ticket, we'll ask George W. to take care of it. Come on. Let me take you upstairs to show you the place we're going to be working from."

Gladys glided like a cat into the Afghan's carpet shop, her Geiger counter slung over her back like a back packer out shopping. She immediately unslung it and took a reading.

"Nothing," she said, "but if there is a bomb in there, they could very well have shielded it with lead to seal in the emissions."

With Gladys installed, T.F. went down the block to 37 32nd where he'd located an underground garage in which to conceal the Special Operations van. He cleared the entrance and as soon as the van arrived, he waved it down stairs.

To his delight, the four officers of the Emergency Services "A" team climbing out of the rear of the van were dressed in a variety of Middle Eastern apparel. One had a turban, another a robe. "You guys look like the old Taliban," he laughed.

"That's the idea," the team leader said. He pointed to the interior of the van. Six rolled carpets were stacked on its floor. "Our stuff's in there. We'll take them up to the shop you're using as your headquarters, one by one, so we don't draw a crowd. Tell me, they got any ATM cameras in that suspect building?"

"Just one. Super says it hasn't worked for six years."

"Figures. We'll have to get the super's master key and take him into custody while the operation's going on."

"He's been pretty cooperative," O'Neill remarked.

"Makes no difference. It's S.O.P.

O'Neill shrugged. These were guys you didn't argue with. A few minutes later, they were unrolling the first of their carpets in the backroom of the Afghan's shop before the proprietor's fascinated regard. The array of Special Operations Division eavesdropping equipment was mind-boggling. It included microphones no bigger than a pinhead that could be inserted into a key hole and would play back every sound coming out of the room or apartment under surveillance. There were cameras so small they were encapsulated in a wire that could be inserted into the building's electrical wiring or that of the apartment next door, high-speed secret drills to pierce in an apartment's wall a tiny hole into which a camera or microphone could be inserted. The team's pride was a flat camera so thin, it could be slid under a closed door surreptitiously, and film everything in the room.

"Bad guys got no secrets from us," the team leader boasted to O'Neill. Nor, on occasion, did their pets. One of the team's most unusual exploits involved a gentleman's pet tiger. The man had died in his sleep and the tiger, roaring out his grief and hunger was roaming the apartment. The team drew him to the inside of the door with the odor of cooking meat, then knocked him out with a hypodermic needle inserted through the keyhole.

"How many people they got in there?" the team leader asked.

"Far as we know, only one. A male."

"Well, let's confirm that." They did it by placing a thermal imaging device against the walls, which picked up the body heat of anybody inside.

"You're right. One person, a male."

Next, a microphone the size of a pinhead was slipped into the keyhole of the front door. It revealed that Khaled was listening to a radio broadcasting in Arabic. Since the photo images being shot by the police cameraman across the street showed he was sitting with his back to the door, the team leader decided to use their newest and sexiest toy. It was the fiber-optic zoom camera planted in a frame so thin, it could be slipped virtually unnoticed under the closed apartment door.

It was rigged to a computer screen in the Afghan's backroom which, in turn, relayed its images over a cellular phone line to the Emergency Response Vehicle parked in the basement garage at 37 32nd Street, from where the vehicle's special equipment flashed it out to the Office of Emergency Management in Brooklyn. There, Kelly, Anscom, and Graham huddled around their computer screen, mesmerized by the technology and becoming, in a sense, a part of the crime scene themselves.

While the photographer across the street kept his camera trained on Khaled to make sure he didn't get up or move, a Special Operations officer, in his stocking feet, crossed the hallway and slowly slipped the camera under the door of Khaled's apartment.

Gladys watched intently as the images from inside

the flat began to form on her computer screen with astonishing clarity. The officer manipulating the camera slowly moved its focus around the front room in which Khaled was sitting, then to the double doors leading into the back room which adjoined it. Just inside the door was the bulky device, of which the cameraman across the street had not been able to get a clean shot.

"Hold on that!" Gladys ordered. She studied the object with all the concentration she had employed as a nuclear physicist, studying its form, its dimensions and then the give-away outline of the detonation device topping it.

"That's it!" she cried out in a voice that carried through the communication circuitry to the OEM in Brooklyn. "That's what we're looking for! That's their atomic bomb!"

A joyous outburst of near pandemonium broke out in the Office of Emergency Management as her words came over its communication system. "Shouldn't we get the President right away?" Paul Anscom shouted over his hook up to the White House Situation Room. "Give him the good news?"

"Wait a minute!" broke in David Graham, the director of NEST. "Don't, for God's sake, go jumping to conclusions here. Until we've gotten in there, isolated the bomb and rendered it safe, this crisis isn't over. Mugniyeh or Osama Bin Laden could pick up a phone, wherever the hell they are right now, and call the cell fixed to that bomb. They do that, and New York will go! The guy in there has to be sitting on it, waiting to set it off if he figures he's in danger. Or who's to know, some passerby down on 32nd Street may have a beeper that can send it a detonation signal, the way these suicide bombers do with cars they've booby-trapped."

"Commissioner," Anscom asked, "what do we do, now that we know where the bomb is? How do we get in there and neutralize it?"

"Fortunately, the best guys in the world to do that, are already over there on the site, the "A" team of our Special Operations Division. They have a device down in their van, called a Porta Power. It releases a huge blast of compressed air that will just blow the door to that flat off its hinges, 'whoosh!' before you can say bingo. The "A" team guys go in right behind the door as it sails across the room. With shotguns. They have orders to "shoot to stop" rather than "shoot to kill", to calm the civil liberty folks. What that really means is, that if that guy so much as raises an eyebrow, they blow him away."

"Can they do all that without alerting the guy to the fact they're on to him?" Anscom asked.

"Sure. The whole thing is designed for a silent operation. They've done it a dozen times. The Porta Power's on felt runners that don't make a sound. Nothing gets fixed to the door they're going to blow in."

"How fast can they do it?"

"Ten minutes, max."

"I say do it," Anscom said. "Right now."

"Shouldn't we get the President's OK, first?" someone in the Situation Room asked.

"He'll agree. Let's not waste time. Let's give Kelly the go-ahead right now."

No one dissented and Anscom gave Kelly the nod.

Less than two minutes later, the Special Operations men were carrying their Porta Power out of their van and up the staircase of 316 Fifth. On the fourth floor, their waiting colleagues had stripped off their Middle Eastern clothes and pulled on black sweatshirts on which were written "POLICE" in large white letters.

The Porta Power was already fully charged and all the team had to do was glide it silently up to the door of Khaled's flat. The huge charge of compressed air it contained was unleashed by a radio signal. There was a quick, sharp explosion. Then the door, literally, flew off its hinges and sailed into the room.

Shouting "Police! Don't move!" the "A" team, shotguns armed, sprung into the room. Khaled lunged for the button next to the bomb to detonate it, but four simultaneous shotgun blasts, jerked him up right, then flung his body, blasted to shreds, across the room.

Gladys Simpson, the NEST girl burst into the room right behind them. She immediately fixed her eyes on the button Khaled had died trying to push.

"You!" she ordered one of the police officers. "Stand

guard on that button. For God's sake, don't let anybody touch it or even breathe on it!" Everyone understood that as the representative of NEST, she was now in charge of the operation.

She pulled back and cast her expert eyes on the device before her. Holy shit, she thought, sizing up its dimensions, no doubt about what that is. The faces of her two young children back in California crowded into her mind. "Don't panic!" she warned herself. Think systematically, the way you've been trained to do, even if fear and awe are threatening to overwhelm you. Panic is the enemy. You mustn't let panic get in the way. Her legs were weak and shaking, perspiration forming on her forehead. This was it, the nightmare come true, the horror she'd been trained to deal with since, against her husband's wishes, she'd joined NEST. She was standing in front of a fully operational atomic bomb, one whose strength surely equaled that of the one dropped on Hiroshima. If it goes off, not only would it kill her, but hundreds of thousands of New Yorkers as well. Somehow, she thought, trembling, I have got to eliminate any possibility of igniting it. I don't dare move it. It might be booby-trapped. And how much time do I have to do it?

Always assume the worse. That was NEST's modus vivendi going into any situation. She quickly called her boss, David Graham, the head of NEST, at the Office of Emergency Management. He, in turn, hooked up a phone link to a pair of senior nuclear weapons designers at the Livermore National Laboratory in California.

"Should we warn the police and suggest they order an evacuation?" was her first question to Graham.

"No," he replied, "that will only get the media involved and generate chaos on top of chaos. What I want you to do is walk and talk us through that bomb, from top to bottom, estimating each of its key measurements as you go along, but without touching anything."

She immediately spotted the cell phone, installed exactly as had been described to Condi Rice.

"Quick!" she called to Graham. "Get me a Farraday Cage."

"One's already on its way. It should be downstairs, by now. What exactly is that cell phone connected to?"

"There's a wire, about a foot long, that runs down to a black plastic ball, a little bit bigger than a softball."

"Yeah," said the voice of one of the weapons designers at Livermore, "that would be the energy source or, what we call, the fire set. Now what that is, inside that black ball, is something called a capacitor which stores up an enormous charge of electrical power. When a call comes into that cell phone, what it does is answer the call and, in doing so, it sends a signal to the capacitor which causes it to release all that power that's stored up in there, in a single blast into the detonator which fires off the bomb. The detonator should be a big cylinder that is wired to your black plastic ball. When that electric charge hits it, it fires off its high explosives which, in turn, start the chain reaction and an atomic explosion."

"Hey!" Gladys shouted to Graham, "two of your guys just arrived with a Farraday Cage."

"Great," he replied. "They'll fit it into place for you. They've done it dozens of times."

As she always did, Gladys thought the cage bore a vague resemblance to the helmets hairdressers employ to fix a woman's permanent wave into place. On its top was a hook that could be fixed to an eight-foot-high stand with which the cage could be lowered over the cell phone. At its base was a copper skirt that could be fixed into place to keep out any signal coming in from underneath the phone installation.

"Careful," Gladys ordered her NEST colleagues as they started to lower the cage over the cell phone. "Don't touch or move anything. That bomb could be booby-trapped."

The pair, flown in from Livermore 48 hours earlier, worked with fast but sure hands. In less than five minutes, their job was done. As they informed Gladys, the cell phone had been completely surrounded by a copper sheath, making it impossible for any telephone signal to reach it and activate the bomb.

"They've done it." she told Graham with a jubilant shout. "The bomb can't be detonated by a phone call anymore. Now what we've got to do is render it safe."

The air of euphoria embracing the Emergency Operations Center in Brooklyn and the Afghan's apartment was short-lived. Now, the most dangerous and unpredictable part of the operation awaited them, rendering the bomb safe. Gladys had rehearsed these operations dozens of times at Livermore and Los Alamos but they were never the same and never certain. Cold sweat now troubling her brow, she listened to Graham's voice.

"Hey!" Graham said. "There's no reason to make life complicated here and time is critical. We'll get the New York Fire Department to bring a water disrupter in to you, as fast as they can."

"A what?"

"It's a high-pressure hose that will blast out a huge stream at that energy source, one that will blow it apart. Even if it releases its stored-up electrical charge, with all that water flooding it, all you will get is 'poof', maybe a blue flash and a massive short circuit. The charge just won't get down to the detonator with the power it needs to set off the bomb."

Graham had, as he was speaking, turned to Commissioner Kelly.

"Gladys," he said, "a fire truck is on its way to you now with a disrupter."

Five minutes later, the firemen in helmets and slickers arrived. "Focus them on that black energy source ball and tell them to blast away!" Graham ordered.

The huge burst of water from their device flooded, quite literally, the small room. The black plastic ball was torn from the base of the cell phone and flung across the room. A blue flash accompanied its flight. Gladys, her voice trembling, described the scene over the phone.

"OK," said the weapons designer at Livermore, "now, take a close look at that detonator to which the black ball was attached. You should see three wires, one red, one green, one blue running from it into the bomb sphere. See them?"

"Yes."

"OK, cut the red one!"

Her hands shaking, the images of her children before her, she did.

"Done," she said.

"OK, now cut the green one."

"Done."

"And now the blue one."

"Done."

"Congratulations, young lady! You have now disarmed the bomb. It has been rendered safe. It can no longer explode."

His words echoed through the Office of Emergency Management, most of whose members had been tuned into the Brooklyn-Livermore exchange. Strangely, the reaction of the men and women in the main room of the headquarters was not a jubilant outburst of shouting and cheering, but an almost reverential silence, a mute expression of gratitude, in recognition of the enormity of the tragedy New York had just, so narrowly, escaped.

"Bravo, Gladys!" Graham said, adding his word of praise to the congratulations of the Livermore weapons designer. "I knew you could do it. Yours is a NEST first. Paul," he called to his colleague Paul Anscom, sitting opposite him at the command console "now you can call the President. This time, you can tell him we have really got good news."

Andrew Card intercepted the President with the news as he was heading down from his living quarters to the Situation Room. He stopped, staggered almost, under its impact, then leaned briefly against the wall. "Thank God, oh thank God!" he murmured.

The members of his Emergency Committee, who had also just heard the news, stood as he entered the Situation Room. They, too, did not cheer or shout in triumphant glee but, instead, quietly clapped their hands to welcome him.

The President acknowledged their gesture with a grateful nod. He took his seat and laid his hands on the table. For a moment, he glanced at his colleagues, a suggestion of tears in his eyes.

"I think it would be appropriate," he said, "if we, each in his or her way, paused for a moment of silence, in thanks for the extraordinary deliverance that has just been given us." Then he nodded in prayer.

When he'd finished, he glanced down the table to the chairman of the Joint Chiefs. "General," he said, "clearly, our first order of business here now is to stand down the marine landing in Gaza and to order the Sixth Fleet to begin steaming west, instead of east."

The officer sprang to his feet and saluted. "Done, Sir," he said.

The President next turned to Andrew Card. "Please convey my personal congratulations and heartfelt thanks to everyone in New York who helped us to defuse this terrible situation."

He paused a moment, then continued. "I want you to appoint a blue ribbon committee to study every aspect of this crisis, what went wrong, where, how and why. We must learn everything there is to know from it, so we can apply those lessons to the future and make sure something like this doesn't happen again. I will want to talk to Mike Bloomberg, but I think, my first order of business has to be to get on the phone to Ariel Sharon. Would you please get him for me?" he asked the Marine duty officer administering the room.

"Arik!" the President boomed into the phone as soon as he had Sharon on the line, "this time, I have good news. Our police and FBI agents have found the terrorists' bomb and rendered it safe. Two of the three terrorists are dead. The third, a woman with false Canadian papers, is trying to escape via Canada, but our Canadian neighbors should be able to intercept her. As a consequence of these extraordinarily happy circumstances, I have issued the order to cancel the marine's landing in Gaza."

"Wonderful, George! Congratulations. Thank God, this ghastly moment is behind us."

"I share your sentiments, Arik, but you and I have

now got to learn the lessons this terrible crisis teaches us and begin to apply them, before something like this strikes us again."

"What do you think they are, George?"

"We must begin, immediately, an all-out, intensive effort, working with the Palestinian leadership, to reach a just and equitable resolution of the Israeli-Palestinian problem."

"But we — you and I — have been doing just that, George."

"No, you haven't. Nor have I. We have, both of us, dithered and dallied, me with my Road Map, you with your refusal to move your settlers and that damn fence you're building, until we almost lost New York as a consequence of our inaction. I am not so naïve as to think that finding a just solution to the Israeli-Palestinian problem will end the threat of extremist Islamic terrorism. But it will constitute a huge step on the road to that goal, and you and I have got to start marching towards that goal right now, not tomorrow, not next week. You don't have to be a rocket scientist to see what the outlines of a solution have to be – they're all out there, in Bill Clinton's December 2000 proposals, in the work Israelis and Palestinians did together at Taba, in the Geneva accords."

Believe me, Arik, for all the sympathy I bear you personally and the state of Israel, I am not prepared to see another American city menaced, as New York was, because of our failure to come to grips with this problem."

"Alright, George, we'll try, however difficult I think it is. *Shalom.*"

"Yes, Arik, *Shalom*, peace. From now on, peace, above all else, has got to be our goal."

For some time, the hidden grotto sheltering the most wanted man on the planet had been gripped with frantic and feverish energy. Clambering up the rocky trail hewn into the cliffs of Waziristan, the Pushtu tribal chiefs who had pledged to shelter Osama Bin Laden, had been bringing the terrorist chief alarming news. The commanding officers of the Pakistani Army, under pressure from General Mushareff, who, in turn, was being pressured by the Americans, were beginning to crumble. Some Pakistan Special Forces units were now prowling the tribal zones of the Northwest Frontier Province, trying to capture ex Taliban fighters and members of Osama's Al Qaeda forces. There were already reports, up to a hundred people had been seized. Bin Laden's safety was imperiled by their tactics. He might, at any moment, be captured. After all, it would only take the American helicopters minutes to fly to his refuge from their bases in Afghanistan, if they could squeeze the information of his whereabouts out of one of their prisoners. Come deeper into the mountains of the Hindu Kush, they urged, and be protected by greater distant and other, no-less friendly tribal leaders. When the

Americans gave up their search, he could return to this hideaway.

Bin Laden reflected on their advice. He knew how much his bitter enemy George W. Bush wanted to capture him, as he had promised to his countrymen. If that traitor Mushareff was giving into Bush, then there was the risk he might succeed. Nothing, no prospect on earth, would be so terrible, so utterly demeaning.

He ordered his followers to prepare for a sudden flight once the depths of night had shrouded the area. But before leaving this grotto for another hiding place, he was determined to carry out one last nightly ritual.

He reached down, twisted a dial which sent the electric power from a simple twelve-volt car battery into his television set. Its antenna was fixed to a tree on a crest of the mountain's flank outside. The precautions were designed to render Osama's TV viewings immune to any electronic detection devices of his American foes.

The light flashed onto the screen, delivering to the Al Qaeda chief not the evening news bulletin of Al Jazeera or Al Arabiya, but CNN's "Your World Today". For the past three days, he had watched the evening broadcast with special attention as the hours to the expiration of his nuclear ultimatum to Washington ticked away. Nothing in the reports of the network's correspondents in Washington or Jerusalem had yet indicated that the evacuation of the Jewish settlements on the West Bank, which he had demanded if the bomb was not to explode, had begun.

This evening's news bulletin began with an update on President Bush's "intestinal disorder". "The bastard!" growled Osama's disciple and doctor, the Egyptian, Ayman al Zahawiyri. "Trying to negotiate with Sharon could make anyone, even Bush, sick."

Then the presenter's tone changed. "We take you now to the breaking news story we are covering in the Middle East and this on-the-spot report from our correspondent on the West Bank, Ben Weideman."

The screen was suddenly filled with the images of a screaming crowd waving the Israeli flag and posters in Hebrew. The camera then cut away to a shot of half a dozen vans and mobile homes. Settlers were industriously wrapping them in a ring of rolls of barbed wire.

"We are here on the flanks of the Jewish settlement of Kedumin, not far from the Palestinian city of Nablus," Weideman, the correspondent, announced, voice over. "Three hundred of those settlers have just laid claim to some sixty acres of Palestinian land adjoining the settlement, and are in the process of setting up their vans and mobile homes to signify that these acres are now theirs."

The camera cut to the image of a man clambering onto the hood of a jeep, clutching a megaphone. A young woman climbed onto the vehicle beside him.

"Brothers and sisters of Israel!" he shouted, as CNN ran a simultaneous translation of his text at the bottom of the screen. "I am Yaacov Levine, the chief of our new settlement, Elon Sichem, our most recent implantation on the land of Judea and Samaria. With this act, we fulfill one of the most sacred obligations of our faith. After 2000 years of absence, we are reclaiming another parcel of the Holy Land granted by God to our forefathers."

As the crowd cheered, the camera cut away to the image of a Palestinian woman in a black chador weeping hysterically. "Our olive trees!" she cried, "they're cutting down our olive trees. How are we going to feed our children?"

"Bastards!" Osama roared, leaping up from his carpet in rage. "That coward Bush would rather see thousands of his countrymen killed, than stand up to Sharon! Mugniyeh's idea that our plan had to be tied to a demand we wanted him to fulfill was crazy! The only thing those infidels understand is terror like the World Trade Center. Well, if it's terror they understand, then it's terror they will get."

Leaning on his cane, he got up and went over to the small safe placed beside the carpet he used as a bed. He took out a cellular phone, stuffed it into the pocket of his djellabah and hobbled out of the grotto to where a mule was tied up. He untethered the animal, mounted his saddle and rode down to the valley where his jeep and driver were waiting with a cluster of armed tribesmen.

He ordered the driver to head for the little community of Oudja, some ten miles away. The action he was about to take could endanger his life if the American's listening satellites were able to pin down the location from which his call came, but then, like the others before him, he would become a *shahid*, a martyr.

When the minaret of the town's mosque came into sight, he ordered his driver to pull over and stop. Slowly, tenderly almost, he composed on the keyboard the number of the cell phone he knew had been attached to their Pakistani atomic bomb, before Imad Mugniyeh's men had smuggled it into New York. He pressed the phone to his ear and listened in what was close to a state of ecstasy, as the number he had called began ringing.

Then to his utter astonishment, he heard not the answering 'sound' he was expecting, but the voice of a woman speaking English. "We are sorry," she said, "but the number you are calling is temporarily out of service. If you wish to leave a message, you may do so after the tone."

THE END

Post Script

A month after the terrorists' bomb was discovered and defused, Detective Lieutenant T.F. O'Neill, FBI Agent Olivia Phillips and NEST's Gladys Simpson were invited to a small ceremony at the White House. Andrew Card welcomed them at the West Gate and took them to a small room adjacent to the Oval Office. Only one other person was present, Gina Newhouse of the Associated Press, a pool photographer for the White House Correspondent's organization.

Shortly after they arrived, the President appeared. In a few brief and well-chosen words, he thanked them all for the services to the nation they had recently provided in New York. Then, with Andrew Card's help, he hung around each person's neck a Medal of Freedom, the nation's highest civilian honor. He shook each one's hand, embraced the two women, and left.

"Hey, Little Pal," O'Neill said, "could you celebrate these trinkets by spending a little off-duty time up in New York with an old widower?"

Olivia smiled. "You know," she said "that might be nice."

Card took them back to the West Gate where a car waited to drive them to Reagan National airport. On the way out the door, the AP photographer turned to Gladys.

"Where are you from?" she asked.

"Livermore, California."

"Wow!" the reporter said, "A long way from New York. What do you do?"

"I'm a nuclear physicist."

The photographer stood gaping as the trio got into their car. Hey, she thought, there must have been a hell of a story up there in New York that somehow we missed.

Acknowledgements

We wish, first and foremost, to express our immense gratitude to our wives, Dominique and Nadia, who shared all the moments of our long and difficult research months, and were our irreplaceable collaborators during the writing of our book.

We also wish to express our thanks to Colette Modiano, Manuela Andreota, Marie-Benoîte Conchon and Antoine Caro, who spent long hours correcting the manuscript and encouraged us with their words and thoughts.

We could also not have written this book without the confidence and enthusiasm of our editors, Leonello Brandolini and Nicole Lattès in Paris, Gianni Ferrari, Massimo Turchetta and Joy Terekiev in Milan, Carlos Reves and Berta Noy in Barcelona, Shekhar and Poonam Malhotra in New Delhi.

The reader will understand that, given the highly sensitive nature of much of the information to be found on the pages of this book, we cannot cite, for security reasons, the names of all of those who contributed to the more secret aspects of our research. We wish, however, to acknowledge the help we received from among others, Dr. Frank N. Barnaby, a distinguished British nuclear weapons designer who now, in his retirement, devotes much of his energy to the problems of nuclear proliferation; Dr. Ralph James, deputy director of the National Laboratory in Brookhaven, New York; Senator Christopher Shays (R – Connecticut) who presided over a sub committee of the Senate devoted to the problems of national security and, in particular, some of those related to certain aspects of nuclear terrorism, as well as his Chief of Staff, Larry Halloran.

We would also like to acknowledge the help of Brian Wilkes, Rick Arkin and Deborah Wilkes of the Homeland Security Department's Emergency Response Team whose challenging task it would be to confront a national emergency of the sort described in this book. We also owe a thank you to Dr. Lisa Holmgren, former director of NEST and, for years, an expert on nuclear issues for the National Security Council, as well as a number of very thoughtful people at the Nuclear Threat Initiative of the Carnegie Foundation.

And special thanks to two old friends, Milt Beardon, who ran the war against the Soviets in Afghanistan for some years and is now a distinguished author in his own right, and Frank Bolz Jr. who was the mainstay of our research at the New York Police Department.

Dominique Lapierre and Larry Collins

FULL CIRCLE

FULL CIRCLE publishes books on inspirational subjects, religion, philosophy, and natural health. The objective is to help make an attitudinal shift towards a more peaceful, loving, non-combative, non-threatening, compassionate and healing world.

FULL CIRCLE continues its commitment towards creating a peaceful and harmonious world and towards rekindling the joyous, divine nature of the human spirit.

Our fine books are available at all leading bookstores across the country.

FULL CIRCLE *PUBLISHING*

Editorial Office

J-40, Jorbagh Lane, New Delhi-110 003
Tel: 24620063, 55654197, 30973793 • Fax: 24645795
E-Mail: gbp@del2.vsnl.net.in / fullcircle@vsnl.com
website: www.atfullcircle.com

Bookstore

The **FULL CIRCLE** BOOKSTORE
5 B, Khan Market, New Delhi-110003
Tel: 24655641- 44 • Fax: 24645795

Warehouse & Sales Office

B-13, Sector-81, Phase-II, NOIDA (UP) - 201305
Tel: 55654198, 0120-3093992

Other titles by **Dominque Lapierre** from **FULL CIRCLE**

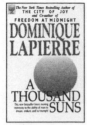

Rs. 295

A THOUSAND SUNS

From Japanese terrorists in the Holy Land to freedom fighters in fascist Portugal; from spread of Nazism to the liberation of Paris; from Mahatma Gandhi to Mother Teresa; Lapierre delves eloquently into the very heart of the history of our time. Most of all, this international bestseller bears moving testimony to the ability of mankind to endure, to dream, to triumph.

THE CITY OF JOY

"The City of Joy is about suffering... Yet even more the book is about words that wonderfully leaven the whole: loyalty, kindness, tolerance, generosity, patience, endurance, acceptance, faith, even holiness."
— **New York Times**

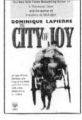

Rs. 125

IT WAS FIVE PAST MIDNIGHT IN BHOPAL

Hundreds of characters, situations and adventures are telescoped into this fresco full of love, heroism, faith and hope. A real tragedy of crucial relevance to our times, which is also a warning to all those sorcerer's apprentices who threaten the future of our planet.
Rs. 250

If you would like to order any of these books and receive them at your doorstep, **postage free**, please write to us at **World Wisdom Bookclub**, J-40, Jorbagh Lane, New Delhi-110003, and send us a Cheque/D.D. for the amount. **For outstation cheques** please **add Rs. 35.** Please make the cheque/D.D. in the name of **FULL CIRCLE Publishing.**

Join the

WORLD
WISDOM BOOK CLUB

Get the best of world literature in the comfort of your home at fabulous discounts!

Benefits of the Book Club

Wherever in the world you are, you can receive the best of books at your doorstep.

- Receive FABULOUS DISCOUNTS by mail or at the FULL CIRCLE Store in Delhi.
- Receive Exclusive Invitations to attend events being organized by FULL CIRCLE.
- Receive a FREE copy of the club newsletter — The World Wisdom Review — every month.
- Get UPTO 25% OFF.

Join Now!

Its simple. Just fill in the coupon below and mail it to us at the given address:

- -

Yes, I would like to be a member of the World Wisdom Book Club

Name ☐ Mr ☐ Mrs ☐ Ms _____

Mailing Address _____

_____

City _____ Pin _____

Phone _____ Fax _____

E-mail _____

Profession _____ D.O.B. _____

Areas of Interest _____

Mail this form to:
The World Wisdom Book Club
J-40, Jorbagh Lane, New Delhi - 110 003 • Tel. : 24620063, 55654197 • Fax: 24645795

Is New York Burning?